AN ORDINARY STAR

AN ORDINARY STAR

a novel

CAROLE GIANGRANDE

Cormorant Books

Copyright © 2004 Carole Giangrande

No part of this publication may be reproduced, stored in a retrieval system or transmitted, in any form or by any means, without the prior written consent of the publisher or a licence from The Canadian Copyright Licensing Agency (Access Copyright). For an Access Copyright licence, visit www.accesscopyright.ca or call toll free 1.800.893.5777.

Canada Council for the Arts **Conseil des Arts du Canada**

ONTARIO ARTS COUNCIL
CONSEIL DES ARTS DE L'ONTARIO

The publisher gratefully acknowledges the support of the Canada Council for the Arts and the Ontario Arts Council for its publishing program. We acknowledge the financial support of the Government of Canada through the Book Publishing Industry Development Program (BPIDP) for our publishing activities.

Printed and bound in Canada

This novel is a work of fiction and the characters in it are solely the creation of the author. Any resemblance to actual persons, living or dead — with the exception of historical personages — is entirely coincidental. Names and incidents are the product of the author's imagination and historical events are used fictitiously.

LIBRARY AND ARCHIVES CANADA CATALOGUING IN PUBLICATION

Giangrande, Carole, 1945–
An ordinary star : a novel / by Carole Giangrande.

ISBN 1-896951-56-2

I. Title.

PS8563.I24O74 2004   C813'.54   C2004-904127-4

Editor: Marc Côté
Jacket and text design: Tannice Goddard, Soul Oasis Networking
Jacket image: "Two Days to North America", by Jupp Wiertz
Printer: Webcom

CORMORANT BOOKS INC.
215 SPADINA AVENUE, STUDIO 230, TORONTO, ONTARIO, CANADA M5T 2C7
www.cormorantbooks.com

This is for you, Phil.

(1943–2002)

I can only say, *there* we have been: but I cannot say where.
And I cannot say how long, for that is to place it in time.
— T. S. ELIOT, "BURNT NORTON"

A story when it's telling, it has no end.
— FOLKSONG

LIGHTNESS

I

The rock hits Sofia, a crushing red explosion of pain, and she remembers everything at once. Feels it, too — her foot inside her mother's shoe as the poor woman stumbles and falls, hitting her head on the cobblestones. Years ago — but it's happening right now, at Burke Avenue and White Plains Road, across from De Lucca's Meats. July so hot you could roast a marshmallow on it, so maybe the heat's made her mother dizzy. Or maybe a paving-block was loose on the road and she's tripped.

Old now, Sofia's gone and done the same thing. No — not true. Life's thrown a rock at her, hurling it across time. She's not at all like her mother lying on that Bronx street, the crowd moving in on her as if she were a trolley running late.

Did she get hit? asks a cop. *No,* Sofia wants to say. *She always lies in the street like that. And now I got hit, too. I fell and hit my head on the edge of the bathtub.* Only at this very moment she's ripping apart, exploding like some galaxy in space. Closing her eyes, she rushes into blackness.

Cousin Chris is taking me to lunch today. Nine in the morning when she got out of bed. Taking her time, she donned her bath robe and slippers, then crossed herself, thanking God for the grace of another day. A summer day, but she's decided to wear her linen jacket and slacks since the restaurant's going to be chilly. She eased herself up from the bed and made her way to the bureau.

Caro Stefano — his photo was beside the jewellery box. Her beloved, gone a year now. She lifted the lid and examined various brooches, selecting the dark amber one in an ornate silver setting. Cheered by its richness, she thought about her two daughters, Petra and Julie. She hoped they'd enjoy her beautiful things when she's gone. Yesterday her cousin Chris flew in from Paris and came by Petra's music store. He gave her daughter something to pass on to her, just in case the two of them didn't connect. A flat packet that she'd left unopened on the bureau.

So open it. What are you waiting for?

After my shower, I'll open it.

Cara mia, *open it.* She shivered. That wasn't Christopher's voice. Warm but commanding, a voice she hasn't heard in decades — not since Uncle Paul vanished. She can feel his hands on her shoulder, his lips close to her ear.

An Ordinary Star

She opened the package and read the letter.

When Sofia got to the bathroom, she couldn't remember walking down the hall. She was pensive. *A silly old letter Uncle Paul never mailed, saying he loved me. I should put some plants in this room. All that light and steam goes to waste.* A memory was jangling her body like that bell that used to go *brrrng* when you banged open the door at Bernie's Deli — *crusty rolls, fresh today.* She knew Uncle Paul was as stale as it gets. *Forget it.*

Putana, said the voice. *I thought you liked it.*
Who said that? she yelled.
Her eyes blurred with tears as she turned on the shower.

Dammit, Uncle Paul. She's hurtling through a black void and the rock's shattered into a thousand pieces. There's no remembering one thing, then another. Her whole life's converging on her like the Big Bang in reverse. *You've always wanted to fly*, says her uncle. *We're going downtown to see the Zeppelin.* She's a child floating inside a spring day bright with forsythia, drifting above the treetops, gliding kite-like above the tulip trees in Van Cortlandt Park and the rumbling el to the east, then south over the twin blue domes of Holy Name Church on Gun Hill Road in the Bronx. She can glimpse her father's turreted house with the huge silver beech on the lawn. Higher she floats, southward over Spuyten Duyvil Creek and the Harlem River — so high that she can see to the tip of Manhattan, its spires tearing holes in the mist. *When are you flying in the Zeppelin?* She's tugging at her uncle's arm. *Will you take me?* He looks flustered by her teasing.

Do you love me, cara mia? he says to her. She's a foolish girl of twenty-five, and she tells him that she loves him, only he says *kiss me*. Something flashes in her hand. Now she hears Stefano, what he said about the past. *You can't see it anymore. That doesn't mean it isn't here.*

Today her uncle's caught up with her. *You pulled a knife on me. It's my turn*, mia bella.

She can taste blood in her mouth.

Petra's kneeling beside her. She holds out her hand, covered with a sticky ooze of blood. Her eyes are shocked.

"Mom, what happened?"

"I got hit."

"You fell. You hit your head." Petra's pressing a towel against the wound.

"What time is it?"

"Twelve-thirty."

Sofia can't remember falling. She remembers getting up at nine o'clock.

Petra looks worried. "I'll call an ambulance."

"I'm not ready to go yet."

"I'll get you ready. The ambulance guys'll help."

That's not what I meant, thinks Sofia.

I'm not ready. There are things I still don't understand.

She isn't about to be killed off by the shock of memory.

Not when she already has a real illness, one to which she's resigned. A few weeks after Stefano's death, Sofia learned that she wouldn't leave this earth with the swift dispatch of her poor husband. For her, something inward and mysterious — a change in the blood, its river current growing weak, its cells ill-formed. *We live longer and odd things get us nowadays*, the doctor said.

Sofia had chosen not to memorize the cumbersome name of her disease. To her mind, it's earned no right to a separate existence. Body and blood — together they grew old. You died then.

A haematoma — a blood-clot on the brain.

She must have heard the doctor tell her daughters that she'd require surgery, but she doesn't remember. She can't recall the ambulance ride or her arrival at the hospital or whether she had surgery and if so, when. She sleeps and wakes. Like a newborn wrapped in blankets, she feels bundled up in the enormity of her body's pain and numbness — panicky, without the words to call for help. She's on a respirator, the plastic mask covering her nose and mouth, tubes feeding a steady drip into her weakened blood. Zig-zagging on the monitor above her bed are the lines that display her pulse and heartbeat. It's all about her — she's there for the reading. The inner details of her body are rising to the surface, the readouts drawing them to everyone's attention — just as a decoy draws a real duck to a hunter's eye. Only time is the hunter, and time has already felled her.

She yearns for inner strength but she's not sure where in

her weakened blood she'll find a current strong enough to push her onward. A trickle of red cells carry scant oxygen and her heart is tired when she needs to do battle. She feels like a soldier who knows she'll have to lay down her life, but who wants to gain ground before she makes the sacrifice. She closes her eyes. *On a dock I sit watching a ship pull into the harbour of Bari, Italy — my parents' city. Night falls with a droning sound, planes of the Luftwaffe dropping their bombs. The ships in the harbour explode and the city's in flames.*

"Mrs. Fiore, how are you doing?"

I'm going to die.

Honey, can you raise your right hand? They're trying to see if her body is still plugged into her brain. *Yes, Your Honour, I swear to tell the whole truth.* She lifts her hand — as heavy as a brick. *God give me time.* The nurse is adjusting the intravenous bags, fixing the needle in her arm. She strokes her hair. One by one, the ships go down. The water closes in.

2

Sofia drifts into a house on Maywood Road in Williamsbridge, the Bronx, near the river that meanders southward toward Long Island Sound. It's 1919, her father is *il dottore*, and he owns the large Victorian house with the shade tree in the front yard, sheltered by a privet hedge from the looks of passers-by. It's a corner lot, one of the nicest on the street. There's no garage, but Dr. Gentile's black Model T is safe parked by the curb. Their neighbours have also prospered in this part of the city — Mr. Giorno, the florist; Mr. Santini, the plumber; and Harry Bernstein, the owner of Bernie's Delicatessen. Most do business on Burke Avenue just south of here, where life still moves at a walker's pace. There are trains for the more adventurous, but the el hasn't yet found its way to Gun Hill Road and trips downtown aren't common.

It's New York City, but in her Italian neighbourhood, fishmongers and vegetable sellers still meander past clapboard houses along gravel roads, and Sofia knows enough of the pedlars' dialect to recognize their chants. *Anil', anil', i ravanil'*, or *i 'broucocc'*, but her mother Livia is seldom there to buy their radishes or apricots. She's a nurse, her dad's receptionist. A tall and ample woman with bobbed russet hair, she dresses with taste and style. She has beautiful hands, adorned with gold — a wedding band, and a cameo ring that Sofia covets.

Her parents' home is a tranquil place, with its carved oak furniture, its sofa upholstered in rose brocade, protected with crocheted antimacassars. Her father's shelves are stiff with leather-bound books in English and Italian, with phonograph albums of Verdi and Puccini, Vivaldi and Scarlatti. There's a piano that her mother plays, her collection of *canzone italiane* lying on the music stand. In the dining room, generations of photographs hang on the wall behind the buffet. There, in the course of endless chatter over *antipasto* and *vitello*, *crostata* and espresso, the living keep company with the dead.

Today they begin with her late Uncle Guido. His photograph shows a handsome young man, his body having the lithe intensity of an athlete's, waiting to leap at the starter's gun. *Yes, he loved baseball*, her father said. Yet in the photo, his hand is resting on a telescope. *He made it himself — he ground the lenses. We nicknamed him Guido Galilei. He wanted to visit outer space.* Sofia's uncle went to France instead and drove an ambulance in the Great War. He didn't return. A neighbour asks Sofia's father how his parents are doing.

"*Così, così*," he says. "They're still sad. They don't want to socialize."

Only they never visit us anyway, Sofia thinks. She's puzzled by the absence of *nonna* Rosa and *nonno* Domenico, but she senses that she's not supposed to ask why they don't come.

Her mother passes the *biscotti*, then glances at the photos of her own dad and her youngest sister. A year ago, they died of influenza, and now she's going to have a mass said in their memory. Sofia listens, absorbing all the details. Almost eight years old, she isn't sure what to make of all this. Her dark, inquisitive eyes gaze at the pictures on the dining-room wall — many of them of family from Italy that no one has ever met but everyone remembers.

The only Italian whose name she knows is the plume-hatted soldier, Salvatore Bruno — her dad's real father, killed in Abyssinia. Relatives keep dying so that the chain of graves grows longer and longer. Someday, she thinks, it will circle the globe. Who will look after them all? There will never be enough masses said for their souls, never enough candles lit or brooms to sweep the gravestones, never enough Mr. Giornos to make and deliver all the floral wreaths to Malazzo's Funeral Parlour. Yet her parents don't seem worried. After every burial, there's always enough food, always enough convivial chatter, none of it meant for her. Now there was this anniversary mass.

"We'll have to go to the cemetery," says her mother.

"Do I have to come?" asks Sofia.

"*Rispetto.* You're old enough to show respect. Yes."

3

Sofia's mother took her to visit the graves with her Aunt Julia and *nonna* Constanza. It was chilly in the Bronx, scarf-and-mittens cold, and her aunt had put on an extra muffler so that *nonna* wouldn't worry that she'd catch influenza and end up in the ground with her father and sister. Woodlawn was a beautiful spot, the cemetery's dark ground snowy, patched with white, like the horse that pulled the milk truck down her street. The spare trees, the headstones, the paths through this place — all of it serene enough to lighten the weight of sorrow. Aunt Julia put her arm around Sofia.

"Look up, *cara mia*," she whispered.

Sofia stared at the wintry sun, dim and tired as an old pearl in a grey sky, and she saw around it a ring of light.

"What's the halo?" she asked.

An Ordinary Star

"Ice, I think."

On either side of the ring were two faint, luminous globes. *From heaven*, Sofia thought. She turned around. "Mom, look at the —"

She's disappeared. Sofia was disappointed, then scared.

Aunt Julia touched *nonna's* shoulder. "*Guarda*, look, ma."

The woman looked, then went back to her praying. Bowed down, a black shawl covering her head and shoulders, she seemed unable to do more than murmur prayers and kiss her beads, as if she herself were mounded into the earth.

Bundled in thoughts, *nonna* didn't see this thing in the heavens — or did she need new glasses? Sofia wondered at the pale and radiant sight, and it seemed to her no accident that it had come in this moment of remembering death. She could sense something filling her aunt, some deep comfort and refreshment of the soul, because as Sofia held her hand, she felt it too. She thought of parched days in summer, of the iceman hacking off chips for the neighbourhood kids, his pick sparkling with light, her tongue tasting the coolness even before she reached out her hand. When the ice shard melted in her mouth, it was almost a sweetness inside her.

A pale reflection of the face of God, but where was her mother?

Her aunt glanced at *nonna*, watching as the woman turned toward her.

"I'm ready to go," said *nonna*.

Aunt Julia looked upward one more time. Sofia noticed that the halo and the two pale orbs were gone. *Come back*, she thought. *Don't leave us so fast.* It was windy, and at her feet an oak leaf scuttled by. Then Sofia saw her mother standing next to the oak tree, her dark coat the colour of the trunk.

"Mamma, where were you?"

"I didn't go anywhere."

"Did you see the circles of light?"

Her mother looked cautious. "No," she said. Perplexed, Sofia watched as Aunt Julia went chasing an oak leaf, then an acorn, then a small, greyish rock, a handful of pebbles, a twig. She was grabbing things, stuffing them in her pockets.

"*Che cosa fa?* What are you doing?" *Nonna* stared at her.

"Souvenirs," she said.

"What, of the graveyard?"

Aunt Julia got down on her hands and knees, snatching up whatever she could, grabbing pebbles, branches, even a broken clam-shell; some gull flying all the way from Orchard Beach had dropped it here one happy summer, long ago. Faithful bits of earth, things that would hold this moment the way a bank holds coins — good things that belonged to the promise that the sky had given her. Her poor aunt was ferreting for twigs and leaves like a frantic squirrel until *nonna* crouched down, took her in her arms and stopped her, gave her a handkerchief to dry her eyes.

Sofia's mother, Livia, looked much like Aunt Julia, but her mother's ample beauty had a worldliness that her aunt lacked. Younger than her sister, Julia seemed more frail and remote, light dancing around her like an out-of-focus photograph. Yet after the visit to the gravesite, she seemed the more substantial. Since Leo's birth a year ago, her mother's colour had begun to fade — not only from her skin, but from her eyes, her hair, her clothing. This was no ordinary illness. It felt to Sofia that wherever her mother stepped, she might drain the colour away from that patch of the world. One morning, she saw it happen. As her mother stood in the living room, daylight eased its way through her body as if it were translucent glass. Sofia could no longer see her. Only the light.

Sofia was afraid to tell anyone. She felt sure that if her mother had a serious illness, her father would know. She drew closer to her Aunt Julia, who was only ten years older. She was more like a cousin, one with peculiar, boyish hobbies. After school she'd work on her collection of dried flowers and leaves, sorting them with care into the White Owl cigar boxes that the druggist downstairs was kind enough to give her. Sometimes she'd meet Sofia and take her home with her. *It's just that Leo makes your mother tired, she'd say. He's only a year old.*

She distracted Sofia from her worries, spreading out specimens on the kitchen table — desiccated spear-like leaves, woolly clumps of dried pink flowers — *See?* Aunt Julia would cup a dead bloom in her hands and its dryness would soften, its colour become more intense and beautiful. Sofia wondered if her aunt could bring dead flowers back to life. Sometimes when Aunt Julia took a dried bloom in her hand, she could smell its fragrance. A faint sweetness, like incense, and then her aunt would murmur the floral names in a language that sounded like the Latin prayers at mass: *Polygonum persicaria* for smartweed, *Trifolium pratense* for clover. She'd speak these words as if the plants were medicine, as if they belonged to a holy rite that might heal her mother's affliction. Sofia would feel hopeful as her aunt put her treasures back in their boxes, fitting them into bureau drawers and the slight, hidden spaces of her closet.

What Julia lacked in her collection, she found in books. She'd speak about them with a delicacy and grace that seemed to lift them off the page. Once Sofia pointed to a drawing and tried reading the caption.

"*Quer-cus pal-us-tris*. Pin Oak. Here's that leaf you went and grabbed," said Sofia.

"You mean at Woodlawn?"

"Then my mother came back."

"I don't understand."

"She fades away. That time she disappeared."

"Sweetheart, she went for a walk, that's all."

"No. She didn't see us. She didn't see the circles in the sky."

4

Sofia was ten when her mother's appearance began to dim and brighten, as ceiling lanterns do in a thunderstorm. She was no longer the child who'd seen her mother vanish at Woodlawn, but she wasn't sure she was old enough to understand what was going on. Her mother seemed afraid. *Take me to the water*, she said once to Sofia's father, and Sofia remembered that both of them had grown up in the city of Bari, a harbour on the Adriatic Sea. Her dad had taken the family for a ride through Riverdale to see the autumn colours along the Hudson. *I want to be close to a river*, said her mother, and as she spoke, sunlight rippled across her face as it does on the surface of the water.

Sofia's father drove her up Gun Hill Road to Montefiore

Hospital. It was a trim brick building, set back from the road. Its newness chilled her.

"Will she come home?" she asked her dad.

"*Figlia mia* — why would you ask?"

"Mrs. Santini says no one ever comes out of Montefiore Hospital alive."

He patted her head. "These are modern times," he said. "Shame on her."

Aunt Julia paid her sister a visit. When she came home to speak to *nonna* Constanza, Sofia was in the room and she could sense her aunt's discomfort. About to leave, she heard Aunt Julia's lowered voice.

"Feminine problems," she said to *nonna*.

Nonna looked sombre. "These are the worst," she said. "My own mother died of them."

Please keep mamma away from the hospital. Sofia's mother had said that.

"Anaemia," said her father when Sofia asked him.

Her mother came home, but a few months later she packed her bag again. It was spring and she was going to take three-year-old Leo to visit a cousin who lived outside the city — in Mamaroneck, in a cottage on Long Island Sound.

"Can I visit?" asked Sofia.

"We'll see," said her mother, which meant no.

"I'm going to miss you."

Her mother peered in her hand mirror. She powdered her nose.

"The air is cleaner by the Sound," she said.

"Will you be back soon?"

"Will I be back." Her mother sighed. "Of course I'll be back."

"When?"

Silence.

"Would you bring me something back?"

Her mother dabbed at her eyes with her handkerchief. "I'll bring you something pretty."

Her Aunt Julia was studying Natural Science and Sofia felt sure she'd be able to explain why her mother was ailing. After school, her aunt would meet her and take her home for supper with her father and *nonna* Constanza, holding her hand as they crossed Gun Hill Road. The weather grew milder and they'd walk after supper — the twilit sky so clear that Sofia could see a few stars twinkling overhead. As they passed the honking automobiles, the vendors' wagons and trolleys, Sofia searched for the words to ask her aunt what was wrong with her mother. The sky was growing dark. Aunt Julia took her cold hand.

"*Cara mia*, is there something wrong?"

"I miss my mother."

Right on the street, at the plaza in front of Holy Name Church, Aunt Julia crouched down and put her arm around Sofia.

"So do I," she said. "So I want to show you something."

"What?"

"Look up."

A gleaming light hung suspended in the southwest sky like a tiny pearl on velvet.

"The planet Venus," said Aunt Julia. "You can only see it now and again."

"Can my mother see it?"

"She's probably watching it right now. In fact —" her aunt paused. "She told me she would be. This very night." She kissed Sofia's forehead and brushed her hair from her face. "Wouldn't you like to learn about the stars?" she asked.

Sofia nodded yes.

This way you'll understand light. What is this radiance shining through your mother as if she were a stained-glass window? Would you like to know why the sun shines and what the air is made of? Sofia was happy to be distracted in this way. The two of them went to the Bronx River Gorge, where they peered at the rock cleft and the rushing water. *The Bronx River is the only true river in New York City. Did you know that?* Sofia didn't. Her mother loved this river as much as she loved the Hudson. She'd taken her on picnics there. *Do you know why the sky is blue?* Aunt Julia did her best to explain the rainbow spectrum of the sun, how its high energy at the blue end was scattered into the atmosphere.

"The sun has blue in it?" asked Sofia.

"The blue escapes into the sky."

Sofia imagined a cake of laundry bluing, dissolving in water. She peeked at her aunt's astronomy notes. *The sun*, said her college instructor, *is an ordinary star, unexceptional in every way. It will not live forever.* Sofia read a few more sentences, then glanced at the top of the page. *Natural Science*, it read. *Instructor: Mr. P. Gentile.*

Uncle Paul?

"What are you looking at?" Aunt Julia asked.

"Your teacher's my Uncle Paul."

"Yes, I know. And he's my brother-in-law."

Sofia took a minute to absorb that.

"I bet you like his class the best," she said at last.

"I like his *subject* best."

Sofia put her hand over her mouth so her aunt wouldn't see her grin. Her Uncle Paul — serious and bookish and staid and *handsome*. Dark-eyed and beard well-trimmed, he had the demeanour of a prince. She thought of the old daguerreotypes in her father's books, the Italian men of letters, sombre and never smiling. These frontispiece portraits would always be covered with tissue paper, as if to protect these men of refinement from the hands of the ordinary reader. That was her Uncle Paul, all right. Yet she knew there was more to him than that. He was Paul and not *Paolo*, said her father, because he preferred a modern-sounding name. He wanted to be a man of science and not the echo of an Italian *professore*. It was her aunt's good luck that this grave and complicated man liked airships and anything that floated, since Aunt Julia herself left a cloudlike impression on the world.

According to her father, her Uncle Paul had been *intelligente*, the kind of obnoxious kid who had to stay after class and write *I must not throw water-bombs* one hundred times. He'd driven Sofia's grandparents crazy. In his own version of Russian roulette, Uncle Paul would take a few balloons, fill the odd one with water, then push all of them out the tenement windows over Orchard Street where the loaded ones would land on the squawking chickens in their crates and in the peddlers' wagons full of apples and pears and bananas. *Pazzo*, some merchant would yell, shaking his fist at the lunatic upstairs. *All in the interests of physics*, Paul would insist, without a smile.

Bad behaviour seemed to run in the Gentile family. Her father's parents sounded less than law-abiding, but Sofia never understood his explanations, since they had to do with politics. *Anarchists*, her father said. She didn't know what that meant. She knew that the police had been to her grandparents' house a year before. *An explosion on Wall Street*, her father whispered to her mother. *Across from the Stock Exchange.* Only they weren't arrested. *They will be if they don't behave*, she overheard him say — a comment which puzzled her, since she'd thought that only children had to behave. Later her grandparents had marched down Lower Broadway with a sign saying *Free Sacco and Vanzetti*. Sofia didn't know why *nonno* Domenico and *nonna* Rosa cared about prisoners, but she was beginning to sense why her grandparents never came to visit. It was part of the tantalizing mystery of her uncle, who just happened to be teaching her aunt.

And her aunt just happened to be teaching *her*.

Aunt Julia invited Sofia and her father to observe the stars. It was late April, ideal for viewing, the night air growing milder. In Van Cortlandt Park, they found an elevated clearing. Aunt Julia asked Sofia to look toward the southwest. "There's your brother's constellation," she said. "Leo the Lion." Its head formed a pretty sickle of stars.

"Is there one named after me?" Sofia asked.

"Not in *this* galaxy," said her aunt. "But surely in some other one." She pointed northward to the tail of Ursa Minor — to Polaris, the North Star.

"The whole sky turns around it," said her aunt. "It's like the hub of a wheel."

"Polaris," said her father, "is the first star Uncle Paul learned."

It was small and white, and it seemed to be very far away.

"Its light takes about three hundred years to reach us," said her aunt.

Sofia could make no sense of that.

"It's true," said her aunt. "There are galaxies that started to shine when Julius Caesar was emperor of Rome. Do you know what else?"

"What?"

"Stars have colours. You see that bright star in Leo? Regulus is *blue*."

"How come?"

"Because it's young."

Sofia smiled. "I'm not blue and I'm young."

"Oh, you are silly," said her aunt, and then she tried explaining about gases and how a star's colour tells its age. Something about these strange, almost nonsensical facts made Aunt Julia's comments delightful. The next day, Sofia made up a star rhyme as she bounced her ball in front of *nonna* Constanza's stoop. *I'm young and blue — and who are you? I'm young and white — and not so bright. I'm yellow-gold —*

and getting old. I'm old and red — and almost dead. It kept her giggling for days.

One evening in late June, her father brought along Uncle Guido's telescope and trained it on the most beautiful star in the southeast sky. *This was Uncle Guido's favourite,* he said to her. *Alberio, the double star in Cygnus the Swan. You cannot see its beauty with the naked eye.* Sofia peered into the eyepiece and she saw not one star but two — a topaz and a sapphire, gold and blue.

"He built the telescope for stars like this," her father said. "Its light is coming from the time of Michelangelo."

"Does Uncle Paul have a favourite star?"

"*Alphecca*," said her father. "The jewel in the maiden's crown, *corona borealis*." It was a circlet of seven stars, the brightest gleaming blue-white. Sofia looked up and counted them.

Her aunt continued to distract her from her mother's absence. As the weeks passed, anxious questions faded from Sofia's mind and a sense of lightness overtook her. The two became friends. Her aunt got A+s and her uncle gave her extra homework. At her house on Tremont Avenue, Aunt Julia papered the walls of her bedroom with astronomical diagrams. "Thank God you want to be a teacher," said *nonna* one afternoon. "All those stars in your head, who do you think will marry you?"

Nonna knew nothing.

Sofia watched everything.

She knew that if Uncle Paul asked, Aunt Julia would go out

and collect stars the way boys scooped up lightning-bugs on summer evenings, in bottles with holes in the lids. Stars in jars — swollen Red Giants bouncing around in outsized canning bottles, White Dwarfs sassy and twinkling in the darkness of empty jam pots, light-years stored on the pantry shelf — the very light that bore witness to the birth of Christ and the fall of Rome dancing among the flour sacks and canned tomatoes, sugar and pasta and beans in *nonna* Constanza's kitchen. *They'll cause a fire, all these stars*, her *nonna* would say before she'd douse their sizzle with a bucket of water.

After school, Sofia and her aunt drifted along Tremont Avenue, down side streets, past neighbours and shoppers and vegetable carts glistening with peppers and *melanzane*, past the baffled stares of peddlers and housewives. Aunt Julia's feet skimmed the sidewalk with Sofia a distance behind, the two of them skipping and floating like dust motes in the falling light. In late afternoon, every brick and cornice was etched in gold, and nothing seemed too small or humble for the sun to overlook. Light glazed the dizzy stripes on the barber shop pole, the edges of the mailbox and the fire alarm, the pushcart laden with melons and bananas, even the row of plucked chickens dangling in the window of the *macelleria*. Her aunt, too, was as bright as a comet and Sofia felt like her sparkling tail. *Madonn'!* Heads turned at the butcher's and the delicatessen. No, they weren't crazy. They were dancing through the modern world, alive as it was with flying machines and telescopes and the spinning top of time and space. Everyone else was moving too slowly.

Sofia watched the passers-by meandering past the squat apartment houses and the small walk-ups with their tiny stoops. It seemed to her as if hours had passed, as if she'd fallen asleep and woken up in another part of the city. The scene reminded her of a street-circus. Young mothers in pretty frocks scooped ice cream into their toddlers' mouths with tiny wooden spoons; an organ-grinder strolled by with a monkey on a leash; a carousel hitched to the back of a truck crawled along the sidewalk, selling rides for a nickel. Kids were playing jacks and stickball, and then Sofia noticed that Aunt Julia wasn't beside her.

She was up ahead, eyeing a man wearing a straw boater and holding up a cluster of balloons — pink and red and yellow. He, in turn, was looking upward, at an apartment window. Moments later, it opened, and a young girl waved at him and smiled.

Sofia hid behind a lamp-post and watched.

"You can't come upstairs," said the girl. "My mother's out."

"Here, catch."

A nudge from a warm breeze lifted the balloons upwards, and the man seemed to float upward with them. Above him, the girl was stuffing the whole squeaking armload of balloons between her shoulders and the window sash. Sofia lost sight of the man, as if the girl had caught him, too.

There was another fellow standing in the shadow of an oak tree. He leaned against the trunk, one arm folded, one hand resting on his chin.

"They seem lighter than air," he said.

"I would think so. Yes," Aunt Julia answered. She smiled and said hello.

"Like dirigibles," he went on. "The principles are the same."

It's Uncle Paul. He stepped out of the shadows.

"Now tell me," he said. "If the girl upstairs let go of a balloon, how high would it fly?"

"Until there's no warm air to lift it," Aunt Julia replied. "Until the air leaks out and it falls."

A stray balloon came drifting toward him and he grabbed it.

"They fly until something stops them, *mia bella.*" He made a bow, then handed the balloon to Aunt Julia.

She smiled. "*Grazie, Paolo,*" she said. "How lovely."

He stood still, gazing at her. Then he said goodbye, tipped his hat, and walked on.

They're in love, Sofia thought.

Aunt Julia caught Sofia behind the lamp-post.

"What are you doing here?" she asked.

Sofia was so stunned that she couldn't speak.

"What do you think your mother would say if she knew you were following me?"

Sofia thought the question strange. She hadn't considered her mother at all. In fact, she was in love with Aunt Julia, and if her mother remained ill and distant — as washed-out as the old chintz couch in the sun room — she intended to live with her aunt and whomever she married, provided it was Uncle Paul.

"My mother doesn't care," she replied.

"Your mother loves you," she said.

"She doesn't love me. She's going to die, and you don't love me, either." Sofia was surprised by the harshness of her own words, and she began to cry. Aunt Julia took her in her arms. She stroked her hair.

"*Cara mia*, be brave. You're ten years old — you're a big girl. When your mother comes back, you can show her the stars."

"When?"

"Soon."

Sofia dried her eyes. "How come you can't tell me anything about my mother?"

"It's hard to explain, Sofia. She's ill, that's all."

"I *know* that."

Her aunt looked exhausted. "That's all you need to know," she said.

Once a week Sofia went to Holy Name Church and lit a candle. *God, please let me know more.* Her own intuitions grew more vivid. She wanted to know everything about everyone — beginning with her mother. Her desire made a hard fist, hard enough to break God's bones. She lit a candle. And another. *Are you listening?* And another, until she'd used up all her change, until the dark side altar was ablaze.

5

Sofia's mother returned from Mamaroneck with Leo. She was tanned and refreshed from the salt air of the Sound, and she looked better than she had in many months. In the evenings she'd sit in the living room doing embroidery while Sofia wondered how to draw close to her mother again. It seemed as if too much time had elapsed since their last conversation.

"Sofia?" Her mother's voice startled her. "Would you like me to teach you needlework?" Sofia's hands felt too large and clumsy, better suited to rolling *vitello* in breadcrumbs and oil.

"I'll make a mess."

"*Figlia mia*, I'll show you how. You can stitch your favourite constellations." Her mother was embroidering yellow roses, shading them with lustrous gold and orange. "No one gets well doing nothing," she added.

Sofia saw her chance. "Did you have influenza?"

"What I had —" she began. She pushed the needle through the cloth. "— is hard to explain to a child." She held up her hoop and began to demonstrate a complicated stitch. Sofia folded her arms across her chest.

"I've just turned eleven," she said. "I'm not a child."

"That doesn't make it easy to explain."

"You want me to learn embroidery before you leave us."

Her mother grew pale. "No one's forcing you to learn."

"Tell me the truth and I'll learn."

She continued embroidering. "I cannot have any more children," she said.

Sofia wished she hadn't asked.

She watched as her mother stitched an imagined flower in peacock-blue, sea-green and gold. As she continued to embellish the design, she became as translucent as the lancet window in the church choir. The late-noon daylight filtered through her body, and her beautiful stitchwork began to disappear.

They had to stop her bleeding, Aunt Julia whispered to *nonna. That's why she had the operation.* Sofia listened.

Aunt Julia dropped by to help her with the housework. "Now I have some good news," she said.

Sofia was starching a collar and cuffs. "Tell me."

"Your Uncle Paul and I are keeping company."

Sofia continued ironing.

An Ordinary Star

"And — something else."

"What?"

"Your mother's feeling well enough to go dancing."

"It won't last. She'll collapse and end up in the hospital. She'll go away again."

"Sofia, don't be so selfish. Let her enjoy what she can."

Sofia heard *for as long as she can*. Over the past few weeks, her mother had grown aloof, and in her look Sofia could see the hard set of *nonna* Constanza's chin, the same chill determination in her eyes. She looked like a soldier preparing for battle, and her distance filled Sofia with an ache of longing. She glanced at a blue silk shift lying on the back of a chair.

"She can go dancing in that dress," Sofia said.

"*Bravo*. That's the spirit."

"I'll iron everything. Don't worry."

Her aunt left. Sofia picked up her mother's garment and ran her hand across it. She lay her cheek against the soft silk.

To her surprise, her mother grew stronger.

For two years Uncle Paul courted Aunt Julia, and Sofia's parents went out with them. Afterwards Sofia's mother would sit with her on the sofa, take her hand and walk her in memory through vaudeville at the Royal Theatre and boat rides in Bronx Park, through fish-fries and picnics on City Island. She'd listen as she described visits to *nonna* Rosa and *nonno* Domenico, the grandparents on Orchard Street, on the Lower East Side.

"Thank God your uncle left home," she said. "And your father."

Sofia was old enough now to understand her grandparents' absence from her life. She began to mull over the rare occasions when they'd come for dinner, when she could almost taste the deep rumble of argument at table, fragrant with odours of orange and crushed almond, cured tobacco and *grappa*. She knew that an anarchist was a radical and that both her grandparents were of this persuasion. *My father calls Paul 'a petty bourgeois,'* said her dad to her mother once. She didn't ask what it meant.

In any case, her anarchist grandparents loved Aunt Julia, and they weren't bad people, said her mother. *They've had too many things go wrong*, she said.

"Is that why Uncle Paul's so serious?"

"He just looks that way. He works at being modern."

Works? Sofia imagined her uncle lining up for vaudeville shows, viewing the movies of Chaplin or Lillian Gish — over and over, as if he had to memorize them to pass an exam. No, worse — with the single-minded push of an asthma patient gasping for air. He'd graduate with an A for Airships and a B for Buoyancy — a youthful fellow in modern times, decked out in smart trousers, a vest and fedora, a tie and double-breasted suit.

Her mother showed her snapshots — dapper Uncle Paul alongside Aunt Julia, her hair in soft waves that were tangled with light, her eyes beguiling and distant. She seemed to be drifting away from herself, tethered to the earth by her thoughts alone. She was wearing a flowing dress sashed at the waist, her hair adorned with a beaded headband, bows on her elegant shoes. Uncle Paul, tailored and handsome, had his arm around her. Sofia imagined that both of them were about

An Ordinary Star

to dance the Charleston. Her aunt's dark eyes were shy and reticent. Uncle Paul looked uncertain, a good-looking man unused to the attention of a camera.

"Uncle Paul took her dancing," said her mother.

"Can Uncle Paul *dance*?"

She smiled. "I think he taught himself."

Sofia imagined her uncle putting a waltz record on the phonograph, watching the disk as it spun around its axis like a starry galaxy. *I must practise asking for a dance*, he'd say. He'd turn to the sofa cushion. *Julia, would you care to dance?* he'd ask. He'd sweep up her aunt into the rhythm of the music, holding her close to him.

Before she went to sleep, Sofia lay in bed, replaying the scene until Uncle Paul at last abandoned the sofa cushion, took her hands and waltzed her around the dance floor. It was a grand ballroom full of elegant women with bobbed hair and long gowns, their cigarette holders inscribing coded messages in trails of smoke. On her arm was Beau Brummel, his suit exquisitely tailored, his polished dance shoes clicking on the marble floor of the Waldorf-Astoria. Together they swirled under the twinkling lights of a hundred chandeliers. *I taught myself to dance*, he said. *Anyone can learn.*

Sofia smiled as she drifted off to sleep — not yet sure what she wanted, certain she'd have whatever it was.

6

Sofia's father left his snapshots on the mail-table for Uncle Paul and Aunt Julia to pick up. Her parents had just bought a radio set and the music of Paul Whiteman's band hop-skipped into the air. Uncle Paul listened to the jazz rendition of "Whispering," his look as grave as a doctor with a stethoscope. He didn't tap his foot or snap his fingers. Instead he lifted the lid of the console, eyeing each of the four vacuum tubes. "That's quality sound," he said.

Sofia wondered if dullness was fatal.

Her uncle wasn't the dapper man in the photos, much less the gentleman who'd waltzed her around the ballroom. His eyes were warm, and she could hear secrets knocking around inside him.

Her mother handed a photo to Uncle Paul. "There's you

cutting a rug," she said.

Sofia looked at it. "Can you dance?" she asked him.

"Nothing jazzy, honey. Just an old-fashioned waltz."

"Like the one on the radio?" Whiteman's band had stopped playing and *The Waltz Hour* had begun. Sofia strode over to Uncle Paul and curtsied. "May I have this dance?" she asked.

"*Che principessa.*" Her father laughed.

"*Basta, Sofia,*" said her mother, but she didn't try to stop her. Sofia felt light as a cork on the ocean, bobbing along on her father's amusement and the rapt attention of her mother and aunt. She turned the radio up.

"What's the name of this song?" she asked.

"*The Skaters' Waltz,*" said her uncle.

"*Bene*, you win a free dance." She grabbed her uncle's hand.

"*Bravo, Paolo*, how are your feet?" said her dad.

Uncle Paul got up. She gave him one hand and placed the other on his waist. He put a hand on her shoulder. She could feel the soft cloth of his shirt against her hand, the moistness of his hand in hers. She wanted him to be certain, not anxious and afraid, yet she could sense that dancing before an audience caused him some anxiety. She didn't care. If he meant to marry her beloved aunt, he'd have to shape up. Something unstoppable propelled her forward — a nameless energy, as if she were the wind and her uncle was a room that needed airing. He carried the musty scent of pipe tobacco and too many books, all of them prefaced by stiff, formal portraits of learned men. She wanted to yank a window open and send herself howling through his soul.

He danced with her. Very stiff and formal at first — ONE-two-three, ONE-two-three — and then his face relaxed into gentleness. He moved with ease, adding a flourish or two as he spun her under his arm. When the music ended, he bowed.

"*Grazie, signorina.*" His eyes looked grateful.

Her parents and Aunt Julia applauded.

"You're *excellent*," said Sofia.

"Now *Paolo*, that wasn't so bad," said her father.

"Not at all."

In her sleep that night, she kept seeing her uncle's grateful eyes, hearing his voice.

For Aunt Julia's birthday, Uncle Paul took her to the theatre in Manhattan and invited her out for cheesecake afterward at Lindy's. It was spring of 1923. Before they left, they dropped by Sofia's house so that her father could take pictures. First with Aunt Julia in her pink shift dress and string of pearls, then with her aunt, her mother and herself. It was a beautiful day, and yellow-blush roses were in bloom in their garden. Livia clipped one and gave it to her sister.

The rest bloomed in Sofia's imagining.

Paul and Julia went to the Palace to see the greatest vaudevillian of the day, the flying man in top hat and tails, white cravat and dancing cane. *Good evening — everything is copacetic* said Bill Bojangles. The man burst out dancing, a tapping of his whole body up and down a set of stairs, then into the aisles, then up and down again, and the sound, the pulse, the tapping of his feet felt like the clickety-clack of the wheels of trains, the click-click-click of Morse code sending messages, the crazy ticking of all the clocks on earth, of a human metronome, of time itself striking him. Afterwards, the two of them walked along Broadway, walked to Lindy's, not saying much.

"I love his name, Bojangles," said Julia. "The sound is full of bells."

"Clocks," he answered.

"I'll keep the program forever," she said. "I'll put it in the box with my leaves."

Uncle Paul smiled. "I'll design an airship and name it for him. *The Flying Bojangles.*" Aunt Julia laughed and he shivered because he knew he was floating in the grace of flight, and he took her hand. There on the street in front of Lindy's, home of fine sandwiches and elegant confections, he looked at Aunt Julia and asked her to marry him. She said she would, and he held her hand tight as if love were in every sense a loss of gravity, as if one or the other of them might scuttle away, like scraps of paper in the wind. Yet his feet heard the dancing of the ground underneath them, and his body felt a tapping, a hand on his shoulder, as if Bojangles himself were talking to him. He smiled at Julia, then did a little skip, then another.

SOMEONE WILL FLY

I

"The airship is coming to New York," said Uncle Paul. He read from the paper. *A brass band saw them off in the town of Friedrichshafen, Germany. Men tossed their hats in the air and women waved handkerchiefs as the last German Zeppelin set sail for America. The plant located in this town is to be destroyed under the terms of the Treaty of Versailles. The LZ-126 is expected to arrive in New York on Thursday, October 15th.*

Sofia eyed the photograph. Her brother Leo grasped the edge of the table and stood up on his toes to see.

"I'm going to sail away," he said.

"It's an *airship*," said Sofia.

Her father frowned. "It's German," he said to Uncle Paul. "Don't tell pop you even *looked* at it."

"It's not German."

"Whose is it, then?"

"America's. Germany had to make it for the Navy." Uncle Paul turned to Sofia and Leo. "Do you children know what an airship is?"

"Yes," they replied.

"Tell me."

"It flies with gas in it," said Sofia.

"*Bene*. When you grow up, the two of you will fly across the ocean."

Her father examined the photo again. "It will take how long to cross?"

"Four days, I think," said Paul.

"What speed. I'm told that photos like this will soon cross the ocean in an hour. By wire."

Sofia looked at her father, perplexed.

"*Figlia mia*, the telephone wire," he said. He put his arm around her and pulled the newspaper closer so that she could look at the airship. Pictures by *telephone*? That puzzled her. Like her uncle, she was more intrigued by the ship of the air. To her it looked magnificent, and she pondered the new idea that both the dirigible and its photo could glide with ease and grace across the ocean. She felt transported by the wonder of it, into another dimension where extraordinary things were possible. For a dizzy instant she stepped outside the constraints of time and found herself present to the whole span of her uncle's life.

"You're going to fly in the Zeppelin," she said.

Her body rang with the words — a pitch precise enough to shatter her uncle's composure. He broke out in a sweat, mopped his brow with his handkerchief and cleared his throat.

"Getting on board would take influence," he said.

"I'll say a prayer that you can go."

Sofia excused herself, unsure of how she'd spoken with such certainty that she'd managed to upset her uncle. She felt as if she'd pried loose a secret that she had no business knowing, much less proclaiming, and she sensed that she should not have done this. If it had been possible for Aunt Julia to fly with him, she might feel less guilty for her intrusion. Although they were married now, her aunt wouldn't be going with her uncle — not on the trip that Sofia felt was imminent. Among the small joys of Sofia's life was the fact that Aunt Julia was her Eighth Grade teacher at P.S. 5. *You won't have her for long,* her mother explained. *She's in a family way. Poor Julia only found out two weeks ago,* she overheard her saying to Mrs. Santini, and by then it was past Labour Day — too late for the school to hire another teacher. Aunt Julia would have to quit at Christmas.

Leo was walking around the room on tiptoe, his arms extended like a bird's.

"I'm going to fly," he said.

Had no one seen Aunt Julia leave the ground?

2

Sofia sat at her desk, hands on her notebook, her eyes on her aunt. The woman seemed adrift in haze, so that you had to blink and re-focus your eyes in order to catch a glimpse as she passed by. It must have been the loose cut of her dresses that made her seem ethereal, but no — that was camouflage, a distraction from something more peculiar. Sofia could sense that her aunt had the power to fly away. Not that she'd do such a thing — just that her relationship to gravity wasn't as secure as everyone else's.

She thought of her mother who could fade from sight (yet never quite did), and she wondered what odd predilection life might have in store for her. Evaporation into thin air (and of course, re-appearance) was a fate to which she'd resigned herself — a useful condition in the modern world where matter

An Ordinary Star

and energy were said to be one and the same. As for her aunt, as careful and orderly as her teaching was, she seemed attentive to another reality altogether, a wind that might lift her up and sweep her out the window.

"The largest airship ever built will fly into New York Harbor this week," her aunt told the class. They'd have the morning off to see the spectacle. Hands waved in the air.

"How big is it, Mrs. Gentile?"

"Are there Germans in it?"

"How many people does it hold?"

"Will we see it in the Bronx?"

Sofia raised her hand. "Who is going to fly in it?" she asked.

Her aunt looked alarmed. *I was right. Uncle Paul is. She knows it, too.*

Her best friend Tina waved her hand in the air. "Can we raffle off a ride for charity?" she asked.

"The student with the highest marks could represent our school," said Gabriella.

"Class, this isn't a boat ride," said Aunt Julia. "You can't just go downtown and line up for tickets." Everyone grew silent. "Who do you think is most likely to ride in the airship first?"

"Sailors."

"Weathermen."

"The President."

"The Mayor."

Uncle Paul. Sofia didn't speak.

"Any of those answers might be right," she said. "Who remembers what's happening in January?"

"The solar eclipse," said Tina.

45

"Someone will fly in the shadow of the moon," said Aunt Julia.

Sofia hadn't imagined this. Now she could feel the chill of the air and see the blackened sun, the sweep of the moon's penumbra darkening the world. *Someone will fly.* Her aunt must have imagined this spectacle — how her husband would float upwards while she'd succumb to gravity, her body swallowed by the weight of her child. Sofia saw the airship hovering over water, rocking in a stiff wind while Aunt Julia gripped the edge of her desk, then eased herself into her chair. She looked pale, as if she might faint.

"It's because she's expecting that she looked ill," said Sofia.

"My mother was like that," said Gabriella.

She's not supposed to be like your mother. Or mine. She's supposed to float and now she can't. Sofia felt resentful, as if her aunt had betrayed her.

"I bet the thought of flying made her sick," said Tina.

"Why don't we stop by church?" said Gabriella.

From time to time they did this, especially if someone they knew was ill. Although they never talked about it, all three of them enjoyed the brief ritual of silence and candlelight. Apart from Sunday Mass, they made visits on feast days, family birthdays, First Fridays, Wednesdays and Fridays in Lent, occasional benedictions (for the incense and gold vestments) and any other excuse that they could invent without appearing as devout as their pious *nonnas*. They never did anything ostentatious — no rosary beads, no Stations of the Cross. Five or ten minutes — but it seemed to Sofia that they'd stepped into a realm of mystery where any prayer might form on their lips, any grace be given.

Who had change to light a candle? Tina stuck her hand in her pocket and pulled out some pennies. "I've got enough to burn the place down," she said. A coin rested on her open palm.

"Heads, it's a girl. Tails, a boy." She flipped it. It came up tails.

"Boys need more prayers than girls," said Tina.

Holy Name Church was on Gun Hill Road, at the foot of the steep grade that gave the street its name. It was set well back from the sidewalk, flanked by two domed towers and approached by an impressive flight of stone steps. On their first visit, Tina had eyed the stairs, whistled under her breath, pulled a spaldeen from her pocket and started bouncing it off the bottom step. *Anyone for stoopball?* she'd asked. They'd all shushed her and made her stop, but nobody'd thought being a tomboy was a sin. Sofia remembered this as Tina pushed open the door, striding down the aisle as if she wanted to file a complaint about an unanswered prayer. She led the way through the shadowy nave to the side altar, where a bank of flickering red vigil lamps sat in a rack before a statue of the Virgin. Beyond it was a stained-glass window which depicted the image of a woman dressed in gold, with light streaming from her head, her hands, her feet. *A woman clothed with the sun*, read the inscription. Sofia had always assumed the woman was Mary. She knelt before the altar, dropped a few pennies into a box, lit a match and then a candle.

The fiery window dazzled her eyes. Something clutched at her stomach, a round, hot fist, a prayer rumbling in the centre of her being, a powerhouse of energy ready to smash the invisible wall between earth and heaven. She was no humble petitioner and this was not just anyone's kin. *God, make this baby healthy and give Aunt Julia strength.* Face in her hands, Sofia felt exhausted, as if she had to rest and gather all her wilfulness for another onslaught at the gates of heaven. *Oh, and one more thing. Give Uncle Paul a ride he'll never forget.* She looked up, eyeing the flames in the blood-red lamps. *Even if it makes Aunt Julia sick*, she added. *I want Uncle Paul in that Zeppelin.*

How could she say a thing like that?

If that is Your will, Oh God, she added.

She wanted to laugh.

3

"Luxurious. The biggest airship on *earth*," said Uncle Paul, stretching out his arms like a singer. "They're going to use it for scientific research and the first to go up will be — the astronomers. For the solar eclipse. For the best view — in — history." He leaned across the table, speaking to his brother in a hushed voice, each word intense and emphatic. Sofia could feel the murmur of her uncle's words against her skin, see his eyes lively with excitement, a few stray curls of dark hair falling against his forehead. Elated, she breathed in the fragrances of cured pipe tobacco and cigarette smoke as if they might lift her up into the clouds.

"I've begun talking to colleagues," her uncle whispered to her father. "I'm qualified as both a professor and a draughtsman and there must be a way I could get aboard."

"*Bene*," said her father. "You must let me know what happens."

Sofia pretended not to listen.

At the other end of the table, Aunt Julia was talking to *nonna* Constanza, their words muted by the roll and pitch of the men's voices.

"My first child was stillborn," said her grandmother. "So was your *nonna*'s."

"I'm not worried," said Aunt Julia.

"Don't be. Another child will come."

Sofia's mother sat at the table, arms folded, eyes on Aunt Julia. *It didn't happen to me*, said her look. *Wise up, sis.* Sofia could see that her grandmother seemed indifferent to her own power, determined to be callous. She looked impassive, her big arms folded, the flesh on them hanging like sleeves. Her hair, still black, was long and twisted in braids around her head. She was as strong as a cliff beaten by gales, and Sofia felt the weight of her gaze, a strength that could break whatever it touched.

"You don't eat enough. The child won't grow."

"I eat fine, ma."

Nonna's eyes were cold. "You listen. Or it dies."

"Ma, I'll be all right."

"You think so," *nonna* said. "In this family, we have no luck."

Sofia listened. *Why don't you tell her to mind her own business?* she thought. *Nonna's an old hag. She's never even been to school and you're a teacher and she's telling you your baby's going to be born dead? She's a witch. You should boil her in oil like a frittata. You should push her in front of a train*. It angered her to see Aunt Julia's face — punctured by grief, like a window smashed with a rock. *She* should have thrown the rock. Her mother looked frustrated. *Pay no attention*, she murmured to her sister. Since her operation, she'd continued to grow stronger, her strength hardening into a stony resistance to foolish notions as well as to disease. Sofia watched her mother's lips move. *Uno, due, tre, quattro ...*

Around them voices rumbled and crashed like waves on the beach — her father and Uncle Paul's laughter. Her brother Leo folded his napkin into a sailor's cap and placed it on his head.

"So you're off to sea," said Uncle Paul.

"Aye, aye, sir." Leo saluted.

Sofia's uncle turned to her father. "I'd like to study the sun's corona," he said. "From the airship."

"If they invite you —" Elio lowered his voice. "Pray your child isn't early."

"Not until February."

"*Veramente*, listen to me. I'm a doctor. It can be early."

"What happens, happens." Uncle Paul downed a glass of *grappa*.

"Your first child." Elio smiled. "Maybe a son."

Uncle Paul filled his glass again. "A son will understand."

"*Sì Sì*."

"Imagine — I may greet my firstborn in the sky."

"*Nonna* says that eons ago someone cursed the women of the family," said Sofia's mother the next day.

"How?" asked Sofia.

"I don't know how."

"Is there really a curse on us?"

Her mother grimaced. "Only if you think there is."

"Aunt Julia does."

"*Figlia mia*, how do you know that?"

"I heard her ask *nonna* what to do about it. *Nonna* said, 'Nothing. Only a blessing can undo a curse.' Aunt Julia told her she'd try to find a blessing. *Nonna* laughed."

"Aunt Julia's trying to show respect, that's all."

No, it's not all. Sofia had been at the table with the two of them and she knew she'd seen something she wasn't supposed to have seen. How *nonna* let her hand rest on her daughter's stomach as if she were about to yank and pull a knot tight, joining Aunt Julia to her as she'd been in the womb, binding her to her mother's loss and her grandmother's also. In *nonna* Constanza's hand was the curse of all those years bearing down.

4

The moon is going to pass before the sun, her aunt said in class. She explained how the gases in the sun's corona would dazzle the Bronx and northern Manhattan with a great fringe of light. For two minutes, the whole world would shift and move and turn on end like the snow in a paperweight. On the blackboard, she'd written the words *total eclipse, corona, shadow bands, Bailey's beads* and *diamond ring*. She explained each term, but it seemed to Sofia as if the sky were already darkening, the temperature dropping, the dark sky alight with the eerie silver of a near-total eclipse, and she'd wondered if her aunt also had the power to rearrange the order of time. Aunt Julia wrote the date on the board. *January 24, 1925* — a Saturday — and the time: *9:10 AM (?)*.

Or thereabouts, she said.

The moon might be early or late, it seemed. No one could be certain of the precise moment.

It didn't surprise Sofia that her aunt was at ease with this idea.

I won't be your teacher in January, so I hope that each of you will begin to plan for the eclipse, she told the class. *The Zoo will be an excellent place from which to see it. Or the Botanical Garden.*

A boring place, Sofia thought.

She imagined Uncle Paul as he floated into the sky.

On the day before the Zeppelin arrived in New York City, Sofia visited Holy Name Church. She'd been coming more often since the evening when *nonna* let her hand rest on Aunt Julia's stomach. Now she knelt before the side altar, saying a decade of the rosary before the woman clothed with the sun. *Hail Mary, full of grace.* Today she couldn't concentrate. She closed her eyes.

A graceful ship of the air went floating through the church.

She drifted away. On their bedroom ceiling, Aunt Julia and Uncle Paul had decals of the stars that formed the Big Dipper and Cygnus the Swan. She knew this only because her aunt had told her.

She imagined Uncle Paul's voice.

Speaking of stars, the solar eclipse is coming, he said. *Lights out.*

In January, yes, said Aunt Julia. *A black sun swinging her fans.*

Ta-da. He took her hand.

Just like Josephine Baker.

Paul laughed. *A chorus-girl? Is that how you teach science?*

I've told my pupils what we'll see. Mercury and Venus and the summer stars. Paul smiled. He hummed a few bars of "Once in a Blue Moon," hopping a little on his dancing feet. *We can watch it at the Zoo*, she said. Paul squeezed her hands. *Where's your sense of adventure, kiddo? We'll watch it from an airship.*

Julia paled. *Not me.*

Why not, sweetie? We'll each study one thing. We'll get to talk on the radio.

I'll expose some film so I can look at it. From the ground.

Paul grabbed her. *I'll expose you. Pick something to look at, or —* He grabbed her blouse.

Shadow bands.

No one ever sees 'em, doll.

There'll be snow, she said. *Perfect conditions to see them.* Just before the total eclipse, alternating strips of light and darkness would appear, so that the whole snowy Bronx would ripple with light like the jerky flicker on the movie screen.

Oh my sweetie, smart as Einstein, sweet as jelly doughnuts, sweeter, said Paul.

She laughed. *We'll fly right now.* He rolled her on to the bed.

Sofia jumped, as if she'd been startled. She was still kneeling in front of the altar. She shrugged. *Who made that solar eclipse in the first place? Who made me and gave me daydreams?* Tomorrow the Zeppelin was arriving in America, an impossible thing of beauty made by man. Just like Aunt Julia's child-to-be.

She left without lighting a candle.

5

A doctor's office doesn't close, said her mother. Sofia would go downtown with her aunt and uncle to greet the first transatlantic crossing of the largest aircraft in the world. She gripped Aunt Julia's hand as they left the subway, carried along by the biggest crowd she'd ever seen. Hundreds of people on their way to work mobbed lower Broadway, filling every space from Canal Street *all the way to the Battery*, said her uncle, although neither of them could see that far.

"You'll have no trouble seeing the airship," he said. "It's over six hundred feet long."

"That's *big*."

"And *light*." He rose on his toes, as if unseen hands were lifting him upwards. "It'll move with the touch of a finger."

"Soon we'll cross the ocean by air," said Sofia.

"In four days, imagine," he said. "It would take a steamer several weeks."

Someday everyone on earth will float, and earth itself will be lighter than air.

Aunt Julia, five months pregnant, looked downcast. Sofia squeezed her hand. "Aren't you excited?" she asked.

Something had begun to unravel in her aunt — the careful knit of reason, as if she'd allowed her mother to take hold of this delicate yarn, to yank at a strand. *Why be so sad*, thought Sofia, when the crowd of people near Broadway and City Hall Park had the fizz and sparkle of seltzer and pinwheels? A sizzle and buzz of people here for the arrival of the airship, the narrow tip of the island so jammed with viewers pausing on their way to work that Sofia imagined lower Manhattan weighted down and tipping into the bay. *No wonder*, Uncle Paul remarked — the papers said the Zeppelin was enormous, longer than Yankee Stadium (longer at least than the distance of the pitcher's mound to centre field) — and what airplane could claim that? This was no putt-putting bundle of wooden slats and bicycle parts; this was a gracious ship of the air, fifteen times the height of a man, a luxury vessel with fine dining, beds and berths.

"One day we'll take the children on a trip," said Uncle Paul.

"One day. Yes," Aunt Julia replied.

"I could fly away just looking," he whispered.

A gentle, unfocused expression drifted across her aunt's face. It was the look she used to have in class, attentive yet distant, her body drifting away.

"There it is, look!" said Paul.

Sofia saw the airship approaching from the northeast — a giant silver lens painted on the blue sky, floating above the East River, drifting southward toward the bay. She had never seen anything that looked as strange, that felt as alien. Like the silvery home of Martians, so metallic was its gleam, so perfect its form and so silent; none of the irregular charm and noisiness of human transport, the boxiness and grumbling of automobiles or the awkward cranking up of a plane's propeller. The Zeppelin was ribbed under its bright aluminium skin, the ribs converging at either end like the lined segments of an enormous melon.

"I feel I could reach up and touch it," said Sofia.

Julia's face darkened. She looked ill.

"It's like a *whale*," said Sofia.

"Then we are standing at the bottom of the sea," her aunt said. There was terror in her eyes, as if she were being crushed under the weight of air.

Sofia stared. It looked strange — true enough. The great dirigible threw perspective out of kilter, turning Manhattan's skyline into a set of toy buildings and bridges. Up ahead, two escort planes were approaching the ship. Against its massive form, they looked like flies. All around them, everyone was going crazy. Factories let their whistles go, steamships in the harbour set off sirens, Model Ts honked their horns — a cacophony of bells and foghorns and cheering. The air spun with eddies of white — a snow-squall of ripped and shredded paper, the pages of phone books torn apart and tossed out of the open windows, coils of ticker-tape snagged on every lamp-post. Down it came, like snow in a paperweight — the whole world turning on end.

"Look, look, look," Paul whispered. "Straight up."

How low it was, a cloud itself, the Zeppelin in the west now, moving northward along the Hudson, hanging in the air like breath, making a cross with the tower of the Woolworth Building. "The world's tallest building meets the world's biggest airship," said Uncle Paul. "Just think, Julia. We can tell our child we saw it."

If our child is born. Sofia saw it in her eyes.

"I'm getting tired," said Aunt Julia.

Uncle Paul stared at the airship until it disappeared from view.

They walked to the subway at Chambers Street, and Sofia could hear the murmur of her aunt and uncle's voices, a humming and then a crackle, like a blown fuse. It must have been the noisy, early-morning crowd, the subway rumbling below their feet, the honking racket of taxi horns that made them raise their voices. Sofia tried to ignore them. *Enjoy downtown*, her mother had said. *See how many landmarks you can spot.* As they walked along, Sofia memorized everything: the decorative height of the Woolworth Building, St. Paul's church with its delicate steeple, the cake-like Municipal Building, a glimpse of the Brooklyn Bridge. *One, two, three, four landmarks. What else?*

They were talking too loud, her aunt and uncle. She tried dropping back a step or two.

"What's wrong?" Uncle Paul's words.

"I didn't like the look of it."

"The greatest invention of the century, and you worry

about aesthetics. Julia —"

"I don't like flying."

"I thought you *liked* adventure, sweetie."

"Paul, I'm —" She put her hand on her stomach.

His face looked as if she'd slapped it. "So?"

"Ma lost her first. It runs in our —"

"Your ma's a real buttinsky. She's got you scared of everything."

Down the subway stairs they went, still talking. Sofia hurried behind them. The train pulled into the station.

"... so I'll fly by myself."

"Paul, I'm sorry if I hurt you. I don't feel well."

"I'll drop you home. I'll have your mother come upstairs."

They stepped into the subway as the doors slammed shut.

Grown-ups never notice that you're in the room. They act like you don't speak English. Or even Italian.

She understood much of her parents' native language, but Uncle Paul and Aunt Julia continued to speak in low and rapid dialect, and she gave up trying to follow the conversation. After a while, they were silent. She and her aunt were seated in the subway train while her uncle stood next to them, gripping the strap, his unhappy eyes scanning the Smith Brothers ad as if it were an important headline on the front page of the *Times*. Aunt Julia pulled out a handkerchief and dabbed at her eyes. Her uncle must have seen this because when Sofia glanced at him, he looked remorseful. She didn't stare. His pain was too intimate a thing for her to see. His thoughts belonged to her aunt, not her.

Aunt Julia's hands were folded on her rounded stomach. Moments later her uncle's hand moved until it rested on her aunt's. He left it there.

Uncle Paul brought Sofia back to school. As she eyed him, she could feel her life funnelling like sand through the neck of an hourglass, down a narrow passage to the end of childhood. Everything had changed.

"When are you flying in the Zeppelin?"

"Honey, I —"

"Will you take me?"

The words were out of her mouth before she could stop them. Her uncle looked troubled, but Sofia felt buoyant in the spirit of the day and she grabbed his arm with a passion that surprised her. "Of *course* you'll take me."

"I don't even know if I'm going. Besides, Aunt Julia —"

"Leave Aunt Julia home with the baby. She doesn't want to come."

Something flashed across his face. *It's possible*, his eyes said. *I like that.* She stared at him, fascinated. *What* was possible? *What* did he like? What had started out as a light-hearted exchange had darkened into sombre colours, enticing and a little dangerous. He must have also realized this. He glanced at his watch.

"You'll be late for school," he said.

"Thank you for the trip."

Her uncle looked flustered. "I'm missing my briefcase," he said. "I may have left it —"

An Ordinary Star

"It's in your other hand."
She said goodbye.

Sofia meandered along the sidewalk, pondering their conversation. Adulthood made her light-headed, that was it — and her feet skittered like leaves in an eddy of wind. She doubted if anyone's inner life was safe from her prowling and scavenging. *My mother disappears and my aunt floats. I rummage through people's souls.* She imagined the soul as a chest of drawers, its delicate garments left in disarray. *I just want to look. I'll put everything back where I found it.*

Only she wasn't sure what she wanted.

Escape. She wanted to fly.

It was still recess. She'd returned to school early, not late — her uncle had wanted to get away from her. Gabriella and Tina spotted her and waved.

"Where's your aunt?" Tina asked.

"She took the afternoon off. She was tired."

"You went all the way to the Battery?"

"Almost."

"I saw it," said Gabriella. "Across from the Palisades."

"It looked like a cucumber," said Tina.

"A cucumber from outer space," said Sofia. In the classroom, she found her pad and tried sketching what she'd seen over Lower Manhattan — the vast airship that glided through the sky and made boats and airplanes into toys; the tallest building in the world, its rooftop peaked and as elegant as a pastry, the sleek dirigible crossing behind it. As she drew, the

63

airship grew larger and the silvery hue of its skin felt warm and almost life-like. In her hands she felt the same furious roiling of energy she'd once called prayer. She drew, and the drawing hummed with the motors of the great ship and made her dizzy all over again.

"That's copa*cetic*," said Tina.

"I've got an idea," said Gabriella. "Why don't we give this picture to Mrs. Gentile as her going-away present? Everyone can sign it."

"That's swell," said Tina.

Sofia said nothing.

"You don't like the idea?"

"My aunt doesn't like the airship."

"She'll change her mind when she sees this," said Tina.

Everyone signed the picture, and Sofia wrote: *Thanks, Mrs. G., for a swell "ride." Your Eighth Grade class at P.S.5.* She rolled it up and put it in her locker.

That night Sofia closed her eyes and drifted upwards as if she were air. Uncle Paul was holding her hand, and in her dream she flew with deliberate slowness above the city. Lower Manhattan opened wide like a lady's fan, its elegant bridges and parapets spread out below her on watery silk, but she was floating away from it, and the city vanished.

6

The day after the Zeppelin had docked, her Uncle Paul met with a colleague visiting from Washington D.C. John Ames was an astronomer, an authority on the sun's corona. The man had requested that her uncle put in writing his wish to view the solar eclipse from the air. In mid-November, Uncle Paul came to visit with a letter in his hand. *There will be a flight that day to the centre line of the path of totality*, he wrote back. *That would be east of Montauk Point, Long Island. I will be in need of a draughtsman to help with my observations on board the airship* Los Angeles, *and I have no one as of yet*. Her uncle had written back again, listing his qualifications.

"Are you going up in the airship, Uncle Paul?" Sofia asked.

"If they invite me, yes."

Aunt Julia's face paled.

"Uncle Paul's gonna sail in the airship!" said Leo.

"Children, we don't know yet if he's going," said their father.

"Or how safe it is," Aunt Julia said.

Uncle Paul spoke to Sofia's father. "Breaking new ground is not for the timid," he remarked.

"The airship's full of hydrogen," Aunt Julia said. "If it caught fire —"

Sofia grimaced. *It's not going to burn. Come on.*

As she looked at her uncle, she remembered that not long ago, her aunt had been fearless. She hadn't worried about blindness the day she'd shown the class how to view the partial phase of the eclipse. On her desk Aunt Julia had placed a straw bonnet and a spaghetti colander — the kind used in every Italian kitchen. *What do they have in common, class? Holes*, everyone said. *So this is a safe way to watch. Stand with your back to the sun and hold one of these so that it catches the rays. There should be a white surface a foot or so away from it. Or you can use the snow. You'll see hundreds of suns being nibbled by the moon.*

What had gone wrong with her aunt?

Her uncle belonged to the new world. Her aunt belonged to *nonna*.

And what is going to become of me?

Yesterday she'd heard her mother whisper to her father. *Mamma feeds her too much. There's no talking to either of them.*

"Why is Aunt Julia like that?" she'd asked.

"Like what?"

"She's *different*. She's lost her spunk."

"That happens sometimes," said her mother, "before a child comes."

"Did it happen to you?"

Her mother paused. "No," she'd said. "Aunt Julia is — not like me."

And it won't happen to me, either, thought Sofia. All around her, the delicious rumble of men's voices.

Later that evening, Aunt Julia fainted.

It happened when Sofia and Leo went outside to look in the telescope with their dad and Uncle Paul. The two men had built a contraption to help her dad guide the scope and camera, so that he could take pictures of the solar eclipse. *It's because the earth is rotating*, he said to them. *The sun drifts out of view.* The men were practising, moving the scope to track the moon, and Sofia asked if she could look. As she gazed upward, she found herself inside a moment that sheltered her in memory. Aunt Julia in Van Cortlandt Park, a fanciful girl of eighteen — *There are galaxies that began to shine when Julius Caesar was emperor of Rome. Stars have colours. Look up!* The luminous orb of the moon was scarred and yet perfect in its roundness. Her aunt had opened her eyes to its beauty.

Her mother yelled at them to come inside.

"*Uno minuto*," said Uncle Paul.
Right this very minute? Sofia lingered, gazing at the moon. Aunt Julia's trouble was nothing serious. Uncle Paul and

her father took her arms and walked her to the car. "I'll let you know," said Uncle Paul to her dad, "as soon as I get word from Washington." Aunt Julia walked between them, her head bowed.

"She worries too much, your poor aunt," said her mother, once they'd left.

"You should tell her to stop," Sofia replied.

"*Cara mia*, it's not so easy. Try to be kind to her."

"I don't know what to say anymore."

"Why don't you go and visit her?"

Sofia had an idea.

A week after her aunt quit teaching, Sofia hurried along Tremont to *nonna's* squat brick house — past the candy store and the grocery and the *macelleria* with chickens hanging in its windows; past the church and the telegraph office, its wires fraying from news so bad that she could almost feel blue shocks from across the street. Never once did her feet leave the ground. The neighbourhood seemed bleak on a chill December afternoon, and she remembered floating like a kite's tail through that spring day when her aunt drifted toward Uncle Paul — when the entire world was etched in gold. She wanted that day back.

More than this, she wanted to know why her aunt had cut the kite from its tail and why she'd abandoned the stars. Sofia felt afraid. Aunt Julia's body was swallowing time — nine months kneaded into flesh and bone and spirit. She had become the opposite of starlight.

An Ordinary Star

The door to the apartment was ajar and Sofia could hear *nonna's* voice. She knocked.

Aunt Julia eased herself out of the chair and they embraced. The woman was as soft as bread. She smelled of the kitchen and moved with the indifference of cake batter poured into a pan. Her body felt as if everything, even her bones, had gone to fat. Sofia pulled away. As she did, she noticed her drawing of the Zeppelin taped to the wall, covered with signatures from her Eighth Grade class.

"Uncle Paul insisted," said her aunt.

Sofia felt excited. "Did he like it?"

"He loved it." Her aunt looked subdued. "And so do I," she added.

Sofia didn't believe her. "Are you feeling better?" she asked.

Aunt Julia gave her a wary look. "I'm fine."

"*Mangia*, eat." *Nonna* brought food to the table. "You eat with us, *figlia mia*." Sofia resented the presence of this woman, her assumption of authority in her aunt's house. She'd wanted to visit Aunt Julia alone, but her grandmother's energy filled the kitchen, moving from stove to table, opening Aunt Julia's cupboards, handling china and glassware with the fondness of a new bride. She went to the stove and began to fill a bowl of soup. The savoury smells of rosemary and oregano filled the room.

"From now on, I cook," she said to Julia. She turned to Sofia. "You see what happened at your house? Fainting. She cannot take care of herself. *Figlia mia*." She patted her daughter's cheek, then set down a bowl of rich meat soup and fresh bread thick with butter. Julia ate.

"A farmer's vine fat with a melon, how you look," said *nonna*.

Why do you put up with this, Aunt Julia?

Nonna put her hand on her daughter's stomach.

Sofia felt she ought to leave. Her aunt was unravelling like an old sweater, its yarn picked up and spun into a ball, the needles clicking in her mother's deft hands. Worse. She could feel the pat of her grandmother's hand, as if it had touched her own cheek. She saw that her aunt was comforted, and she felt the stirring of great loneliness and fear. She got up to go.

"So soon you're leaving?" asked *nonna*.

"Mom's expecting me."

Sofia left, but she kept the apartment door open a crack. From the hallway, she watched and listened. A moment passed in silence, and in that moment, she could almost feel the strength of *nonna's* hands criss-crossing Aunt Julia's abdomen, of her aunt's acquiescence to their power. It was the same paralysing gesture she'd witnessed a few months ago at the dining-room table. *Only a blessing can remove a curse, said nonna.* Maybe her aunt had decided that this was a blessing.

The hands stopped moving.

"So how is the child?" her aunt asked.

Nonna stroked Aunt Julia's hair. "I know how the child is, but not the words to say. I am here to care for you. Only God says."

7

"I will be flying on the *Los Angeles*!"

"*Bravo!*" said Sofia's father.

"Can I come?" asked Leo.

A week before Christmas, the letter had arrived from Mr. John Ames. "A special recommendation," said Uncle Paul. "I'm the only civilian."

Sofia's mother and *nonna* were preparing for Christmas, frying *struffoli* while she and her brother trimmed the tree and hung garlands over the stairwell. Aunt Julia sat on the couch, knitting.

"I'll be sketching the solar corona," said Uncle Paul.

"And will someone be taking photos?" her dad asked.

"A motion picture and stills, also. My job is to be more precise."

When her uncle glanced at her, Sofia felt as if he could see inside her head.

"Your turn will come," he said. "There's a woman astronomer at Harvard now. Miss Annie Cannon is also going to observe the eclipse."

Sofia could feel Aunt Julia listening.

"She does something called solar spectroscopy," her uncle continued.

"She must be *smart*."

"*Brilliant*. Dr. Ames will introduce me."

Aunt Julia was knitting, row after row, a furious clicking of her needles. Sofia sat down next to her. "Did you hear that?" she asked.

"I'm not deaf."

Sofia lowered her voice. "You should be careful. If you don't dress up more, he might —"

Aunt Julia glared at her. "I think you should mind your own business."

"You're not worried about —"

"You are a selfish brat," she said.

Sofia was stunned.

"You think I haven't noticed. Staring through a crack in the door. Not visiting me. *Spying*."

"Aunt Julia —"

"So what trash were you collecting in that head of yours?"

Sofia didn't answer.

In church, she knelt.

Her mother had reprimanded her and sent her off to

confession. She told the priest she'd provoked her aunt and had harboured unkind thoughts. Her mind, she explained, was a room full of open windows, and images flew in and out — dancing with her uncle on the Zeppelin, her aunt slipping on ice, a stillborn child. It wasn't that she wanted these things. She tried not to dwell on them — well, maybe once or twice she'd mulled them over. As her penance, the priest told her to say a rosary. He also asked her to do one more thing.

I want you to imagine your aunt and uncle happy, he said.

She struck a match to light a candle. In the gritty rasp, she heard their voices.

Dear Julia, you used to be so happy, said Uncle Paul. She put her hand on her stomach. *In here I'm happy*, she replied. He knelt in front of her and took her hands. *Tell me what's wrong*, he said. She told him that she was anxious, that she knew he had more than the unborn child on his mind.

The world is a dangerous place, she said.

Julia, he answered, *the world is also lighter than air.*

Paul took his handkerchief and dried her eyes. *Don't be afraid*, cara mia. He rocked her in his arms, so that Julia would feel his thoughts embracing her.

Julia, remember these days for both of us. Collect the sunlight in your hair, spin its corona into golden silk, clasp it in place with ruby brooches, gems on fire. Pin and stitch and gather time. Remember the eyes of heaven, the stones, the leaves. Write this.

At home later, Sofia wrote the words down.

Maybe she'll forgive me if I ask her.

In church, in the still twilight of the side altar, she'd seen her aunt and uncle in a single moment, as if she'd been asleep and dreaming. Later, when she remembered it, the story had duration — a beginning and an end. If it did happen, Sofia felt sure her intuition was something less than grace. It was, if anything, the curse of her family to know so much: to wander, homeless, through the souls of others, unwanted and unseen.

Only that's what I asked God for once, wasn't it?

She remembered that she'd loved Aunt Julia.

Two weeks before the eclipse, Sofia's father handed her a worn brown leather case with a strap. It contained her late Uncle Guido's military binoculars from the Great War. Sofia was elated. On the clear nights remaining before the eclipse, she turned the binoculars on the craters of the moon. Indoors she studied her father's astronomy books, musing over the moon's cone-shaped umbra, the inverted cone of its penumbra. Then she drew pictures for her brother Leo, so he'd understand what was about to happen. On the day of the eclipse, her father would drive the family, along with his telescope, to the Mosholu Golf Course at Van Cortlandt Park. He'd found a good viewing spot where the land rose at Gun Hill Road on the south side, where at nine in the morning, the sun would hang above the bare trees on Jerome Avenue to the east. Her mother invited neighbours back to the house for hot chocolate after the eclipse, including Tina and Gabriella and their parents. Her father continued to refine his camera mount, fine-tuning the controls, then practicing outdoors in the cold to see if the moving parts would stiffen in the chill air.

Sofia prayed that her parents would not invite *nonna* and Aunt Julia.

"I will not have either of them here," her mother said.

"Even if they ask?" said her father.

"My sister will understand if I say no."

Her mother seemed in good health. Sometimes in quiet moments, her colour would fade so that sun would pass through her skin. Yet when she went to work and did household chores, she looked strong enough to resist even God. *I'd better stay well*, Sofia overheard her say to her dad. *Who'll help my sister when the baby comes? Not some backward* cafone, *if you'll pardon my language.*

Sofia waited. Something extraordinary was about to happen in the alignment of heavenly bodies, in their revelation of God's mighty laws. If the universe could be so generous with its gifts, then maybe her aunt would forgive her. She'd have to find the courage to ask.

Imagine your soul has eyes, the priest had said. *Close them when you feel temptation.*

She took one last look.

My uncle belongs to the new world. He'll fly away on a Zeppelin, and even when he comes back, he'll never return. And my aunt? I can see her on that early morning. She's climbing the stairs to the roof, lifting her arms up to heaven. Look! Look! At any moment, the sun will go out. At any moment, anything can happen.

Sofia drifts into their souls. She begins to see with their eyes.

WHAT THEY SAW

I

Everything took place just as she perceived it — of that, Sofia felt certain. She entered the souls of her aunt and uncle, as if her own spirit were unmoored from her body and she had no existence of her own. It was in the grace of that extraordinary time, she thought, to receive such a gift. She understood them and their hearts became hers.

"Read to me, *Paolo*."

The sun, Paul read aloud from his text, *is an ordinary star in size and mass. There are no doubt many like it in our vast galaxy of a hundred billion stars. While it was worshipped by Egyptians and Sumerians, we know it to be of no particular moment, except for the fact that it provides us with the warmth and light that make life possible on earth. It is no doubt for this very reason that eclipses were so frightening to primitive man.* Julia listened, a pensive look on her face. Paul leaned over and ran his tongue over her lips.

"Pass my quiz and you get more," he said.

"Test me."

"How long will the eclipse be?"

"Two minutes it will last," Julia said. "That's not counting shadow bands."

"Are you going to time them?"

Julia looked hesitant. "Ma's gonna get hysterical. Me outside in the cold."

"You let that woman stop you, I'll give you an F. So help me, I'll never sleep with you again."

Julia fell silent.

Paul took a deep breath, then reached for her hand and held it between his. "*Cara mia*, listen. Climb to the attic and stand on the roof. I'll show you how."

"Ma's afraid for me." She felt Paul kneeling beside her.

"Sometimes I'm afraid for you," he said.

"I don't understand."

"Julia, I'm your husband and this is not your mother's child." She was crying and he took her in his arms. *Julia, I want you to see the sun go out. I want you to hold it in memory as no one else can*, but these were thoughts that he didn't speak as he put his lips on hers.

He led her to the attic door and gave her the skeleton key. He showed her the steps — how to climb them with a cat's grace, with the silence of a ghost.

Sofia knew that her aunt was pondering Uncle Paul's life and the two extraordinary things that would cross its path — the moon's shadow, the airship's flight. While he waited for this day to come, Julia found herself desiring him again, as if she were waking from a long sleep. She'd wanted to show him kindness, to do what would please him. She bought a scrapbook and began to read the papers with care, clipping out the solar diagrams, the path of the total eclipse. *A proof of nature's orderly ways*, the newspapers said, and she found this reassuring. The first eclipse ever beheld by the white man in Manhattan. *No man will live to see the next one*, wrote the *New York Times*. She began to count. When the moon's shadow fell again on this city, her unborn child would be ninety-nine years old. She shivered, resting her hands where she thought his head might be, his eyes.

"God made the sky good," said Julia to her mother that evening. "The cold will not harm my child. Neither will the eclipse."

"God has never given birth," her mother said.

Nonna Constanza couldn't forbid her aunt to do anything — Sofia knew it. Until the moment when Uncle Paul asked Julia to climb up to the roof, her aunt hadn't realized the danger to her marriage posed by her sudden terror of the unknown. Since her pregnancy, fear had seeped into the depths of her like a moist trickle leaking into a basement. Her life swung between anxiety and lassitude, as if the unborn child were an opiate that tied her up in cravings, then left her in a stupor. All Aunt Julia cared about was holding on to the child. Normal — that was how she thought. She'd nod off, dreaming of her courtship, hearing the tappety-tap of a dancer's toes *keeping time* — an odd phrase when she realized that she couldn't hold on to anything, including the man who'd married her.

Thank you, Sofia, she'd think, *for telling me to dress up. You see everything and understand nothing.*

"Julia, these are modern times," Paul had said to her more than once. "Men are flying in airplanes, sending telegrams, making moving pictures as they fly. Nothing is going to be lost from the world, not ever again." Yet inside Sofia's aunt was a child, the only thing that mattered: a calendar, a timepiece, a human clock, the bearer of memory, a mortal being. It puzzled Julia that Paul, who'd lost a brother, didn't understand this.

2

The huge airfield stretched across the pine barrens of southern New Jersey — almost a desert. To Sofia, her uncle seemed as empty.

Inside the hangar, he was a dust mote in a vast cathedral, its huge archway letting in light. He was still astounded at his luck in being here. He was glad to be away — from Julia's moodiness, from her mother's interference, from his own father who muttered threats at his traitor son for flying on an airship built by the government of the Boche. Before they'd left New York, John Ames suggested that they stay overnight in New Jersey after the flight. *A little celebration*, he said. *A sailor's pleasures. Care to partake?*

He hesitated, thinking of Julia. Then he realized what he

wanted and that it was wrong and that he'd do it anyway.

By all means, yes, he said.

On the night before the eclipse, Sofia dreamed this, and when she opened her eyes, she felt as if she were still watching her uncle. She saw him standing in the gondola beneath the huge airship, watching the massive doors of the hangar as they opened outward into darkness. It wasn't yet dawn and the sky was indigo blue, the stars still visible. John Ames was standing next to him, peering out at the airfield.

"I like the feel of this," he said. "A thing that hasn't been done."

"Of being first," said Paul. "My wife'll listen on the radio."

"Have a look at the mob out there," said John. "We're royalty."

She saw a few hundred sailors in the ground crew — enough to launch this ship into the still air. Now they were guiding the huge Zeppelin through the doors, loaded with a cargo of several dozen men and a raft of scientific instruments. The crew was walking it outside, its engines rumbling, and her uncle could feel the momentum, the grand sweep of the dirigible as it began its passage out of the building. Around them, hundreds of men were alert for the mooring officer's yell, *up ship!* to loosen their hold on the guide-lines. Under the control-car at the front were sailors ready to toss it upwards; under the engine car in the rear, another crew would attach itself, running out toward the field, heaving it forward into flight.

As the nose of the Zeppelin slipped out of the hangar, a swaying cross-wind hit it from the side, lifting the sailors up

An Ordinary Star

on its guide-lines, floating upwards into the sky like flies in a spider's web. Straining hard, they pulled themselves back down again, and Paul could hear their officers shouting *don't let go!* Paul shivered. *Almost as if it has a mind and wants to fly on its own.* The pilot was struggling to force it down. Her uncle was chilled, his fists clenched tight.

"A few bumps," he said.

"They'll write it in the papers," John remarked. "*A near-catastrophe*, just wait."

"Blown out of all proportion."

"Of course."

Not an inch of the flying ship went to the wind. The force of the sideways gusts of air couldn't tear its skin or bend the ribbing underneath. In her waking dream, Sofia knew that it could have been a disaster. It felt as if *nonno* Domenico and Germany had, for quite different reasons, cursed this ship — its modern beauty, aluminum-skinned and gleaming. Someone had built death into its tubular inside, ribbed and cross-braced, girdered end-to-end — and yet it was an object that like the eclipse itself, could be compared in form and shape to nothing on this earth. An ineffable wonder; even so, it was frail enough to be swayed and toppled by a nudge of wind.

"Remarkable," said Uncle Paul as the ship floated into the air. "No cause for alarm."

"Expertly done. Yes. "

Awake and dressed, Sofia felt witness to a dream that wouldn't end. Six cameras and a spectrograph, the *Los Angeles* moving northeast along the Jersey coast before heading out to sea on a frigid morning; the rising sun a golden fleck in a vast blue eye that would soon blink it out. New York City was holding its breath, crouched and waiting for the moon's shadow as her uncle moved out to sea and toward Long Island Sound. The world below him grew formless, then disappeared.

Oh, Julia.

"Lighter than air, indeed," said John as he adjusted the spectrograph. *Lighter than the weight of trouble, yes,* Paul thought.

He'd set up his drafting board, the black disc in place for the sun.

He imagined Julia giving birth alone.

I want you to see the darkness. They would know each other then.

The airship crossed the north fork of Long Island, moving eastward past Montauk Point, to the south of Block Island. Forty-five hundred feet above the ocean, they waited.

If he weren't *nonno's* son, he would give thanks for so much grandeur — how it was that the sun and the moon conjoined in darkness like lovers. He would bless it all.

He didn't know how.

The subways were rumbling up from Manhattan and into the Bronx, their passengers bundled in shawls and caps and muffs, their white breath like car exhaust against the flame-blue sky. These people would stake out spots along Coogan's Bluff and Morningside Heights, on the rooftops of Williamsbridge and Belmont. Below him was water, a cloud bank, the horizon.

Julia, be with me. Climb on the roof.

An Ordinary Star

The airship was rocking, nudged by a soft pillow of wind.

"There it goes," said a voice. A black razor, nicking the sun.

3

"You will not forget this beautiful day," said Sofia's father.

Bundled up in capes and leggings, caps and scarves and gloves, Sofia and her brother Leo and their parents gathered at the southeast corner of Van Cortlandt Park at half past seven in the morning. Along with them were a crowd of friends and neighbours, Bronxites and folks from Manhattan who'd come here for one of the best views in the city. Parents were fiddling with cameras and smoked glass; kids were stomping and shuffling and rubbing their mittened hands to keep them warm. A few boys had climbed the oaks and sycamores beyond the clearing in hopes of getting the best view. Sofia patted her binocular case. She could feel the static crackle of excitement, everyone's breath chugging white steam, as if this crowd were a giant locomotive, anxious to depart for the eclipse.

Sofia and Leo were watching their father, his graceful hands adjusting the levers on his wooden contraption that would keep his telescope and camera tracking the rotation of the earth. *Dottore, che cosa fa Lei? What are you doing?* She heard it said over and over, as if her father were setting a broken bone — so mysterious and beyond the ordinary was everything a doctor did, including his recreation. Her mother stood beside him in her long beaver coat that she only wore on Sundays, her hair tucked under a knit cloche hat. From her pocket she pulled out a gold watch on a chain which she pressed into her gloved hands. She glanced at it.

"It's about to begin," she said. She beckoned to Sofia and Leo. From her purse, she pulled out a doily of fine crocheted stitchwork. She held it at arm's length and looked down at the snow. Through the doily's holes, dimming sunlight fell. Scattered at their feet were hundreds of tiny lit circles, a black nibble in each.

"Look, Leo, on the ground. See?"

"Those little black cut-outs are the moon?"

"They'll get bigger," said Sofia.

Along came Tina and Gabriella, waving bonnets.

"Pinhole doilies, you beat us to it." Tina rolled her eyes at Sofia. "You've got bi-*noc*-ul-ars. Big league."

"The light's starting to get *strange*," said Gabriella.

"Where's your aunt?" Tina asked.

"At home." Sofia felt a twinge of sadness.

"Your uncle's in the blimp, huh?"

"Near Montauk Point. Right on the centre line." Sofia felt proud again as she stared at her father's silhouette. Doctor Gentile looked like the captain of a ship, his hands steering the great wheel of the heavens. Silence gathered around him as he tracked his camera on the black disk, its crescent a dazzle of gold.

"He's driving through the *u*-ni-verse," said Tina. "In his Model T."

"A grand touring car," said Sofia.

"Daddy's rocket ship," said Leo.

"Look for stars," said her mother.

The sky began to darken.

4

As she rose that morning, Sofia could also feel Aunt Julia getting up, putting on her warmest clothing, tiptoeing down the hall to the attic door. Her aunt's movements were trance-like, as if she were falling into an old, familiar habit, one that her body knew how to perform without the consent of her mind. It felt as if Paul's hands were moving her upward, as if Aunt Julia were afraid. *God help me. If ma comes upstairs, she'll be furious, spotting me out on the roof.*

The night before, *nonna* Constanza had told Aunt Julia that she'd watch the eclipse from indoors. They said the rosary for Paul in the airship

"One I had stillborn," she said again.

"You told me. Yes."

"The air is bitter cold outside."

"I promised Paul."

Nonna shrugged. "Do what he tells you, then. *Solo in Dio si trovo sicurezza.* God will watch."

Let us celebrate, Uncle Paul had said. *The moon is going to pass before the sun.* It would be a holiday with rituals all its own — the rooftops crowded with families, with newspapermen and photographers. As for Aunt Julia, she was wearing Paul's old watch with a second hand. In her pocket was a notebook and a pencil. She'd told Sofia's mother that she hoped to write down the time when the shadow bands appeared and how long they took to make their ghostly ripple across the whiteness. *What a story for our child*, Sofia heard her aunt say. Scared she was, even so.

5

The sky turned ink blue and the wind rose.

To Sofia, the crowd of people jammed in the park was starting to feel like the ticket line-up at the RKO: whole families, capped and mitted, bundled up, stomping their feet — hey, there was Mr. Bernstein from the deli. *How'ya doing, honey?* He'd brought some fresh-baked crullers rolled in sugar and his own thermos full of hot coffee, and he passed his treats around to the neighbourhood kids. *Mom, is it OK to have one? If I split it with Leo?* The two of them sank their teeth into the warm dough, coated with sugar that had melted into the crust. *Yum.* It was so *cold* out. It would take another half hour for the moon's black disc to cover the sun. She and Tina and Gabriella finished their crullers and stood shivering in a huddle, their arms around each other.

In the noise of the crowd, there was silence where her father worked, oblivious to the cold. Every ten minutes, another photograph, a constant adjustment of the camera drive to keep the sun in view, safety checks of the filter over the lens. Her mother made notes.

As he worked, *il dottore* was attracting a crowd of onlookers.

"Che cosa fa?" "What's he doing?"

"He's taking pictures of the sun."

"The sun moves, so he has to move the camera."

"È meraviglioso." A wonder it was.

Mi scusi. A man moved through the crowd. He was carrying a large square camera with a huge flash, and Sofia realized that he must be a newspaperman. Earlier her dad had been interviewed by someone from the *Bronx Home News*, but he'd wanted to complete his photographic record of the partial eclipse and he didn't have much time to give the reporter. Sofia expected him to dismiss this new fellow, but her dad was gracious. The man was speaking Italian — he must have been from *Il Progresso*. He asked a few questions, took her dad's picture and handed him his card. Her father looked delighted.

"Figlia mia, he wants to see my photographs," he said. "They may publish one of them."

Sofia was awed. "Do you believe that?" she said to Tina.

"Of course. The sun's a bigger star than Gloria Swanson."

"And moonstruck, too," said Gabriella. They started giggling.

"There it goes!" yelled Harry Bernstein.

"Look up!" shouted her mother.

Ahhhh, a breeze of voices, and Sofia gazed at the silvery pearl of light swelling out of the black disk, and darkness fell. Blue darkness as the sun slithered behind the moon, its black face framed in a pinwheel of gauzy light. She stared the bright gleam of Venus in the sky and then she lifted the binoculars to her eyes. Grand and enormous the black sun was, all feathery halo and gems of ruby fire on its rim. *Look! Look! Look!* In her throat was the cry of all their voices, and into herself she gathered the eerie light, as if she were the lens of her father's camera and the shutter exposing his film. She passed the binoculars to Tina and Gabriella. *Quick! Look!*

She glanced at her father who'd darkened into a lone shadow at the edge of the earth. Everyone in the park had vanished and the sky was crowded with stars as her family drifted through the heavens and into a new world. Somewhere in this vast and empty sky was Uncle Paul in his airship. And Aunt Julia?

Up on the rooftop, raising her hands.

In the grace of this moment, Sofia knew that it was so.

6

Sofia also knew that by nine o'clock in the morning, the sky had begun to darken as the airship hovered, high above the sea. With men and cameras and instruments at their stations, Uncle Paul waited. She watched with his eyes. Darker it grew, night-dark and very cold, and as he looked toward the northwest, he'd see the train of the moon's shadow sweeping across the water and the face of the clouds. It was speeding at hundreds of miles an hour, a dark canopy, only moments ago over Julia's rooftop in the Bronx, over northern Manhattan, Connecticut, Long Island. He was tangled inside of it, clad in a robe of darkness.

Julia, look up.

The sky was a bird, a blue-black cormorant rustled by air; the clouds became gemstones, lit by opalescent flashes of yellow and purple, orange and red. Best of all, the sun was a vaudeville star with a vast, obsidian face — a star that thrilled the earth when it tossed out a boa of silken feathers and began to dance. *Coronal rays at twice the diameter of the sun.* Paul made estimates, sketching, his hands full of light.

7

Don't be afraid, Aunt Julia. Her aunt had recalled that the stairs weren't steep, not for anyone of ordinary size, but she was wrapped in a woollen coat and scarf, and she felt too ungainly for the narrow stairwell leading to the roof. *Just hold on to the rail,* she heard Paul tell her. *Up you go now, slow. Take care.* She took a deep breath, imagining the silence of the panther's step, and she began to climb. *Little one, someday I'll tell you this story, how I went out on the roof to see the eclipse for both of us.* As long as her mother didn't come up here, but she'd latched the attic door from inside. *You are twenty-four years old,* she heard Paul whisper, as if he were standing next to her.

Julia opened the door at the top of the stairs to a tiny rooftop porch, the kind of place you stood and hollered *fire!*

An Ordinary Star

Gripping the rail against the wind, she stepped outside. There was ice on the rail, on the floorboards; her foot, her gloved hand slipped. She gripped a metal rung in terror and she crossed herself. No, this was dangerous. She shouldn't be here.

She heard Paul's voice. *You let that woman stop you, I'll give you an F. So help me, I'll never sleep with you again.*

Tears froze in her eyes. Then she looked down.

It was early morning, and below her in the chill Saturday dark, thousands of people were crowded along the sidewalks and lined up on the snowy roofs of houses and apartments. There were crowds jamming Tremont and the Grand Concourse — enough for a parade, as if they were waiting for President Coolidge in his automobile, for flags and bands and the city police. It had been like this downtown when they went to see the Zeppelin, but now the dull weight of fear had fled, and she felt as if she might fly herself. Down below, hawkers were selling smoked glass. People were practising with Brownie cameras, scarved and mittened tots piggybacked on their fathers' shoulders, cold youths tugged on their caps, chugged steam, stomped and shuffled and jigged in their boots, clapping their hands in rhythm. Julia held the excitement in her hands, tasting its richness. A double scoop's worth packed into a cone — that sweet it was.

Bless this world.

She felt giddy with a lightness of spirit as if she might drift into the sky and she thought of her husband, hovering over the ocean, feeling at that moment as if she were about to untie some invisible rope and send herself floating above the city. If her neighbours looked, they'd see her. *Constanza's crazy daughter, what a disgrace, so big now, too.* She giggled, knowing that when she came down from here, her mother would be hysterical.

Oh, but forget it — the shadow's coming.

A bolt of fabric dragged along the ground, falling into the pleats and tucks of darkness in the hills — that's how the moon's shadow looked to her, billowing across the frozen expanse of snow until it touched her eyes. The sky fell into twilight, the colour of laundry bluing in the water, and when she cast her eyes around she saw a grey-and-white rolling and tumbling in the snow, like a motion picture of the ocean waves. Shadow bands — there they were — and every snowbank in the Bronx was alive and flickering in the light of them. Julia glanced at her watch, then saw the shadows fading as the sun blinked out.

She saw Mercury, then the morning star Venus, and then she heard people clapping and cheering below as the moon's disk sashayed in front of the sun — a stately, courting lover of a moon. Around the blackened sun was fire, and she stared. There was almost a taste to what she saw, cold and sweet to the tongue, as it was in childhood with the iceman's chips of light. She watched the corona fading into a silver circlet around the sun's occluded face. Hanging from it was a glittering solitaire, a diamond.

How can I hold you? She lifted her hands in the darkness.

There were cheers and applause below her, and Aunt Julia imagined the racket echoing across the hills of the Bronx and the flat beaches of Long Island Sound and rolling down the heights and slopes of Harlem. In her mind's eye she could see thousands of faces turned to the darkness, to the majestic sweep of the moon and the flaring cape of its shadow, to the sky as a grander stage than any on Broadway, with the moon an actor in the role of Night. *Everything is copacetic —* Bill Bojangles' face in the moon, the words the vaudevillian always said before he danced, the show they saw the day Paul asked her to marry him. *Yes, I will, Paul.* She was electric: a humming wire, a human telegram, Morse code clicking. *Saw sun go out stop Grand Concourse packed stop shadow bands diamond ring corona stop a splendid gift of God stop.*

She could feel her child. One kick after another.

Alive, alive!

Wanting to be born.

Too soon.

LIGHTER THAN AIR

I

"You have a new cousin," said Sofia's mother.

What a shame that Paul wasn't home, she whispered. *Two weeks early and such a difficult birth.*

"I warned Paul it could happen any time," said her husband.

"He didn't believe you?"

"He'd planned to stay out there overnight. They got back too late as it was."

After the eclipse, Sofia felt that a profound strangeness had entered the world. She began to realize the depths of nature hidden from her eyes, the mysteries she could only glimpse. How could the sun reveal its most splendid light in darkness?

And the moon's shadow — frail and ephemeral — how could it come barrelling into the Bronx at five hundred miles an hour? Nothing was quite as it appeared. In the special dispensation of that day, she'd had the gift of seeing and knowing what her aunt and uncle saw and knew. She wasn't convinced it was altogether a gift, that she'd realized her Uncle Paul would be celebrating like a sailor and that he'd chosen to do something wrong. Even so, it stunned her, that she was able to know it. For days she felt like whispering, as if the entire world had become a church.

The whole family came to baby Christopher's baptism — Aunt Julia, Uncle Paul, *nonna* Constanza and even *nonna* Rosa and *nonno* Domenico from Orchard Street. She noticed her grandparents entering the back of the church, glancing with trepidation at the candles, the baptismal font, the jar of holy oil and the priest in embroidered vestments. Apart from Mr. Bernstein, Sofia had never met anyone else who didn't attend mass or receive the sacraments. *They don't have one*, said her mother when Sofia asked what her grandparents' religion was. Her mother's tone of voice said that the question was no more polite than asking about an amputee's legs. Later Sofia found out that her Uncle Paul thought faith was unscientific, but he went to church from time to time to please her aunt. Her dad was the dutiful Catholic — the only one in his family. *Your father alone of the brothers was born in Italy*, her mother remarked. Sofia remembered that her real grandfather had been a soldier loyal to the king, a man no doubt quite different from the anarchist Domenico.

Rosa e Domenico — she'd never seen them happy. Their very names breathed sorrow as pungent and lasting as the odour of their foreign cigarettes. She knew that they'd brought their politics to America, along with melancholy she could almost taste. Sofia imagined them with their comrades downtown, declining sugar for their espresso so that it would be as black and as bitter as their conversation. Just the same, she found them more interesting than her other relatives.

Domenico was a shoemaker, a wiry man with alert, intelligent eyes and a voice like a watchdog's growl. He'd sit slumped forward, his rolled-up sleeves showing the knotted muscles of his arms, one hand gesturing with an unlit cigarette, the other making a fist to slam down. He had no use for *i Fascisti*, and Sofia never heard the word without feeling the *thud* of his hand, the rattle of china on the table. Today, so far, he'd said nothing. He looked uncomfortable in jacket and tie, clutching his cap, as if he wasn't sure what else to do with his hands.

"*Fa bene a scuola?*" he asked her. "Are you doing well in school?"

"*Sì*. Did you see the eclipse, grandpa?"

"It was beautiful. Yes." He paused. "And no one charged admission."

Unlike her husband, *nonna* Rosa could read, and sometimes when she thought she was alone, she'd open the newspaper, her finger slow in its pace along each line, as if she were about to sneak up and pounce on some unsuspecting insight. She was as gaunt as a feral creature used to hiding and stealing food, a dark-eyed woman with an angular face, unsmiling in the way of people who live from one crisis to another. It didn't surprise Sofia that she'd taken as a second husband a man so at odds with the world, so unlike her late Salvatore in his plumed hat. Unlike *nonna* Constanza and the other women, *nonna* Rosa seldom left the room when the men's conversation began. On weekdays she worked as a seamstress and on weekends she'd go to Union Square to hand out leaflets on birth control and get herself arrested. *For once I won't argue with them*, Sofia's father said to her mother. *Contraception is my parents' only good idea.*

Aunt Julia walked into the room with Christopher in her arms.

"*Che bello*," said *nonna* Rosa. She reached out and swept up the baby in a gesture as large as the room. "Julia, *cara mia*, are you well? Did they take good care of you?"

"Very. He was born on the night of the eclipse." She looked proud.

Nonna Rosa drew close to her. "If you need any help, come talk to me," she whispered.

Aunt Julia's eyes sparkled. "Soon."

"What are you two whispering about?" her mother asked.

"I am damaging her brain," said *nonna*.

"We're discussing the modern world," said Aunt Julia.

Nonna's *going to pass along some of Mrs. Sanger's leaflets*, thought Sofia. Her mind spun itself a fantastic cocoon of thought, as if some colourful insight might emerge and take wing. *Aunt Julia saw the eclipse from the roof. Uncle Paul flew in an airship. They're made of something different from the rest of us. They're lighter than air and they float.* They weren't afraid to pull the cork on life, to let it froth and bubble over into the world.

Except that you insulted your aunt. Sofia went over to her.

"I wanted to say — I'm sorry."

Her aunt pulled a stray hair from her baby's bunting. She straightened his blanket.

"I hope you can baby-sit for us."

You have nonna *to do that*, Sofia thought.

At least her aunt was speaking to her. She let Sofia peer at the baby. When he opened his eyes, Sofia shivered.

"*Che luminoso.*" Sofia's mother held the child. As if to cast a shadow, she passed her hand back and forth above his wide-open gaze. He didn't seem to notice.

"He's a dreamer, that's why," Aunt Julia said.

Uncle Paul had also changed. Gone was his beard and his wary look. The clean, sculpted lines of his face named him as a modern man — an aviator, goggled and helmeted, striding toward his airship. That older, Italian soul of his had gotten lost — a diaphanous thing, torn from his body the day the Zeppelin skirted New York and headed out past Montauk Point. She wondered what had become of the moment she'd asked him to dance — as if it, too, were lost forever. Once it had been easy to camp out in his soul. She sensed things were going to be different.

He grinned. "How's school, kiddo?"

"Fine, thank you." She frowned.

He gave her the thumbs-up. "Keep watching those stars at night." He turned to her father.

"I've been asked to publish a paper on the eclipse," he said.

"*Bravo.*"

"On my next flight, I'll take my son."

Aunt Julia stood up, waltzing the child around the room. "Not without me," she said.

"Cara mia —" Paul looked astounded.

"I have decided the time has come," said Julia.

"Brava!" Livia clapped.

Elio raised his glass. "To the first mother and child in flight."

"To female bravery," said Paul.

He loves her, thought Sofia. *Did the eclipse do that?* She felt a pang of hurt.

Imagine your soul has eyes, the priest had said. *Close them when you feel temptation.*

She did. But not for long.

He was out with the sailors, the night his son was born.

"Now I'll show you my pictures," said Elio. *Nonno* Domenico took the prints in his hands as if they were glass. He pondered each of them in silence.

"Well done," he said at last.

"A new camera," said Elio. "Made in America."

Nonno turned to Paul. "And you, did you take pictures also, up in that German airship?"

"Pop, it belongs to America now."

"Never mind." He continued talking to Elio. "The Boche kills your brother and sends us an airship. He's fool enough to fly in it."

No one said a word.

An Ordinary Star

"But you, Elio, have had these pictures in the paper."

"More than that, grandpa," said Sofia. "They're going to be published in *Rome*."

Silence. Her father looked distressed.

Domenico eyed him. "One son with the Germans, another with the Fascists."

"You should give Rome a chance, pop," said Elio.

Domenico slammed his fist on the table. "Have I no children left?" he asked. Paul went to put his arm around him, but he brushed him off.

"Papa," said Paul. "This is America."

"America's full of liars. You come with me, I'll show you what lying feels like."

"I will not."

"I will kill you."

"That's why I'm staying where I am."

"Excuse me, this is my house," said Elio. "There are women and children present in this room."

All the women got up to leave, except *nonna* Rosa. The men resumed their shouting. In the kitchen, the women sat down at the table, helped themselves to coffee and *biscotti* and continued their conversation. Sofia felt subdued, knowing it was her fault that the fight had started in the first place. After a while, the yelling stopped. Sofia tiptoed into the corridor, flattened herself against a wall and eyed the men from the entranceway. Her father and uncle were sitting at the table on either side of her grandfather, their arms on his shoulders. The old man's face was buried in his hands. Sofia wondered if he was still upset because of Uncle Guido. *Nonna*

Rosa was speaking, her voice low. *You still have Paolo and Elio*, she whispered.

When Sofia returned to the kitchen, her mother was rocking baby Christopher. Then she heard *nonna* Constanza's voice.

"He doesn't look at me, that child. He sleeps too much."

"Mamma, he's fine," said Aunt Julia. "I —"

"I am your mother. Don't answer me."

"I'll answer as much as I like!" Aunt Julia screamed. "Whose child do you think this is?"

Good for you, Aunt Julia.

Sofia's mother was trying not to smile. *Nonna* turned her chair so that her back faced both her daughters. With her big arms folded, she looked like a massive boulder, impervious to storm and wind. Her aunt walked around to face her. She took the woman's hands.

"Mamma, listen to me."

"Not when you talk like that." *Nonna* pulled her hands away.

"I'm sorry I shouted. You must realize —"

"You are not worth hearing."

"The child is having tests," Aunt Julia said. "Elio has found a specialist."

"Specialists cost money. You'll end up in the poorhouse."

Julia stroked her hair. "Mamma, you are so contrary."

"My feet are killing me. Do I go see a doctor?"

"Here — rest your feet." Aunt Julia pulled up a stool. "What would you like? More coffee?"

"*Sì*. Not too much sugar. You always put too much."

Nonna *in English is spelled n-u-t-t-y*, thought Sofia.

After the guests had left, her mother spoke to her. "Your father should have told you not to mention Rome," she said.

"How come?"

"Because *nonno* doesn't like the Fascists."

"*Nonno* doesn't like *anybody*."

"Be respectful," said her mother.

"Last time it was the imperialists. Before that, the Bolsheviks."

"Sofia —" Her mother paused. "His life has been very hard."

She explained that Sofia's dad had invited her grandparents to come and share their home, thinking that trees and a backyard garden in the Bronx would lift their spirits. Only *nonno* had told her father that their true comrades were on the Lower East Side, not in the bourgeois north end of the city. "Along with their memories, what few they have in America," her mother added. "And poor Uncle Guido, his memory, too. So they will stay where they are."

Sofia heard what she didn't say: *Thank the Good Lord.*

Sofia overheard a lot of things, including her dad telling her mother that the specialist's report would come in mid-week. It was a few days later that Dr. Gentile came home from his office, his footsteps as quiet as snow falling on snow. He didn't speak at the table, and his silence was a tight thread in the soft weave of their conversation. After dinner, Sofia went upstairs and heard voices coming from her father's study. She tiptoed up and put her ear to the closed door. She knew she wasn't supposed to do this, but she told herself she'd walk away if it were none of her business. She didn't like feeling shut out of her own home.

She heard her father's voice. *The ophthalmologist's report* and *blind* and *she didn't seem troubled, your sister.*

Impossible, Sofia thought.

Her mother spoke. *We have to convince mamma that it wasn't the eclipse.*

Sofia felt disgusted. She remembered the sight of *nonna's* hand bearing down on Aunt Julia's stomach, and she thought that if anything had cursed the child, it was that ignorant old woman. She tiptoed downstairs to her room. *How could baby Christopher be blind?* she wondered. He looked as if he'd swallowed the sun, as if light were dazzling his eyes.

The following day her mother told her what she already knew.

"He'll have to go to a special school," she said.

"Where?"

"I don't know where."

Sofia had never travelled further than Manhattan, and so she imagined a special school in the *terra incognita* of Upstate New York, the same bleak wilderness where Sing Sing Prison was. Poor Christopher would be sent to live in an institution, without the comforts of home and family. It sounded like a lunatic asylum. She felt chilled.

Not so long ago, she'd confessed to the priest that she'd imagined her aunt slipping on ice, the baby dead. She'd realized that her soul was a dirty mirror and that the sacrament washed the dirt off and let her see who she was. Peering into it, she'd seen that she was like *nonna*. Slights and insults she chewed on like bubble gum, then blew up to enormous size. Then she'd imagine revenge. So she knew how satisfied *nonna* would feel when she heard about baby Christopher — how smug she'd be. Only first she'd get hysterical.

Except for *nonna*, theirs was a normal family.

She didn't want to be like her grandmother, or to see her aunt and uncle stricken with grief. Her father had said something strange to her mother. *She didn't seem troubled, your sister.* Sofia was puzzled. *Maybe the test didn't work on Christopher*, she thought. *Too much light coming from his body. Maybe she knows that.*

I guess we're not so normal after all.

Then she saw her aunt fly.

Time ebbed away, two or three months of it, into a morning when Sofia was walking up Gun Hill Road, near the edge of Van Cortlandt Park. She felt a stirring of wind, then saw a smudge of light, an apparition coming into focus — a woman with a green cloche hat and dark, rippling hair. It was her Aunt Julia and she looked like spring, here to sprout grass and prod the trees into leaf. *All the way up from Tremont Avenue*, Sofia thought. *Maybe spring comes there first.* It was early May and Saturday — too early for strollers in the park and spring was late in coming, but just the same her aunt wore a green tunic and skirt and a yellow scarf around her neck. She was pushing Christopher in the carriage and as she approached the park bench, Aunt Julia stopped. With a graceful sweep of her arms, she scooped up baby Christopher and then — flew.

Like a leaf in the wind — spinning, then floating — her colours the same as the tulip-tree flower with its waxy green leaves and golden inner folds. Sofia recalled the grand pleasure of collecting a skirtful of these fat, messy blooms in the grass before her mother yelled *basta!* She laughed, then started running.

"Aunt Julia!"

Sofia chased her for a few yards, but her aunt and Christopher vanished into air. Puzzled, she went back to the park bench. The baby carriage was still there, her aunt's green cloche hat on the blankets, so she sat and waited for the two of them to return. The warm sun seeped into her bones and she felt drowsy. She dozed off, and when she opened her eyes, she glanced over at the carriage, at her aunt's hat lying on the coverlet. Something was wrong with that hat — it had grown larger. She went to look and she saw that the carriage was overflowing with tulip-tree blossoms — their green petals birdlike, as if they, too, were about to fly away. *They're not even in bloom yet. They don't even grow in this part of the park.* Mystified, she looked up at the bare trees.

As she sat on the park bench, Sofia recalled telling her friends that Christopher was blind.

"After all those prayers?" Tina paused. "Maybe it was my fault. My smart-aleck remarks about burning down the church."

Sofia didn't think that had anything to do with it.

Gabriella agreed with her. "He may be gifted," she said. "Maybe *we* can't see *him*."

"He looks all lit up," said Sofia. "He just doesn't look — *blind*."

"Maybe he isn't," said Gabriella.

"The specialist said he was."

"Who knows? He might see something we can't."

Sofia mulled over Gabriella's words as she sat waiting for her aunt, and she wondered what part Christopher might be playing in these odd events. She thought to sit and mind the baby carriage, but she'd promised her mother that she'd shop before the stores closed, and it was now three o'clock. Had she been here since this morning? She made her way down Gun Hill Road to Burke Avenue, and the long shadows of the day troubled her. It had seemed no more than an hour ago that Aunt Julia had drifted away in the park, and now there she was up ahead, dressed in soft green and yellow, pushing her baby carriage through the door of the Budget. *Why is she shopping here?* Sofia followed her inside, but by the time she'd bought sugar and eggs and flour for her mother, her aunt and the baby had vanished, as silent as air.

AL NUOVO MONDO

I

A framed newspaper clipping of the sun in eclipse hung on the dining-room wall, flanked by photographs of two dead soldiers — Sofia's late Uncle Guido with his telescope and her dad's lost father, the plume-hatted Salvatore Bruno who died in Abyssinia in 1896. The photo of the black disc surrounded by a feathery halo was first published in New York's *Il Progresso*, then transmitted to Italy and printed two weeks later in *Il Popolo d'Italia* in Rome. Its caption read *L'Eclissi del Sole, 24 gennaio 1925 alla città de New York. Questa fotografia di dottore Elio Gentile* ... Sofia knew the words from memory. *Cittadino americano che è natto a la città di Bari.* An American citizen, born in the city of Bari.

She could feel her father's eyes on her.

"Italy has *blossomed*," he said.

Sofia was fifteen years old and she pictured the crocuses by the front walk, their strength and resilience after a winter's sleep. It was a Sunday afternoon, and her dad sat at the head of the table in suit and tie, a tiny garnet on his tie-clasp, a gold ring on his finger. Behind his glasses, his eyes had a probing, gentle look, as if he were sorting through a patient's symptoms. He addressed Sofia.

"*Dimmi, Sofia*, the father of Italian music."

"Palestrina."

"*Bene.*"

He opened the anisette, poured it into a tiny spoon, then stirred it into his coffee. He spoke to her younger brother.

"Leo, your turn. *Il nome del Duce d'Italia.*"

He grinned. "*Troppo facile, papà.* Too easy."

"*Signor Troppo Facile?*" Their father laughed. "Can you name one of his achievements?"

"*Sì, papà.* He printed your picture."

"*Figlio mio —*" Elio tried not to smile. "It was printed in *Il Duce*'s newspaper. He's not the editor. *Signor* Mussolini didn't send me a telegram. You mustn't brag."

I wish he had, Sofia thought. At work on a project for her history class, she knew that a telegram from *Il Duce* would have impressed her teacher. There was no need for his comment, said her father. It was praise enough that Italy's leader had seen this photograph, since the pursuit of science had deep Italian roots.

"Tell me about Galileo," he said to her. "What did he discover?"

"The moons of Jupiter," said Sofia.

"Leo, what else?"

"Sunspots."

Her mother was listening. Although she came from the city of Bari, Livia had been brought there for adoption after losing her parents in an earthquake. She'd been taken to America, yet she seemed to be drifting back toward that long-ago calamity, its fires still burning, light and shadow flickering in her eyes. *We have no graves to tend*, Sofia's father often said. *We cannot show respect.* Even their American dead were buried elsewhere — Uncle Guido, born in Manhattan, was laid to rest in France. Sometimes her dad would reach out, as if to grip an invisible railing on a flight of stairs. How surprised he'd look — horrified to find nothing there. It was as if he had no history, as if he were falling through the sky.

"Shall we continue the quiz?" he asked. "Italian literature."

Leo grinned. "It's Sofia's turn."

"Dante's great work, *Inferno*," he said. "Can you quote the opening lines?"

Sofia began:

> *"'Nel mezzo del cammin di nostra vita*
> *Mi ritrovai per una selva oscura*
> *Che la diritta vita era smarrita …'"*

She felt as if she were in the shadowed woods, lost on the path that had disappeared. *Who are we?* She glanced at the photos — at her parents' shattered mosaic of the world, its cracks repaired with painstaking care at these Sunday dinners. Only now there was also the image of the solar eclipse on the wall and the portrait of baby Christopher in his mother's arms — the strange child who could upend gravity and trouble the order of time. She felt awed that he could do this and that she could apprehend it. *I have decided the time has come*, Aunt Julia had said. Not long afterwards, she began to leave the ground.

Perhaps she'd imagined everything.

"You recite very well," said her father.

"*Grazie.*"

"However, *figlia mia*," her father continued.

She sat up straight, her hands folded in her lap.

"You've been lost in the woods for the past ten minutes."

Everyone laughed, including Sofia. Only she felt troubled that it was so obvious.

Every Sunday, there'd be another short quiz about Italy and its restoration to a place of honour in the world. Sofia was always prepared, but she found it difficult to stay with the conversation, to leave her tangle of contradictory longings. Hoping to become a teacher like her aunt, she'd stare with anticipation at the books that lined her father's shelves — medicine and history and Latin. As she heard the magnificence of Caruso's voice in her parents' recordings of Verdi and Puccini, she felt as if she dwelled in the heart of a great longing, a desire that was destined to be satisfied. Yet because she was born in New York City, she was haunted by an ethereal thing — the silver airship, the avatar of progress, the vessel that would carry humanity from the old world to the new.

Only she had no idea to which — or what — world she belonged, for as she learned facts, she saw ineffable wonders. Nothing was as it appeared, as if massive boulders were made of wool and the limpid sky were a sheet of glass. Everything partook of a strangeness so absolute that she'd step back from a bud about to bloom, knowing it might flower in a baby carriage if it chose. She thought of Christopher pulling her aunt above the ground, wondering if that were connected to her uncle's flight in the airship and her own father's photograph and its voyage by wire to Rome the Eternal. *I did it because Italy is our mother*, he'd said. *She waits for us to return.*

It's not so simple, she thought.

The following week her mother's face would begin to grow pale, evaporating like the mist of rain in sunlight. Yet on that Sunday, Doctor Gentile was pouring everyone wine, raising his glass in a toast *al nuovo mondo*, to the new world. *To the real world*, thought Sofia. *Whichever one that may be.* Yet she was grateful for her family, and she savoured the taste of this moment when neighbours dropped by after church, when the children sat in silence, absorbing the talk of politics and history along with coffee-sugar, spooned from the bottoms of their demitasse cups. Many years later, she remembered this day. She recalled how, long ago, the life of the world was as fragrant as a ripe fig, as rich as *cannoli*. How once they were almost happy.

2

Aunt Julia and Uncle Paul and Christopher came by after dinner. Under her uncle's arm was the *Journal of Aeronautics*. "Look at this!" said Uncle Paul. The periodical had printed his eclipse studies. Navy officials were delighted, he said. They wanted more publicity — they'd invited him on board again. Aunt Julia swept Christopher around the room.

"We're flying around the *world*," she said.

"Not with the Navy," said Uncle Paul. "*Cara mia*, we'll find a ship that'll take you, also."

"*Et tuo figlio.*" She glanced at Christopher.

"*Et mio figlio.*" He tickled his chin.

"Are you going to fly to Italy?" Sofia asked them.

"The *Los Angeles* is a model commercial airship," said Paul.

That's no answer, she thought. Perhaps they didn't *want* to go to Italy. She couldn't imagine why not.

Afterwards, Sofia asked her father if her aunt and uncle were going to fly to Rome.

He smiled. "That wouldn't surprise me."

"Will they take us?"

"Some day. Maybe. Yes." He said all of these words, each more certain than the one before, as if the contours of a hidden dream were taking solid form as he spoke. Sofia imagined flying across the Atlantic, a four-day journey to the heritage of her parents. Her thoughts came in Italian, and she pictured herself reading at an ornate desk in the Villa Medici in Rome, immersed in the grandeur and power of the ancient city, then donning a commoner's clothes and meandering through piazzas and churches and the labyrinth of alleyways and back streets. It embarrassed her to be so lost in imagining, as if some real Italian might peer into her mind, then expose her as a befuddled tourist, an American *poseur* with no claim at all to this heritage. After all, she'd arrived in Italy by airship, and how could anyone with a passion for speed belong to so civilized a culture?

With some relief, she returned to the world that knew nothing of this inner life.

At Evander Childs High School on Gun Hill Road, they expected even the girls to do well. Sofia decided to prepare an Italian scrapbook for her history project. Her father let her read his magazines and journals until she decided on her topic: *The New Garibaldi*. She wrote these words on the cover in fancy script, and underneath them she pasted a photograph of Benito Mussolini which she clipped from the front page of

New York's *Il Progresso*. For a caption, she wrote: *La Religione, La Patria e La Famiglia.* She described *Il Duce's* March on Rome in 1922, citing the dictator's achievements, quoting praise from *The New York Times* and *The Saturday Evening Post*. "Italians are proud of their country's return to stability and order after the chaos of the World War," she concluded. She showed it to her father.

"I'm glad," he said, "that someone in this family is paying attention to world events. To reality."

He must be mad at Uncle Paul, she thought. As she imagined her uncle floating off in his airship, she had an idea.

"May I include a copy of your photograph?" she asked.

"Of the eclipse?" Her father looked hesitant.

"To show how Italy reaches out to America," she said.

The photograph went on the last page.

On Sofia's report, her teacher noted: *An Italian leader who knows the meaning of hard work. Laziness has been a problem for his people.* Miss Walton gave her an A+, then asked her to enter her work in a citywide essay contest. At home, Sofia showed the mark to her dad. He seemed tired. He'd come home that evening carrying a carton of eggs and a chicken.

She'd never heard him say *My patients don't work hard enough. I can't buy coal with eggs.*

"*Felicitazioni!*" said her dad.

"Don't Italians work hard?"

Her father smiled. "She means *Il Duce* is running Italy with American common sense."

"Does America have such a thing?" asked her mother.

"As common sense?"

"Life is too fast in this country," she replied.

"Common sense is back in style," said her dad. "The Twenties are almost over. *Figlia mia* —" He looked at Sofia. "*Tu hai fatto bene.* Just do me a favour, please. Don't tell your grandfather what you've written. Not a word about Rome. Do you understand?"

She glanced at the picture of *Il Duce*. "*Sì.*"

"Promise me."

"Will Uncle Paul be angry if I tell him?"

He paused. "No. He will not be angry."

He sounded puzzled, as if he wasn't sure. *My brother doesn't care enough to be*, his eyes said.

Sofia said nothing to her grandfather. Miss Walton entered her essay on *Il Duce* in the city schools' competition and it placed first. Then Sofia learned that the president of the Sons of Italy was going to present her with a citation. She knew it would be a great honour, but Signor Roberto Castelli was a colleague of her father's, and she felt certain that his presence at the ceremony would have as much to do with her subject — and her father's photograph — as with her award.

Sofia's mother was making a dress for her to wear to a celebration party. *Classmates only*, she promised her. *Nonno will not be there. The Castellis may drop by, so I want you dressed up.* Her mother looked frail and drained of colour. She was sitting on the edge of the chair, her lips pressed together, her eyes intent, a sewing basket beside her.

"Hold still."

She measured the length from shoulder to hem, from the

hem to the floor. This was a pretty garment made of white organdie, a sash at the hips and no waist to measure. Sofia didn't breathe as her mother adjusted the tape, folded the fabric, inserted each of the pins. She felt like a mannequin, as if she herself were half-finished, as if her mother were patching her together out of scraps of fabric.

"Am I standing still enough?"

"*Shhh*. Talk makes everything move."

Within this enclave of silence, Sofia was measured and pinned, then chided for the occasional imperfection, for the alterations to the pattern that her shape required. Few things caused Sofia to feel so poorly made as her mother's fitting her for a dress. She wondered if it were possible for the human form to meet the standard of these patterns, to conform to their arcane code of dots and arrows and broken lines. She pondered the meaning of *absolute*, as in *absolutely still*. She held her breath.

"Just relax. As you would stand."

She wasn't sure how she'd stand. At school assembly, everyone stood with eyes ahead, shoulders back. Along the Concourse, working girls strode like boys. As for herself, she preferred to float down Gun Hill Road, her feet skimming the ground. Maybe these dress patterns no longer conformed to the modern world, where time and space were all tangled up. She'd never told her mother how she'd seen Aunt Julia shopping on Burke Avenue, adrift above the sidewalk. Her mother was sewing for a girl who walked on earth.

Sofia imagined herself in three dimensions — standing, sitting, drifting through space. With her mother's help, she slipped her arms into a half-made garment bristling with pins. She learned attentiveness.

"I began to sew when I was a child in Bari," her mother said.

Into the pieces of the dress, she pinned her recollections of a narrow, hilly street not far from the Basilica of St. Nicolà: a stucco house, its inner garden fragrant with oleander and jasmine; a harbour full of fishing boats and the blue Adriatic. *Which is why I love the rivers of New York*, she said. *I see my home in them.* Sofia listened.

"If it was so pretty," she asked, "why did you leave Bari?"

"Because you don't ask questions at the age of eight," she replied.

"Will you go back and visit?"

"Leo might," she said. "He wants to go to sea."

"Will you let him?"

"Your father says that first he goes to college. If he earns enough to buy a steamship, maybe then."

"He cannot leave us."

"We will not be together always," she replied.

Sofia went to her room and began to remove the fragile chrysalis of paper, fabric and pins. She began to feel a shifting of the world as she imagined their home empty, their table abandoned to cobwebs and dust. The pins caught in her bare flesh. She brought the dress back to her mother.

There was a cleanness to assembly at Evander Childs that Sofia liked — students attired in shirts and middy blouses, washed and pressed and starched crisp as a sea breeze. The girls wore neckerchiefs and the boys wore ties, both of these in navy, adding sobriety to the blaze of whiteness. All right arms rose to salute the flag; then everyone sang "The Star-Spangled Banner." Sofia felt part of the American eagle, about to lift its wings.

First woman President of the United States, Tina whispered. *I can see it coming, ta-da.*

Will you be Vice-President? Sofia whispered back.

Depends on the vice, kiddo.

For this occasion, there were two speeches, one from a Mrs. Grady on the Board (who referred to Fascist Italy's fine example of civic virtue in a decadent world) and the other from Mr. Castelli. He was fair and well-dressed, of medium stature with a noble profile that reminded Sofia of Caesar Augustus. In front of the audience he turned to her and said, "You're a daughter of Italy, and your learning will one day be an inspiration to your husband and your children." She received a certificate and five dollars from the New York City Board of Education, along with the medal and citation from the Sons of Italy. "Oh you are so *smart*," whispered Tina. Gabriella had made her a card from scraps of coloured paper and ribbon. After school, they took Sofia to Bernie's Delicatessen and treated her to an ice cream soda.

Her mother was in the audience. That evening she gave her the gold ring with the cameo, the one she'd coveted.

"So you'll always have me with you," she said to her.

"I'll never take it off," said Sofia.

On the mail-table in the front hall was an envelope addressed to her. Inside was a note with a picture of the airship *Los Angeles* pasted to one side. *Dearest Sofia*, it read.

Congratulations on your own "high flight," for you've made us all proud of your achievement. With Love and Fond Wishes, Your Aunt Julia. Uncle Paul had also signed his name. Sofia thought of *nonno* Domenico. She could hear the thud of his fist crashing down and then her father's voice in her head. *Cara mia, not a word to him.* All the same, her dad was very proud of her. She'd brought great honour to her family.

"Later I'll have something to give you," he said.

Her father often said that Benito Mussolini would restore the legacy of ancient Rome. Mindful of this, Sofia was puzzled when her dad pulled down a volume from the shelf by the Englishman John Burckhardt, who in the early nineteenth century had discovered a lost city. He showed her the map. *Arabia Petraea*, a great Roman province sprawled across Palestine and Syria. The next page showed the ruins of Roman Petra carved in the rock cliffs, its beautiful colonnades still intact.

"Lost for a thousand years," her father said.

A once-prosperous desert city founded by the Nabateans, conquered by the Romans. Lost, then rediscovered.

"It didn't fall apart?"

"The Arabs built it in the Roman style. The Romans were brilliant engineers."

Sofia promised she would read the book.

"I would like you to read all my history books," he said.

"I will. *Grazie.*"

"When we leave this world, this will be your inheritance."

Sofia felt troubled, as if the gravity of his wishes were a

thief, there to steal away her unlived life. The new world with its elegant airships and marvellous inventions receded into the background, and she felt encircled by a high wall, like a tiny seedling in a Roman garden. Trapped by the earth, she looked up to see her aunt and uncle, enamoured of the sky, drifting away. She didn't want her parents' legacy — not yet. It was too soon to tend to their burial plots, sweeping the stones and weeding the grass, placing flowers on the graves on their birthdays, lighting candles on All Souls' Day. She didn't want to see her father's hand shaking as he held Mr. Burckhardt's famous book. She didn't want to hear the sorrow in his voice.

"Everyone is leaving us," she blurted out. "Mamma gave me her ring."

"That doesn't mean she's leaving us," he said.

"Aunt Julia is. I saw her fly."

She waited for her father to laugh, but he said nothing. He looked sombre, as if Sofia had raised a subject of the utmost gravity. At last he spoke in his most gentle voice. "No," he said "You only think you saw her fly." Knowing he could sense her puzzlement, she didn't contradict him. He was silent, and then he spoke again.

"Your aunt and uncle are in pain, *figlia mia*."

"Because of Christopher?"

Her father didn't answer as he handed her the book.

"They suffer from their illusions," he said at last. "What you see is illusion and suffering. *Capisce?*"

She didn't understand, but she thanked him for his gift.

Her father always read after dinner, and it had seemed to her that in the lamplight, his face was transformed into a younger man's, the lines softening into a calm recollection of a lost world. His book felt like a holy thing, its solid weight a comfort. What was written here would last. Only Mr. Burckhardt's words would never float down Tremont Avenue, never be gripped by the outstretched hand of a child, never invite her to gaze at the stars, never fly away.

4

Uncle Paul would fly. Not once, but several times with the *Los Angeles*. What they did on those flights remained a mystery to Sofia — the fine-tuning of radio compasses all along the eastern seaboard at Manasquan and Fire Island, Amagansett and Cape May and Bethany Beach — but Uncle Paul did none of that. He flew and wrote. *Workaday science*, he explained to his family. Sofia found his reticence unsettling. *One has only the pleasures of flight and experimentation*, he insisted. *The layman wouldn't enjoy these trips.* Maybe he was trying to discourage Aunt Julia's interest. *Your aunt and uncle are in pain*, said her father. She wondered if Uncle Paul's restlessness was the cause of their suffering.

It's our interest he wants to discourage, said her father. *Uncle Paul does serious writing and he doesn't trust the papers.*

They turn the ordinary into a spectacle. Uncle Paul even discouraged them from travelling to Lakehurst, New Jersey to view a launching. *I have to be modest with the privilege they've given me,* he said. *I'm a civilian flying with the Navy.* In due time, there'd be a special airship flight to garner the best publicity, he told them. A grand occasion — they could come and watch the launch.

Then for a moment in 1927, everyone forgot about airships.

"*Bravo!*" her father shouted when the radio announced Charles Lindbergh's crossing of the Atlantic. He leapt up, grabbed her mother and swung her around the room. "*Bellissima*, we're going to fly to Rome," he said.

"I'll lend you my kite," said Leo.

"*Figlio mio*, you should think about a career in aviation," his dad told him. "One day, man will cross the ocean in twelve hours."

"Too fast," said Leo.

"Everyone in my class wants to fly," said Sofia. "Even the girls."

"Centuries ago, Leonardo Da Vinci worked on flight," said their father.

"*Il Duce* can claim it for Italy." Leo stood tall, clenched his fist and thrust out his jaw.

His dad frowned. "That is disrespectful."

"Yes, sir."

He sighed. "Read, please, so you don't talk like a *cafone*." He handed his son the latest issue of *Il Progresso*. It had a two-page report on Italian industrial achievements under the Fascists. Leo took the paper and sat down.

"Italy has no need to lie," said his father. "The article lists many accomplishments. Memorize five."

Sofia wondered why her brother had been so provocative. By now he was a compendium of *Il Duce's* achievements learned under duress. On the other hand, she was struck by her father's untroubled look, as if he didn't realize the futility of his efforts. A new wind was stirring the air — no more than a breeze of ideas and inventions, but she sensed that one day it would blow into a fierce storm and then a hurricane. In the midst of it, Leo would leave home, she'd marry and her parents would grow old. The family's table of respectful conversation, of Italian culture and learning would end. Life, it seemed, was a kind of flying. Everything flew away.

"Will and Discipline take to the air," said her brother a few days later. "Meet Leo Lindbergh, Fascist Flyer." He clicked his heels and saluted.

Sofia shushed him. "Are you trying to get killed?"

Leo smirked. "I'm trying out. For the circus."

Their father came home that night with a newspaper from Italy which reported that Mussolini was thrilled by Lindbergh's feat. He'd written to America's ambassador in Rome: *A superhuman will has taken space by assault and has subjugated it.* 'America and Italy have linked arms and are marching forward together: progress joined to tradition,' said the editorial.

"What a magnificent insight," said their father.

"What hot air," said Leo later to his sister. "Lindy could fuel his airplane with it."

An Ordinary Star

"Shhh."

"It's true, though."

Sofia felt troubled, knowing it was.

Early in the following year, Uncle Paul was invited on a flight to the Panama Canal Zone. *The Navy needs some good publicity*, he'd explained to her father. *They've set up a new mooring mast in Panama — a short one.* The previous summer, there'd been a near-disaster at Lakehurst. Wind caught the *Los Angeles* so that it swung around its tall mooring mast in a huge circle like a windmill blade. *Now they want the public to come to view the launches*, said her uncle. *They want everyone to see for themselves that the ships are safe.*

The family travelled to New Jersey to witness the launch of the enormous dirigible, its silky pleats inflating into a beautiful ship of the air. Christopher, now three years old, was clutching Aunt Julia's hand. She crouched down beside him and let her arm rest on his shoulders, as if she were trying to weight down his slight body against the force of the wind. As she watched the airship, Sofia could sense her cousin growing lighter. Then Aunt Julia scooped the slight child up into her arms with effortless grace, as if she were lifting air. The two were dancing, their feet above the ground, swirling like a pair of leaves caught in an eddy of wind.

At that moment, hundreds of sailors were leading the ship from its hangar, and in the gondola she could see the figure of Uncle Paul. The sailors yelled *up ship!* as they let the great Zeppelin slip out of its tangle of cables and rise upward. Uncle Paul waved, then disappeared as the airship drifted, cloudlike, into the sky. To Sofia it looked as if Aunt Julia and Christopher were being pulled along in its wake. Faster they swirled, in an invisible spiral upward, until they, too, had vanished. Sofia waved goodbye to the air.

"When you see Aunt Julia," Sofia said later to her mother, "ask her where she went."

Her mother looked puzzled. "She was with us all morning."

"But *afterwards*."

"Afterwards we went home, *cara mia*."

Time had collapsed on itself, crushing years into the dust of a single moment. That's what happened. Sofia had no idea why, or what it meant, but she felt certain that Christopher had something to do with it. Afterwards, everything was different, and the movement of time was changed forever. Time flew faster than Lindbergh, slower than winter, then cranked itself up to varying speeds, then down again: an automobile, a motion picture, a train on the tracks. What happened when? As Sofia's mother weakened, her father's hair began to grey, and he became old in a few short weeks. Time bounded ahead, fell like snow, slipped like water through her cupped hands. One evening, she heard her father on the telephone. "I cannot come to the meeting," he said. "I have urgent family matters to attend to." She wondered what year it was and whether the war had begun. There were fewer quizzes on Italy. Maybe the war was over. Her father's papers and journals piled up, unread — thick with dust and spun with cobwebs, until the paper crumbled into a fine white swirl, then disappeared into the dust of Babylon. Her father grew old, a brittle leaf. The wind carried him away from her. She is old now, and the wind blows him back.

LIVIA

I

Figlia mia, no one has forgotten Rome, said Sofia's father. *Remember these names: Gaius Julius Caesar. Marcus Tullius Cicero. Horace. Ovid. Virgil. Catullus. I will teach you and you can teach your brother.*

"Doctors *have* to know Latin," said Leo. "And their handwriting has to stink."

"*Leo Caesare*, keep your voice down."

He opened his Latin book. "This beats Benito."

"Quiet. Tonight we're doing defective verbs."

"Infected," he'd grin. "With what disease?"

"Amputated endings. Serious."

"Doctor Sofia, this is not your field." Fifteen year-old Leo had mischief in his eyes, a mess of black curls, freckles and a smile that never left his face, the kind that lingers after a good laugh. When he walked into a room, he almost danced, and the air seemed to crackle with electricity, then music, as if a radio had turned on by itself. Sofia thanked God for his joviality, for without him there were not many laughs to be had. In 1933, the banks and the stock market were fraying like bad wool, and almost none of her father's patients could afford to pay him. Even so, Leo wore his sailor cap and bold striped shirts. He tried not to think about breadlines. He managed to do well in school.

"Tonight I can't concentrate," he said. "I'm planning a trip."

"To the poorhouse?"

He laughed. "To Montreal."

Sofia had never heard of the place.

"It's in Canada," he said. "A beautiful old city. They speak French, but some Italian, too. Closer than Europe." He dropped his voice. "I would like to leave home," he whispered. "Breathe some fresh air."

"But Leo, there's no *money*."

"I can work as a porter on a train," he said.

Sofia was shocked. "You don't listen to the news? There's no *work*."

"I can find a way. *Imperator navis*, that's me. *Caesare*." He grabbed her hands. "There's a shrine up near Montreal," he said. "Maybe the church will organize a trip."

Did Leo have a fever? Puzzled, Sofia scrutinized her brother's face. His lightheartedness had faded as daylight does before a storm. She felt afraid.

"One day," she told him, "we'll go to Italy."

"Italy's a mess," he said. "There's gonna' be a war. I'll see Italy from a battleship. Mom's gonna' die, we're gonna' get old real fast, and we'll never even get to Long Island, let alone Montreal. We'll never be young again, don't you see that?"

"Mom's not going to die," Sofia whispered.

Leo put his arm around her. "I didn't mean that."

It was too late. Her mother, still alive, became a ghost.

What did he mean, there was going to be a war?

Sofia stopped teaching Leo and decided to be more attentive to their ailing mother. She suffered from a weakness in the blood (or so she'd gathered) and Leo didn't understand that for a woman, this was commonplace. Their mother, more fatigued than usual, had decided to quit work for now. Sofia became her father's receptionist. At night she'd read in the living room, joining him in the lamplight. She followed *Il Progresso*, its headlines praising *Il Duce* and Italy's grand *risorgimento*. Leo stopped joking with her.

2

Sofia's mother looked as chilled and brittle as a bottle of milk left out on the stoop. She was at times almost invisible. She wasn't supposed to tire herself, was instructed by her husband not to run too many errands, but she couldn't bear to be in the house all day. Doctor Gentile's office was on Gun Hill Road, and, at noon hour, Sofia would walk down the hill, sometimes heading south on White Plains Road toward Burke Avenue. On this particular day, she saw her mother from across the street. Her bonnet, in any case — its fistful of red cherries. She'd just stepped out of De Lucca's Meats. In her hand was a small parcel wrapped in brown butcher paper and tied with string. *Cold cuts — I could have picked them up on the way home*, Sofia thought.

Her mother was standing halfway under the awning, half

of her sun-bleached, as if the rest had already dissolved in the heat. She was carrying her cloth shopping bag, and Sofia hoped she wasn't planning a run to Leone's for rolls. She decided to catch up with her. She crossed the street, following the red cherries on her bonnet, moving through the crowd, looping back toward the intersection at White Plains Road. The bakery was a block away. Just as she was thinking *it's too warm a day for her to be walking at noon*, the light changed and the hat with the cluster of cherries sank down into the crowd of shirtsleeves and padded shoulders like a rock in quicksand.

Someone yelled *police!* A crowd had gathered where her mother had collapsed and fallen face-down on the cobblestones, her hat askew, blood oozing from the side of her head. A man was kneeling beside her, daubing at the blood with his handkerchief. A cop hurried into the crowd. *Did she get hit?* he asked. *She fell, that's all*, said a woman's voice. *Like a brick*, said another. *Stepped off the curb and down she went.*

Sofia struggled to get to her. *Excuse me, I'm her daughter*, she said as the crowd parted to make room. All these strangers would wonder why she didn't stop her mother's fall, why she'd let her run that errand, why she didn't see ahead that her mother might exert herself in such a foolhardy way. She hurried over to the officer, who went to a call box and phoned for an ambulance. It arrived a few minutes later, a squat black vehicle as sombre as a hearse, the word *Ambulance* painted on the side in bold and careful letters, like a proclamation of some sort. Sofia didn't like everyone watching her distress, didn't like the thought of a hundred or more people sitting on their stoops tonight, shooting the breeze with *yeah, I was there, I saw it. A woman whacks her head on the cobblestones, blood like you wouldn't believe.* Then they'd gripe about the Yankees' losing streak and the mess at City Hall. Her mother's suffering should have more weight than this.

They took her north to Gun Hill Road, then west to Montefiore Hospital. The policeman drove Sofia. She was still clutching her mother's shopping bag.

That was all she remembered of that day.

Sofia asked her dad why her mother had gotten so dizzy that she'd tripped and fallen unconscious. More than this, was it such a serious blow that she'd have to stay in the hospital? He seemed uncomfortable, as if she'd asked him about some private female matter. *Her blood's weak*, he'd say. *It's always been that way and even so, she's never been one for sitting still.* Or he'd say *she needs more iron. The hospital can provide that. So can I*, Sofia thought. *I cook liver and onions and greens.* She told Tina that her mother was in the hospital.

"What's wrong with her?" she asked.

"Anaemia," Sofia replied. *But I don't want to know what's wrong.* The thought kept spinning and flashing, warning her of danger.

Tina lowered her voice. "I'll say a prayer."

Remembering their school days, Sofia had a better idea.

In the plaza at the front of Holy Name Church, Tina stopped, dug into her bag and pulled out a matchbook. She held it up in front of Sofia. "All the candles you can light," she said. "For free."

"*Tina.*"

"C'mon, Sof. It's your *mother*. This is *big*."

"But we should —"

"Pay? Get outta here."

Sofia couldn't imagine it. She dug in her pocket. "I have some change —"

"And God needs nickels for what — the trolley?" Tina yanked her arm and pulled her up the stairs.

The stand held fifty vigil lights. Tina stabbed the air with her finger, counting.

"Thirty unlit," she whispered. She handed Sofia a matchbook.

Will anyone stop us? Sofia wondered. Father Mario or the sacristan could stride in and demand payment from two working girls. She looked around. There was no one in the church. She knelt, then struck a match. She lit one vigil light, blew out the match, then lit another. Each struck match made a gritty scratching noise, the sound echoing and swelling through the nave of the church, the loudness rumbling in Sofia's ears like a load of coal making its way down the basement chute. She worried that the sacristan would hear the noise, that someone might come running in to stop them. Yet the more matches Sofia struck, the braver she got, and for each of hers, Tina lit two. Sofia was enthralled.

Mamma, you are going to get well. She felt a chill

determination but she couldn't think of a single prayer. She clenched both aching fists as if they might otherwise explode. Her mind conjured up a newsreel image — *Il Duce* and the Blackshirts' march on Rome.

She wondered if God had left the world.

"I said a decade of the Rosary for your mother," said Tina.
"Thank you." Sofia laughed.
"What's so funny?" asked Tina.
"What we did."
"Didn't I tell you it would be OK?"
"Do you think anyone will notice?"
"Only God."

The following day, Sofia dropped by the church alone. As she approached the side altar, she noticed that all of the vigil lights had been extinguished.

Sofia make her way down the white-tiled halls to the room where her mother lay under a sheet, her head wrapped in a gauze bandage. She was as white as the enamel bed frame, as the bedpan by the wooden table. The skin on her cheeks was translucent, and through it Sofia could see the frail blue patterning of her veins. Her mother's face made her think of a wilderness map, blank except for the blue of the rivers. Afraid of that thin, veined net, she imagined a thing her mother loved: the Hudson flowing into Spuyten Duyvil Creek and the creek flowing into the Harlem that became the East River before it met the sea. In them she saw the true map of her mother's life, its path through her adopted city. Yet the boats had left the river and the sun bled in the west. Her mother's colour was seeping away.

Her mother opened her eyes and smiled at her.

After each visit, Sofia spoke to Leo. "Mom's fighting hard," she'd tell him.

One day her mother was conscious enough to speak. "I'm proud of you," she said to Sofia.

She wanted to touch her mother, but she felt afraid of her brittle skin and its blue etching of rivers, as if her body had begun its return to the soil from which she'd come. Sofia didn't want to put her hand to such a mortal creature, one so ready to embrace the earth.

She made herself do it. Hesitant at first, she let her hand rest on her mother's forehead, touching wisps of her auburn hair, absorbing the pallor of her skin. Such a thin covering, this snowy whiteness, yet it felt as if her mother's skin were dissolving into the warmth of her hand, drawing in sun as the soil did in early spring. Nothing stood between them — nothing at all. Her mother's breathing was even and she slept.

That evening, Tina called to ask how she was.

"She's full of hope," said Sofia.

The following day, Sofia opened the office without her father. He'd asked her to cancel his morning appointments so that he could visit the hospital. An hour later, Father Mario arrived. She understood why he had come, and then he told her. Early that morning, her mother had passed away.

Sofia paused. "I never guessed how sick she was."

"She didn't want to scare you," he replied.

"I don't even know what she died of."

The priest looked perplexed, but his eyes were kind. "You never asked your father what was wrong?"

"I tried. I was too scared."

"Do you know what cancer is?"

"I think so."

"It spread very fast," he said.

The visitation was at Malazzo's Funeral Parlour on White Plains Road. There were candles by the bier where Sofia stood with her father and brother, flanked by the wreath of chrysanthemums sent by the Children of Mary and the bouquet of white roses from the nurse at her father's office. One by one, the mourners approached — distant cousins, parishioners, patients — most of them weeping. The only dry eyes were *nonna* Rosa's. After she embraced Sofia, she stood back and held her at arm's length.

"*Figlia mia*, I see you're brave," she said to her. "Like your mother."

"*Grazie.*"

"The world is full of suffering. Don't spill your tears too soon."

"I don't cry much."

"Your mother served humanity. You can be proud." *Nonna* Rosa gripped her shoulders like a comrade's.

Nonno Domenico greeted Sofia also. None of the men looked at ease. The only exception was Uncle Paul, tanned and confident, striding right up to the bier to pay his respects.

A few moments later, he turned to one of his cousins. *I've just bought a house on Long Island*, he whispered. *For almost nothing.* The words didn't register on Sofia. She could still feel her mother's dissolving into the warmth of her hands.

Aunt Julia embraced her and stroked her hair.

"Are you going to fly?" asked Sofia.

She'd heard her father say that her aunt and uncle had wangled places on the *Graf Zeppelin*, of all things. In the midst of the Depression and bereavement, her aunt and uncle were going to sail on the most luxurious airship on earth — from Lakehurst to Rio de Janeiro, then back to Chicago for the World's Fair. They'd relax in plush seats, in a dining room with fine china and crystal, crowded with celebrities and champagne. *They're not Mr. and Mrs. Hearst*, said her father. *Just the hired help.* Even so, it felt wrong, so soon after her mother's death.

Uncle Paul would write for his science journal and send dispatches to the *New York Times*. Aunt Julia would tutor two schoolchildren. They were taking Christopher.

"But he can't see," said Sofia.

"Not as we do. No."

"*Nonna* is going to have a fit," Sofia replied.

"I will not let *nonna* rule my life."

Aunt Julia was shedding her own mother like a winter coat in spring. While Sofia mourned hers, the air was astir with the rumble and purr of the airship's engines, with the old world passing away.

3

Mornings were no longer beautiful. Yellow with sunlight, they cracked open, spilling her into a day's hard work. Time didn't pass in the ordinary way. It moved like a disgruntled passenger in the subway, pushing Sofia from behind, shoving her through the turnstile from one day to the next. Otherwise she wouldn't have moved at all. She had no idea what to do with herself, other than her mother's tasks — cooking and shopping, keeping house and doing mending, making the most of her job as a receptionist, putting aside money for Leo's education. She read little and worked hard, sometimes moving with lumbering slowness like an older and much larger woman. From time to time, she'd remember that moment of grace when she melted through her mother's skin and nothing stood between them. Little by little, the memory began to vanish.

Then she'd remember Aunt Julia and Uncle Paul.

The mail came with a postal stamp — *Graf Zeppelin — A Century of Progress* — pressed into paper as brittle as a moth's wing. Sofia read.

> *August 12, 1933*
> *... I cannot begin to tell you what a wonderful experience this is. Imagine the great slanted windows of the gondola, affording fifty-mile panoramas of land and sea. On board are twenty passengers ... First Mate Ernst Lehmann is a delightful man who plays the accordion. Christopher is wild about him because he gave him a lesson or two ... he loves the sensation of floating in the air. High in the clouds we dine on linen tablecloths — with flowers and crystal and silver and china edged in cobalt blue and gold. Such tasty German food — roast goose, steamed apples, boiled potatoes and custard. We float in silence, with no sensation of speed, although we are traveling at eighty miles per hour. In this lightness, we cast enormous shadows.*

Before leaving, Aunt Julia and Uncle Paul had moved to Long Island, but *nonna* Constanza decided to remain behind until she could sell her house. Times were bad and there were no buyers, so she settled for renting out the upstairs flat. *Two daughters in the ground and one up in the air*, she'd complain to her tenants as she swept the halls. *I am the only one who walks on earth.*

At least *nonna* was keeping busy.

So was Sofia. Life grew quiet as it tiptoed past her. She feared that if she waited long enough, she'd become as passive as her aunt had been before the birth of Christopher. Or as nasty and unkind as *nonna*. At the age of twenty-two, she had no boyfriend and little hope of meeting one. She was poor at small talk, worse at dancing. Her friends who'd watched her win honours at assembly had long since gone on with their lives, including her best friend Tina, who was now a nurse. When Sofia went shopping at the Hub, she'd see girls in stylish dresses flirting with boys at the RKO or shopping at Alexanders. She thought they were featherbrained. In her honest moments, she knew it was their lightheartedness that made her ache, and not their weightless thoughts.

As for herself, she had no thoughts at all. Lightness had disappeared from her life. Her aunt no longer floated across Tremont Avenue or flew in the park or crushed the seeds of time into the fine dust of a single moment. There was no money for her education and she couldn't finish high school. She felt like a heavy loaf of bread, chewed and eaten by every passing day.

Aunt Julia wrote her another letter.

August 16, 1933
... As we approached Florida this morning, we were made mindful of the troubled state of our world. Because of the change of German government, Adolf Hitler has compelled the Graf Zeppelin to fly with the

swastika emblazoned on her portside fin. Dr. Eckener (our captain) disapproves of this, but he cannot say a word ... Thousands of people approached the airfield to see us land today in Florida. We have more than adequate police protection, so don't be concerned about rumours that the airship might be attacked. As it is, whenever Dr. Eckener shows off the Zeppelin to the public, he flies clockwise so that the port side with the swastika cannot be seen.

She showed the letter to her father.

At dinner, he ate little. He tried her soup and *insalata*, a small helping of *vitello*. His face seemed like a barren field, its topsoil blown away by twisters.

"Hitler disgusts me," he said. "This time, *nonno* is right about the airship."

"Because of the swastikas?"

He nodded. "And now Italy's playing along with Hitler. How foolish."

Leo almost dropped his spoon into the soup. Sofia watched as his thoughts floated above his head like a word balloon in a comic strip. *Italy — foolish? Did I hear right?*

"Italy has better things to do," her father continued. "In Africa."

"That disgusts *me*," said Leo.

Don't start a fight, thought Sofia.

Her father spoke in a quiet voice. "Britain, France, Germany, Belgium," he replied. "They've all made claims."

"Stealing diamonds," said Leo. "Gold, too."

Sofia cleared the table, brought out coffee and *biscotti*.

"Italy deserves her share," their father said.

"Not exactly a light to the nations," said Leo.

Elio shrugged. He picked up the newspaper and went back to his reading.

Sofia cleared the dishes. She'd begun to imagine herself as one of those indulgent women with swaying hips and an enormous bosom, her legs in black stockings, her swollen feet in laced-up shoes. As if lassitude were her true inheritance, she began to feel at home with the softness of her flesh, her rounded stomach, her slowness getting up and sitting down. At night, she oiled and perfumed her body and her thick, black coil of hair. *Some man is going to love this. But who?* She stood with regal bearing, like a queen.

She imagined Aunt Julia and Uncle Paul returning from their voyage, her uncle trim and tanned, her aunt smart and elegant in suit and leghorn hat. She herself would be dressed in black, the curls of her dark hair escaping from combs and hanging loose on her damp, warm skin, her voice soft with teasing and idle laughter. She'd run her tongue across her lips and gaze at Uncle Paul who'd flush, trying to pretend he hadn't seen. She'd make them supper, shuffling in with the hot food and out with the dirty dishes. *You work too hard, cara mia*, her aunt would say — excusing herself to go to the *powder room*, as if this were a luxury airship. Uncle Paul would smile then, leaning over to kiss her lips. She'd pull away and laugh.

Afterwards Sofia would get out her sewing basket and begin to open the seams on her dresses. *What are you doing?*

Aunt Julia would ask. *What does it look like?* she'd say as she undid her mother's work.

We will be returning next week, her aunt wrote, but Sofia felt sure she'd meant some other kind of week, not the one described by calendars as seven days in length. They'd come back, the two of them, but they wouldn't return. She had lost them. From time to time she'd imagine making love to Uncle Paul as the sound of engines faded in the distance.

STEFANO

I

Time fled, and the loss of her mother ebbed away into other sorrows. Sofia felt certain that her own suffering was nothing compared to the parents of the Lindbergh child. She was beginning to feel resigned to such unfairness, as she was to her more ample size, her soft breasts and thickening legs, her slowness in climbing the stairs. Now and then she read about Hitler's Germany as the *Graf Zeppelin* went humming across the Atlantic toward the tropics, bearing vacationers and sacks of mail and the swastika on its portside fin. Her aunt and uncle would fly that route from time to time. Letters came from Aunt Julia, and also from her uncle. *Cara Sofia, I think of you often,* he wrote in his cramped hand. Sofia took her time savouring his words as she read and reread his airmail letters, tying them together with a scented ribbon, kissing the packet and hiding it in her bureau drawer.

One Saturday morning, Sofia came home with a load of groceries. She emptied the bags, made tea and buttered herself a fresh biscuit. Just as she bit into it, Leo walked into the room.

"Don't say hello," he said. "The food comes first."

She made a face. "You work like I do, then you'll eat like I do."

"Pop doesn't eat at all. He's so depressed, he doesn't even give the Fascist salute."

Sofia glared at him. "Don't you speak that way about your father."

"Hey sis, you're getting to be like *nonna*." He held out his arms in front of his stomach. "*Mangia*. Next you'll be wearing black all the time."

Sofia stood up and stared him in the face. "Who cleans for you?" she asked. "Who shops? Who makes the food?"

"A miserable sister, that's who." Leo socked one fist inside the other. "*Madonn'*. One day I'll be gone and Pop'll be dead. The house'll be your grave."

Sofia swung with her hand and slapped him as hard as she could. He looked stunned as he touched his cheek. Then he started to laugh.

Sofia was crying. "You have no respect."

"Not if you want to ruin your life, no."

"My life is fine."

"Hey, Joe Louis. Heavyweight contender." He started hopping up and down, sparring with his fists. "One, two, three ..."

"You aren't funny."

An Ordinary Star

"You aren't *happy*."

Sofia couldn't argue with that.

They called a truce and Leo invited her to a concert at the church hall. "Your kind of music, sis," he'd said with a wry look. "Nice and sweet and refined."

Sofia didn't apologize.

She was sorry she'd lost her dignity by striking him. That was all.

As she dressed for the concert, she saw that she was striking in her roundness — the curve of her hips, her soft eyes, her clear skin fragrant as summer. She'd styled her gleaming black hair in an elegant twist, put on gold earrings and heels with ankle straps. She felt strong — grounded and resolute, round as the earth. *I'd like Uncle Paul to have a look at me.* This time she imagined him patting her hip while Aunt Julia, pregnant and swollen like a ripe melon, stayed home with *nonna*. The thought of sex with her uncle came rumbling through her, vanishing like summer thunder that brought the relief of rain.

Just once. I could borrow him, like a library book. She wondered where she'd get the nerve. She put the thought aside.

The parish hall was a basement. Its walls were unadorned, except for portraits of Saint Francis and Saint Anthony and a framed photograph of *Il Duce*. At the front of the room was a crucifix alongside a lithograph of Pope Pius XI. Below was a rise flanked by the flags of the United States and Italy. Facing it were rows of wooden folding chairs. *Not exactly Carnegie Hall*, she thought. She looked at the programme.

Stefano Fiore, Violinist. Born in Apulia, Italy, he was awarded a scholarship to study music at the Julliard School in Manhattan.

When Stefano Fiore made his entrance and began to play, Sofia listened, rapt. He was playing Mozart, Haydn and Brahms and the music drew her into a light-headed trance. She began to imagine her uncle's touch, but she pushed the thought aside. She felt like an insect moving toward a flower of great delicacy and beauty. She felt sated and content.

"Did you like that?" asked Leo.

Sofia's mouth was dry. "I think it would be polite to thank that man," she said.

He grinned.

She found herself walking toward the front of the hall, a damp handkerchief clutched in her hand. *I wanted to tell you how much I enjoyed your music*, she thought. *My father also loves the violin.* Stefano Fiore stood up to greet her as she approached him. He had thick, black wavy hair and his eyes set in an angular face were tranquil and kind. Sofia opened her mouth to speak, but courage melted on her tongue. She tried again.

"Your music was beautiful."

He thanked her, but his smile was rueful. "I would like to do this more often," he said.

"Aren't you a performer?"

No, he was only a student, he told her — one who was grateful for his night-watchman's job so he could study music by day and maybe teach when times got better.

"Do you have a favourite composer?" he asked her.

"Verdi."

An Ordinary Star

"*Bravo.* Do you know the *Requiem?*"

Of course she did; her father used to play the recording. Her mother had loved Italian songs — the works of Caldara and Scarlatti. Long ago she'd sing and play them on the piano — *Sebben, crudele* and O *cessate di piagarmi.* As a child, Sofia would hear them in her sleep.

"You're fortunate," he said, "to have music around the house."

Sofia was puzzled. He seemed to be saying he'd missed this in life.

"Don't your parents like music?"

Stefano hesitated. "My mother does."

Sofia told him that she'd lost her mother.

"You're lonely for her, yes?"

She felt in his calm and steady gaze an immense compassion. "Yes, I am," she answered.

He'd found himself that music gave comfort, and there were concerts in the city that were free. Maybe she'd like to join him sometime, if her father didn't mind, and of course, he was welcome to come, too. Sofia said she'd like that, knowing that she meant something beyond music or even his interest in her friendship. Something about his reticence invited her to draw close, as if her inner life were a hearth that might warm them both. She'd caught his hesitation, seeing in his pained eyes a careful man, spare with words, as a cook might be with a rare spice. Born in Italy, Stefano Fiore came with a bandage wrapped around his soul. She found it disconcerting that it made her want him.

2

Sofia and Stefano would often picnic by the Bronx River with Tina and Gabriella and their boyfriends. At other times they ferried alone around the tip of Manhattan where they'd sometimes see airships floating above the earth. They made her think that lightness — like prosperity — was just around the corner, in some grassy field, waiting to lift everyone into the skies. On bright blue days, the dirigibles cast enormous shadows, longer and darker than any skyscraper's. They drifted with a kind of stately indifference, and Sofia imagined that the airships were the gnomons of giant sundials, casting shadows that didn't tell ordinary time. While they hovered overhead, life stopped going anywhere. Everything stood still.

Sofia wasn't sure how she felt about this.

The largest objects ever made, she'd heard her uncle say.

Whales play with their shadows, wrote her aunt on one of their voyages. *Cara mia, what could be more beautiful?* Sofia recalled how afraid Aunt Julia had been at the first sighting of the *Los Angeles*. Now it was she, Sofia, who was fearful.

Safety, after all, had fled from their lives. It had turned out that the suspected murderer of Charles Lindbergh's child was a neighbour. A Bronx resident, he'd lived on East 222nd Street — right across from Tina's grandmother. Hauptmann would go on trial that summer — ten years after the solar eclipse that held New York like a candle in the dark. So much grace was given, and where had it gone? She said this to Stefano.

"You don't have to make sense of everything," he said.

"But I want to."

"But you can't." He paused. "For myself, I trust in — magic."

"Magic?" Sofia felt sure this was a mistake in English. It puzzled her that a man who'd come to America as a child would still have an Italian accent, could still get the occasional word wrong.

"You don't mean 'music?' " she asked.

"*Magia*, magic, *sì?*" He took her hand. "So I'm going to show you, because you doubt."

He invited her on an excursion downtown — not far, as it turned out, from where *nonna* Rosa and *nonno* Domenico lived. From the subway stop at Spring Street, they walked a block or two east to Mulberry, a name Stefano had liked as a little boy. He took her down narrow little roads, shadowy even in daylight — storefronts and stoops jammed together, noisy trucks wheezing and coughing exhaust, deliverymen yelling *andiam'!* at their buddies, throwing crates of fruits and vegetables down on the curb. There were cages full of squawking chickens, and the air reeked with the nauseating warm-blood smells from the butcher's, the rancid stench of garbage and motor oil. Too much traffic, too many people — all of it foreign and yet enticing in its rawness. But not magic.

Stefano Fiore had come to America in 1918 with his Uncle Vito and Aunt Francesca. Today he stopped in front of a tenement building. "My uncle helped me up this stoop, see?" He touched the concrete, and then he touched her cheek, and she thought of the priest putting ashes on her forehead in Lent. *From dust we have all come*, she thought. *Over the places where the dust arose, we hover in the air still.*

"Have you been downtown before?" Stefano asked.

"My grandparents live on Orchard Street."

"*Veramente?* We are lucky. Shall we go and visit?"

"If you like to argue politics." She made a face.

"Are they socialists, your grandparents?"

"Anarchists."

Stefano laughed. "*Povera* Sofia. Do they plant bombs?"

"*Shhh!*" She looked around. "They were suspects once, but the police let them go," she whispered. "My dad's still embarrassed. They still get arrested now and then."

"*Si, capisco.* But should they embarrass *you*?"

Sofia paused. "They don't embarrass me," she said.

"*Bene.*"

"Neither do my parents."
Stefano was silent.

A mild day, a spring breeze blowing west off the river, so they walked across Canal Street, then south on Broadway, past the clothiers and haberdashers, jewellers and shoe shops, past the occasional pushcart-peddler selling red-hot frankfurters and ice-cold lemonade, roast corn and chestnuts. It was a cluttered part of town full of strollers and the piquant smells of street food, along with sidewalk bins crammed with used books and household bric-a-brac. This neighbourhood held nothing wondrous or unforeseen — only the comforts of things that never change much. Sofia liked that.

As they approached Chambers Street, the buildings on Broadway were taller and more polished, as if they were dressed for Sunday and there were seven Sundays to a week. Ten years earlier she'd stood here with her aunt and uncle, looking west at the enormous airship gliding behind the Woolworth Building. Afterwards the office windows opened wide and out of them rippled paper snow, drifting down in dreamlike slowness, as if the city were a crystal paperweight, turned by an unseen hand.

"Now *that* was magic," she said to Stefano.

"And I will show you more magic. Come." He took her hand and they strolled eastward through City Hall Park and toward the Brooklyn Bridge. "Here, look," he said. "When I was a child, it was solace, this bridge. Better than church." He'd loved its gothic arches, its air of serenity. He said its cables were a lyre for the wind.

"You have a wonderful imagination," she said.

"But you've seen miracles."

"Never."

"That solar eclipse of yours? It was a miracle."

"It wasn't," she answered. "There's a scientific explanation."

"You're very hard to convince."

They walked to the ferry terminal at the south end of Battery Park. Stefano grabbed her hands. "Sofia," he said, "There was a miracle that happened that day, or a great act of magic, I'm not sure which. The twenty-fourth of January, 1925. Right here, on this ferry dock at the tip of Manhattan. I was here and I saw it."

She was perplexed. "The eclipse wasn't even *total* down here," she said. "What could you see?"

"A great bulge of quicksilver light, near the moon's disk."

"The diamond ring?" Sofia was baffled.

"*Sì.*"

"Not with a partial eclipse. That diamond would have been invisible."

"Then what did I see, *cara mia?* Believe me — I saw it. So did a reporter with *The New York Times*. He was standing next to me and he wrote it up in the paper. I've checked astronomy books. You are right. No one's written of such a thing — ever."

"And you missed the total eclipse."

"I know. All my friends saw it and I did not."

"But why?"

"I'd come here early, to meet the ferry from Ellis Island," he said. "With my aunt and uncle."

"And on it were —"

"My parents. They got off the ferry, they were standing on this dock with their valises, right over there and before I could run to them, they became *nebbia* — fog. Lifting over the water, into the sun."

"But Stefano, that's —"

"Crazy, *sì*, I know. They are in Italy. But I *saw* them. They did come."

"They sent me on ahead," he told her. "They had influenza and could not travel."

"That's a long time ago. 1918."

"What are years?" he asked.

In his words, she could feel time folding backwards, then looping across space like a bolt of cloth drifting this way and that in the wind. Then she understood that time was a garment that would gather you up in its length and breadth, that would warm and protect you and never disappear. All tangled up in a mesh of years was Stefano — pulling away from a dockside in Italy, watching his parents vanish.

"They are always before my eyes," he said.

For an instant, she wondered where she was.

How peculiar everything felt, as if Sofia didn't know the Battery at all, as if she had to acknowledge some new-found strangeness in the ordinary grass and the wooden park benches and the ice cream stand next to the line-up for the boat ride where kids yelled and laughed and begged their parents for a scoop of chocolate. It felt as if she were seeing this scene through someone else's eyes. She could feel the ghostly presence of Stefano's parents emerging as a skyline does when the fog clears. Whether or not his words were true. Whether or not they came.

They bought tickets for the ferry that sailed past the Statue of Liberty. Stefano wanted Sofia to see how that beacon looked when he'd arrived by ship in America. As the boat entered the bay, he leaned against the rail. "You have to understand," he said. "Italy is going to war. That is why I am thinking about my parents."

Yet here it's safe, she thought. *That's what he wants me to understand. Water slapping the sides of the boat, water dousing fire.*

"My father would like me to fight with the Fascists."

"But you're an American."

He shrugged. "He says it's because he loves me."

"Then why has he abandoned you?"

"I tell you, *cara mia*, he has not. My parents dissolved into the salt air." Stefano reached into his pocket and pulled out a letter. "This speaks better than I can," he said.

Mio Caro Stefano, figlio d'Italia,

> *My Dear Stefano, Son of Italy. How good it is to hear an account of your life. You told me that you admired the police in New York City. As you know, that is my job, also. This is why I am not able to be with you. I have important work to do for Italy. I hope that one day you'll be at my side to help me. Remember that you belong to the noble history of Rome, and it is to*

us that the world will look for guidance in these times of peril.

"When did he send you that letter?" Sofia asked. He showed her the date.

"Nineteen *Twenty-Five?*" She was astounded. "Ten *years* ago, he asked you to fight."

Time had Stefano all knotted up, like yarn in a cat's paws.

"I have not forgotten my own father," he said.

"Maybe you should."

"Forget him? *Cara mia*, a parent's love is for always. And a son's." He pulled from the envelope an Italian flag pin and a cloth Fascist emblem. "My mother sent me these," he said. "On Mulberry Street, I was the envy of my friends."

"Does she want you home, too?"

She could hear waves lapping at the boat, but its gentle rocking felt like the undertow of something terrible and hidden. On the deck, passengers were chattering, but the noise drifted off into an odd and angry buzz, like a telephone left off the hook. The buzzing grew into a loud, insistent drone. She thought of a warplane, of a noise that swallowed sound itself.

"My mother is dead."

"I'm sorry," she whispered.

"I think I should go home to Italy. But they will draft me if I do."

"Maybe one day, you'll go."

"I couldn't go to her burial. It's two months since she died, and no telegram did my father think to send. *'Found dead in the woods,'* according to his letter. Then I got another letter from my cousin. '*Never mind what your father says. He had another woman. He also had a pistol.*' So I have lost my mother. I cannot even pay my respects."

Sofia felt chilled, as if this secret threatened her, too.

"I brought you here to tell you," he continued," so that I could throw these words into the sea. The wind will blow them back the way they came."

It doesn't work that way, she thought. *No wind can take them back.*

He leaned against the ferry rail, took the pin and the Fascist badge and threw them into the waters of the bay.

"Are you keeping that letter?" she asked.

"I cannot part with it."

"Do you miss him?"

He looked away. "I don't want to believe about my mother."

Day was fading as the ferry made its way back. The city lights were not yet on and the bay was calm. "Sometimes I cannot remember the year," Stefano said. He embraced her and kissed her lips, and she parted them so that she could taste the salt of his tongue, the very air he breathed. She could feel his arms gripping her as if the boat were about to capsize, as if they might drown.

3

Sofia went to her room in the evening, and from her trunk she pulled out a folder. In it was her essay, *The New Garibaldi*, its title inscribed on the cover in a large and childish hand. She found the certificate from the Board of Education, then the medal from the Sons of Italy. Nine years had passed since she'd received it, and its weight felt insubstantial, as if it had grown smaller over time. No — it was she who'd distanced herself, moving away from the safe harbour of her own life. She picked up the essay, holding it close to her face, breathing the fragrance of those Sunday dinners, laden with Italian food and lore. Gone forever was that moment when everything was just about to happen and yet at the same time would always remain as it was.

Yet she'd been drifting out of this harbour for a long time.

Its most recent escapee was her aunt, floating across the sky with Uncle Paul and their luminescent son; and now Stefano, whose lost parents were with him in light and the taste of salt air. She hadn't considered that life might blow with a stiff wind, sending her out on a perilous ocean, away from a place of safety.

Even now the thought was only a vague intimation. What other world *was* there? The great airships flew over the shade trees and clapboard houses of Barnes Avenue and Maywood Road where passers-by, worn down by bad times and empty pockets, would lift their eyes, smile for a minute, then return to the cares of everyday. The women who walked to The Budget and De Lucca's Meats would look up at the passing shadow as if it were a cloud, and so would the hot chestnut peddler and the seltzer-man and the fellow who sold Sofia chickens from his truck for almost nothing because he had so little business. Who knew what thoughts passed through their minds, preoccupied as they were with so much trouble? Those men in the neighbourhood who were lucky enough to be employed worked in the familiar stores on Burke Avenue or Gun Hill Road, except for those few who rode the el into Manhattan, a place where time — by Stefano's reckoning, at any rate — moved in dizzy collisions, or not at all. When change came to Williamsbridge in the Bronx, it was supposed to be as unobtrusive as a leaf unfolding in early spring. It hadn't been.

Doctor Gentile said little. In the evenings he'd read *Il Progresso* and listen to the news from Italian Somalia, in conflict with Ethiopia. Sometimes he'd stare at the photograph of his dead soldier father, but for the most part, he avoided politics. After her downtown excursion, he talked to Sofia. From behind his glasses, he peered at her, as if she were a patient with a puzzling symptom.

"Stefano's father," he said. "Didn't he care for America, that he returned to Italy?"

"He never came."

Her father looked concerned, and Sofia wondered how much to tell him.

"Stephano thinks his father had another woman," she said.

He pondered this. "Perhaps Stefano is not his father's son."

Sofia was perplexed. "His father calls him 'son.'"

"And his mother?"

"She's not alive." She told him Stefano's version of events.

"That is a serious accusation," he replied. "Where is the proof?"

Sofia had no idea.

"Consider this," said her father. "What kind of mother abandons her child? *Figlia mia*, nothing is simple. There might have been another man. *Capisce?*"

She told him she understood, yet she wasn't sure she did.

"*Suo povero figlio,*" he whispered. Her poor son.

Perhaps Stefano had imagined the whole thing. *Fog lifting over the water into the sun* — she was tantalized by this strange world in which he'd become her guide. Stefano's life was a stopped clock. When he took her hand, she could feel in its grip the bond that connected him to the place of his mother's death.

"*Cara mia*, I'll never go back to Italy," he said.

"Not even for the music?"

"There is no music."

In the land of Palestrina and Scarlatti? She found this hard to believe. "One day your music will be heard," she said. "Even in Italy."

"You forget my father's with the police."

"So?"

"Imagine what they'd say if Captain Fiore's son picked up a violin."

"They'd be proud, no?"

He laughed.

The problem went deeper than his father. Stefano detested the Sons of Italy and the Jesuits and that capitalist Generoso Pope and his wretched *Il Progresso* and all the other supporters of *Il Duce* in America, despised with equal passion the likes of William Randolph Hearst and his press, along with Henry Ford who wrote cheques for the German anti-Semites. Although he wasn't involved in politics, Stefano counted among his acquaintances more than one Italian anarchist who lived in Manhattan. *Don't tell my father*, thought Sofia.

"I must talk to your grandparents downtown," he said. "We may know the same people."

"Don't. My dad'll throw you out of the house."

"I will not say a word, *cara mia*. The anarchists I know are different. They support Trotsky against —"

Sofia couldn't absorb it all. She felt like a switchboard operator, listening through her headset, her small hands plugging in the vast hum of life itself, compressing its wild electricity into simple chitchat for the telephone. The gap between the power of Stefano's words and what she could grasp of them seemed enormous. Ford and Generoso Pope were two of her father's heroes. *Trotsky?* You weren't allowed to *think* that man's name in her father's house. Nevertheless she listened. *Think about what you have seen in the sky*, he said to her. *It is no less important than anything I tell you.*

She heard him.

They strolled along the Bronx River, the sky like a big pocket showering coins of light through the sycamores along its bank. Hoping Stefano would enjoy simple things, she took him on picnics and boat rides with her friends from Holy Name Church. She didn't take him to Mass.

"The priests are all Blackshirts," he said. "The Fascists have caused enough pain as it is."

"You think they're no good?"

He paused. "They'll get tangled up with Hitler. You wait."

"Italians are too cultured for Hitler."

"A Fascist gang beat up Toscanini," he said. "Four years ago. For refusing to play their anthem."

"My father told me," said Sofia. "He said the anthem was not up to the standards of Italian composition."

"He thought the Fascists should write a better one?"

"I don't know what he thought," she said.

It was true — she didn't. Sofia's father hadn't tried to impose his views on her. Since her mother's death, he attended Sons of Italy meetings in the same dutiful way that he went to Sunday Mass. There were no more quizzes at dinner. Apart from the Italian press, he read novels and plays by D'Annunzio and Pirandello. Every evening at eight o'clock, he listened to the news on the radio. On the table beside his chair was Livia's photograph. He gazed at it as he listened.

Autumn was coming and Sofia felt concerned about her father's introspection, its dark edge of melancholy. She'd ask Stefano to bring his violin and play for him. *Pop needs something to cheer him up*, she thought. She looked in her change purse and found a few coins.

"I'm going to buy some pastry," she told Stefano.

"*Bene*. You are an extravagant woman."

They headed first for Bernie's Deli. All along Maywood and Barnes Avenue, tiny gardens were still in bloom — vines heavy with squash and melons and ripe tomatoes. They grew in front of brick or stucco houses with Spanish-tile roofs and chain-link fences, their last pink hollyhocks nodding like sleepy children. Tonight Mr. Santini was sitting with Mr. Leone, talking about their harvest — *enough to feed the neighbourhood, my friend* — and the grapes for the wine that would have to be made and the fig tree with its abundance of fruit, the finest in the Bronx. As he said this, he waved at Sofia, said good evening and asked her how her father was.

"I love this street," she said to Stefano. "It's so everyday. But there are hidden things."

"Tell me."

"You'll laugh."

"I won't. I promise."

"You see Mr. Leone's house? In back he's built a grotto with a statue of the Virgin, and a little pond. They say he did it because a prayer was answered. Mrs. Santini says there was an apparition."

"*Magia*," said Stefano, and he laughed.

"See? I knew you'd laugh."

"Only because I understand," he said.

When she and Tina and Gabriella were children, she told him, they'd kneel by the grotto and pray that they'd see the Virgin. Certain that the water of the pond was blessed, they dipped their hands into it, then crossed themselves. Birdsong vanished. They'd drifted like water lilies into an enveloping silence.

"I thought that the silence was a person," she said.

"Perhaps it was."

"Everything's so mysterious when you're small."

"And now that you're grown up?"

"The world doesn't change that much. Strange things break in."

They turned onto the main street. Most of the stores were closed at this hour, but Sofia liked peering into De Lucca's with its fat salamis and link sausages dangling in the window, sawdust on the floors and the giant steel slicer on the white countertop over the glass display. Next door was the Budget Grocers. In front of the store stood the bubblegum dispenser, and a smaller, square one full of salted pistachios. Her mother hadn't allowed her to buy the nuts because the pink shells stained her fingers. Even now she could feel Livia's hand in hers, pulling her away.

Apart from the drugstore, the delicatessen was the only shop that stayed open late. Under the counter at the front,

Sofia noticed a plate of raspberry *rugalah*. Later she'd ask Harry to wrap some up for her father. They sat down and looked at the menu.

"Pistachio ice cream, there are no shells in it," said Stefano.

"*Bene.*" She scanned the menu.

"What are you looking for?"

"Salami ice cream." Sofia started giggling. "Italy's gift to America. *Il Duce's* favourite, Leo says."

"A smart-aleck, your brother. I'm amazed he's still alive."

Sofia looked up. Harry was standing next to them, ready to take their order. He looked weary.

"I guess you haven't heard," he said.

The radio was on. Sofia strained to hear. Harry ran to turn it up.

"Italy's marched on Ethiopia," he said. "Wait'll your dad hears this."

Stefano hid his face in his hands.

"In Harlem there'll be riots," said Harry. "Just wait."

"All the Italian stores," said Stefano.

"All that glass on the sidewalk." The man looked tired. He left to fill their order.

Sofia chose her words with care. "There's a photo on our wall of a man named Salvatore Bruno," she said at last. "A soldier who died in Abyssinia, when my father was eight years old."

"And he was —?"

"My real grandfather."

Stefano looked at his hands. *Povero uomo*, he said.

When they got up to leave, Sofia glanced at the plate of *rugalah* under the counter.

"You're buying some?" asked Stefano.

Sofia felt pensive. "It can wait," she said.

In the living room, they saw Sofia's father silhouetted in the lamplight. He looked meditative, seated in his chair, listening to the news. The hush in the room was like a chapel's, at a moment intimate with prayer. She listened. A murmur came from the radio, a sombre voice intoning the news. She was glad she hadn't bought the pastries.

Her father beckoned them to sit beside him. On his lap was a photograph album. Stefano peered at the daguerreotype of a uniformed man.

"This was my father, Salvatore," Elio said.

"Sofia has told me. *Mi dispiace*," he said. "I'm sorry."

"It's all right, thank you. Now he's avenged."

Stefano's voice was quiet. "So now there is justice," he said.

"My father sleeps in peace tonight. Yes."

"I should go home."

"Please, *figlio mio*. May I offer you a glass of wine?"

"*No, grazie*. Wine disturbs my sleep."

Elio put his hand on Stefano's violin case. "Then will you honour this occasion with music?"

Stefano hesitated. "If you wish," he said. He began to play the stately *largo* from Tartini's Sonata in G Minor.

Elio listened. "Why so sad?" he asked.

Stefano stopped playing. "Because I *am* sad, *dottore*," he said. He began again.

4

Doctor Gentile no longer talked about politics. When Stefano came to visit, he'd ask him to play his violin. As he did on the night of Ethiopia's invasion, he'd listen to the music, the look in his eyes as remote as a distant sea. He didn't insist on Italian composers, nor did he seem annoyed when Leo would dance into the room whistling a Gershwin tune for Stefano to play. Instead he paid attention to the jazzy riffs, adjusting his glasses as if he could observe the beginning of a syncopated rhythm before it crept up on the music and jumped it from behind. He never hummed or tapped his foot. He never sang.

In the evening he'd sit in his chair and read, looking up from time to time at the photo of Sofia's mother's on the table beside him. Tucked in the frame were pictures of Livia as a child in Italy. When Sofia entered the room, she'd feel the air stir, as if moved by a sound beyond her range of hearing. She sensed what it was: some lost Italian words, their graceful procession like the rolling of waves that began in the port of Bari on the Adriatic Sea and washed across time to America. Her mother was here, sitting on the arm of her father's chair, humming *Caro mio ben*. Sofia's dad sat transfixed. One evening he touched the gold band on his finger, twisted and turned it, took it off and pressed it to his lips.

Sofia asked him if he was thinking about her mother.

"I think now," he said, "only one thing." Her father paused. He seemed like a jeweller, sorting through his precious words, holding them one by one up to the light. "Love is meant to live beyond us," he continued. He placed his gold ring on the palm of his hand. "This is for Italy," he said. "In your mother's name."

"You're going to give it away?"

He was. More than that, he wanted her to go with him to the rally at the church. They were collecting gold for his embattled homeland, condemned by the world for protecting its interests in Africa. Any gold would help: rings, watches, medallions, cigarette cases, crosses. It was an edifying ritual, said her father, to dedicate this precious metal to a higher purpose. Sofia wasn't sure what she thought of this idea, but she knew she'd have to go to the rally. Leo, who was working nights, would be excused. Stefano, she knew, despised these events. He thought they were rackets run by Fascist mobsters. *You can't trust those crooks*, he said. *They'll steal the gold or sell it for bullets. You wait.*

She couldn't object, but her father's generosity saddened her.

"Your mother would understand," he said.

"Do you think so?"

"Our souls are joined forever," he replied. "They have no need of gold."

On a chill December night, they walked down White Plains Road to the church. It was snowing, and overhead the el rumbled like a tiger, its stripes of light flickering and jumping through the train tracks, rippling on the pastry shop below, the jeweller's, the florist's, the candy and liquor stores. Sofia squinted as they passed the newsstand. *Thousands March in Harlem*, the headline read: Negroes petitioning for the right to enlist and fight for Ethiopia. What luck — right at the stoplight on Gun Hill Road, who should be crossing but Stefano? He had a newspaper under his arm. He'd noticed them.

He strolled over. "Will you be home tonight?" he asked her.

"Later," she replied. "We're going to —"

"A rally for Italy," her father said.

"I have something I must show you both." Stefano pulled out the paper.

"Later you show us," said her father.

"Just don't give them gold," Stefano said.

Elio looked at his watch. "We haven't time." They started walking. Stefano followed them.

"You're *Americans*," he called out. "You owe them *nothing*."

Elio stopped. He turned and glared at Stefano. "We owe them *everything*," he said, and then he strode away. Sofia took her father's arm, and just as the el came rumbling overhead, Stefano yelled that he'd drop by later. They didn't hear him.

At the front of the parish hall was a podium, flanked by the flags of Italy and America. Facing the centre aisle was a table where Father Mario had placed a large basket lined with red velvet cloth. The framed photograph of *Il Duce* that had been on the wall was now standing on the table beside the basket. The priest came forward and begged for his parishioners' generosity. *Think of Italy's gifts of art and culture to the world*, he said. *Let us give in equal measure to our mother country.*

I wasn't born there, thought Sofia. *Stefano's right.*

Sofia understood what the priest was asking. It hadn't occurred to her that she ought to contribute something. She touched the ring that had been her mother's, the gold band with the cameo. *Italy's suffering*, her father said. In his voice was pain that was also a kind of yearning.

She watched as he felt in his pocket, then pulled out a small velvet box and opened it. On the white satin was a circlet of gold, her mother's wedding ring. *Not just his own. He's going to give away hers, too.* Clutching it, he got up before anyone else and walked with a measured pace toward the front of the hall. She noticed everyone's eyes on him: Mr. Santini, the plumber; Rafaela and her husband Tony from the florist's; Mr. Malazzo, the undertaker, and Mr. De Lucca, the butcher, and his wife, and Mr. and Mrs. Leone, who'd been granted some mysterious favour from the Mother of God; neighbours and patients, parents of Sofia's former schoolmates. One by one they got up and stepped into line.

Elio walked to the table and placed the two rings in the basket. His face showed nothing as he strode to his seat, head erect, shoulders back.

It's my turn, Sofia thought.

You're a grown woman now. It was her mother's voice Sofia heard — and for one terrible moment, she remembered the first time her clothes were stained with blood. Now, as then, she heard the terrifying *slam-slam-slam* of all the doors of girlhood, then the heavy sliding of the bolts upon the doors. As she touched her ring, the noise ceased and she passed into a realm of inner silence. She felt alive with the energy that drew all of them to the front of the hall, the current that powered a burning light of generosity and sacrifice. She remembered the students in uniform, their white arms lifted to the flag. Once a good student, she'd been honoured by the city. She'd done nothing brave since.

She pressed her lips to the ring, then yanked it off, as you'd pull dressing from a wound — quick, so it wouldn't hurt. Before she could change her mind, she joined the line moving toward the front of the hall.

Home again, her father received a call asking him to attend to a sick patient. As he was about to leave the house, the doorbell rang. It was Stefano, and her father let him in. The younger man stomped into the hall, shook the snow off his coat and stood in the doorway. He still had the newspaper under his arm. His face was white. His eyes were matches lit with fury.

"Now you can tell us what is wrong," said Elio.

An Ordinary Star

"The more I read this, the angrier I get. Forgive me, but you might not like hearing this so soon after your rally," he said. He opened the paper. "Here are the words of Vittorio, the brother of *Il Duce*. In his plane, he bombed the Africans and even the Red Cross, and he wrote: 'One group of horsemen gave me the impression of a budding rose unfolding as the bomb fell in their midst and blew them up.' What savages."

No one said a word.

Stefano spoke again. "*A budding rose*. When have you heard of such indecency?"

"Such imagination." Elio's voice was bitter.

"A good Fascist insults the dead with a good imagination." Stefano stared into Elio's eyes, his intent look softening into a gaze of sorrow.

Elio's face paled. "Why are you looking at me?" he asked.

"I am not looking at *you*," said Stefano.

"Then who?"

"I am looking at your misery," he said at last.

Elio was silent.

"*Dottor* Gentile, how you have suffered because of this."

Her father looked stricken. "I must go," he said.

Stefano tossed his newspaper aside. He took the man's coat from the hook and held it as he slipped it on. He said goodnight, his voice so gentle that only Elio could hear him.

When her father had left, Stefano took Sofia's hand. "How warm it feels," he said, and then he kissed it. His lips stopped at her bare finger.

"You gave up your ring?"

"I wanted to be brave."

"*Cara mia —*"

"I wanted my father to be proud of me. I'm sorry."

She eyed her bare finger and remembered Stefano's wrath when he came to the door. "Are you angry at me?" she asked him.

"At the Fascists, I'm angry." Stefano let go of her hand. From his wallet he pulled out a photo of his own father — Camillo Fiore in his captain's uniform. Behind wire-rimmed glasses, the man's eyes were penetrating, in a way that suggested menace. Yet his face was as opaque as marble, and she was unable to see into him.

"This is a Fascist," said Stefano. "Not your father."

"It doesn't upset you to show me this?"

Stefano sighed. "I have only one father. I understand how you love your father."

"And you still love yours?"

"Marry me, Sofia. I'll tell you everything." He kissed her.

"I don't need to know everything," she said.

"But will you —"

"Yes, Stefano. But put your father aside."

"It is impossible. His kind are ruining the world."

"But not *our* world."

Stefano took her hands and kissed them. "Our world, too, *cara mia*. We are going to marry it all."

THE GOLDEN SKY

I

They had to wait a year to marry because there was no money and not enough work. *How fortunate your uncle is,* said Stefano. *A professor, and even in these bad times he can teach a little and float above the clouds.* Sofia pondered the man who was able to leave the earth, who carried around him the aura of one who could escape at will from the gravity of ordinary life. Whenever she was near her uncle, she felt like a planet tugged by the pull of an enormous star, swinging into an orbit from which there was no escape. Soon to be married, she didn't feel quite ready for the solid ground of earth. She felt adrift in space, trapped by her uncle's attraction, never far from him, yet never close.

Uncle Paul was keeping a distance from the relatives on Maywood Road. He'd taken to pronouncing his surname as

Genteel, and one of his contacts (who thought he was French) suggested that Aunt Julia might try to write an article about airship travel suitable for the modern woman of refinement. With this man's encouragement, she wrote and sold a piece to the *Women's Home Companion.* The editor wanted more, and *Recipes from Above the Clouds* was followed by *Décor and Elegance Amidships.* The magazine got a pile of mail. *You and your husband must try for a flight aboard the airship* Hindenburg, said the editor. *Their kitchen has one of the best chefs in Europe. Barvarian Duckling and Venison Beauval. French and German wines.* Uncle Paul would fly on the *Hindenburg,* but not with Aunt Julia. In any case, the new airship was already booked solid for its first year. *Next year,* he said to her.

Sofia dreads this recollection of flight, her knowledge that her uncle wanted to leave them. *I know exactly where this story is going,* she thinks. She closes her eyes as the walls dissolve into blue sky. Cloudlike, she hovers and drifts over memory. She doesn't dare look down.

2

"Can't you see where this is going?" Sofia's father glared at Uncle Paul.

"Where, precisely?"

"Straight to hell. Zeppelins are a tool of Nazi propaganda."

"You sound like Pop."

"This time the old man's right." He waved a newspaper in his brother's face. "*Seventh of March, nineteen-hundred thirty-six*," he read. "They flew the *Hindenburg* across Germany to drum up support for their occupation of the Rhineland. Your friend Lehmann" — he spat out the words —"so eager to please Minister Goebbels that he rushed the ship into a crosswind and tore the tail off. Did he care about the weather? About safety?"

"Yes, but —"

"They haven't the decency to care."

"No, Elio." Paul's voice softened. "Dr. Eckener cares. He designed the *Hindenburg*. Goebbels asked him to change the name to *Hitler*. He said no."

"Hitler's a sissy, that's why," said Leo. "Scared to fly."

"No one asked you," said his father. "How would it look if the *Hitler* crashed?"

"For twenty-five years the Zeppelins have flown," said Paul. "None have crashed."

"Try telling that to Hitler," said Leo. "The big sis —"

"Kindly stop repeating yourself," said his father.

3

"At last you're getting married." *Nonno* Domenico raised his glass to Sofia and Stefano.

Apart from *nonna* Constanza (who by now had moved out to Long Island) and Christopher (at home with a cold), the family was celebrating. Sofia could feel Uncle Paul's eyes on her, as warm as charcoal bricks. She smiled at him. He was wearing a tweed jacket with a tiny *Hindenburg* pin on its lapel. He looked distracted and handsome and ridiculously attractive. He smiled back.

Nonno scrutinized the pin. "A wedding is better than most of our family news," he said.

Uncle Paul's face reddened.

Leo strode in, wearing his sailor cap. He did a little jig

in the centre of the room, turning to face his uncle. "*Buon viaggio,*" he said.

"*Grazie.*"

Sofia's father glanced at *nonno*. "We are all on the voyage of life," he said. He poured more wine.

"Let's drink to our health," said Stefano.

"To your beautiful fiancée," said Uncle Paul.

Leo raised his glass. "Up ship!" he said.

Silence.

"Bravo," said Uncle Paul. He downed his drink.

Nonno Domenico's eyes crackled with a blue flash. "I will not drink to Hitler's airship," he said.

"I will not put up with insult," said Paul.

Sofia and Aunt Julia left the room. *Nonna* Rosa joined them.

"A petty battle," she said. She lit a cigarette. Sofia could hear the rumble of men's voices, the crash of a fist on the table. *Nonna* Rosa looked disgusted. "Small skirmishes do not advance the cause," she continued. She blew out a column of smoke, behind which Sofia imagined the wreckage of the German armies in retreat.

"All power to the workers," said *nonna*.

Sofia poured everyone coffee. She passed around a tray of *dolci*.

"Now tell us about your wedding," said Aunt Julia.

Moments later, Stefano strode out of the living room. Elio followed him toward the front door. Leo went upstairs.

"Why are *we* stepping outside?" asked Stefano.

"It's hopeless," said Elio.

"You cannot ask them to leave?"

"Let them fight indoors. Otherwise they'd fight on the stoop. Our neighbours would call the police." Elio slammed the door behind him.

The women listened as the voices rose to shouts.

"You have learned nothing," said Domenico.

"Papa —"

"Even the capitalists see what is going on. The Boche is strong again."

"But what's that got to do with —"

"Flying in a Nazi airship? I'll tell you what."

"Dr. Eckener built it. He hates the Nazis."

"They're going to kill him. Or haven't you figured that out?"

Sofia inched her way into the corridor and watched. Her grandfather's face was like a fast-changing storm, the grief in his eyes twisting into a hurricane of rage. Uncle Paul grabbed the man's shoulders.

"Pop, listen. Please."

His father pulled away. "I lost a son to the Boche. Now you to the Nazis."

"There you go, old man," said her uncle. "Stewing in your juices, like tough meat."

"*Non hai rispetto*. I'll show you tough meat."

Nonno grabbed Uncle Paul by the collar, then drove his fist into his stomach. Paul fell to the floor, his head smashing against the table leg. *Nonno* was about to kick him.

Sofia screamed.

4

An hour later, Sofia's father came down the stairs, gripping his doctor's valise. He looked exhausted. Nothing was broken, thank God, he said. Scrapes and contusions — Uncle Paul would need ice on his jaw, would have to rest. *Worse is the humiliation*, he whispered to Stefano. *My brother will never forgive him.*

The men had come running into the house when Sofia screamed. "*Basta!*" yelled her father, and Stefano yanked *nonno* away from Paul. Domenico's taut body went as limp as a doll's. He stared in shock at his fallen son as if he had no idea what happened and no control over what he'd done. *Che stupido*, he kept repeating, but it wasn't at all clear who he meant — himself or Uncle Paul. Her father helped her uncle up and led him out of the room, and Stefano loosened his grip on *nonno*. He got him to sit down. *Perché?* he whispered. The man sat, his shoulders bent, his large hands hiding his face. Later, *nonna* Rosa apologized, but *nonno* appeared to be as much in shock as her uncle. *I will not come back to this house*, he murmured as the two of them left. *I am sorry. I will not come back.* No one was certain if that was an apology or an assertion of his honour.

Later, Uncle Paul came downstairs, holding an ice-pack to his face.

"The old man's a fool," he said.

"*Basta*," said Aunt Julia. She made him tea.

"You may stay here tonight if you wish," said Elio.

"There's no need," said Paul.

"There is," said Aunt Julia. "Mamma will get hysterical when she sees you." She said she'd return by herself and keep the woman company. Chris would be expecting her at home.

When Sofia glanced at Uncle Paul, she saw his faraway look grow sharp and attentive. A good idea, he told Aunt Julia. He'd stay.

"Sofia."

He said her name with a hushed intensity that silenced everyone. "Do you remember the *Los Angeles?*" he asked.

"Of course." She wondered why he was bringing it up.

"I want you to come to Lakehurst for the launch of the *Hindenburg* on May 11th. You and the whole family. Leave that old man to stew in his juices."

Her father looked weary.

"You don't like this idea?" Uncle Paul asked him.

"Not if you're travelling on business," said Elio.

"When we sail next year," said Aunt Julia, "we can make it more of a family occasion."

Sofia felt her uncle's gaze. *You'd like to go*, his eyes said. *I would. Oh yes, I would.*

Sofia couldn't sleep. Moonlight fell on everything like spilled milk. She stared at the wallpaper — nosegays of blue flowers, white lace, pink ribbon, cream background. Hoping for drowsiness, she began to count the fussy bouquets, then stopped. She could hear her uncle's breathing on the other side of the wall. She listened, but he grew quiet, as if he'd turned over in his sleep. So close they were — their beds separated by a layer of plaster and ridiculous printed flowers. As she closed her eyes, she heard a muffled cry. Her uncle's voice —"Sofia!" as if he were in pain and calling her. No, he must have been dreaming. He was quiet again.

Poor Uncle Paul. Despised and injured by his own father. No wonder he flies away so much. She imagined running into the room. *I'm here — it's all right.* Before the thought could take over her body, she pushed it aside. She felt uneasy that she found the fantasy so pleasant.

She'd have to look in on him tomorrow.

That would be good of you, said her father the following day. *If you wouldn't mind.*

She knew that her father would expect hospitality for an ailing relative under his roof, that he considered her gesture appropriate. Her uncle would need someone to change his bandage and to make him tea. At lunchtime she walked home to Maywood Road, and once in the house, she tiptoed into the corridor and stood, listening to the silence, smelling the morning's fresh-ground coffee and almond *biscotti*, eyeing the polished gleam of furniture and the crispness of curtains and linens. Her house — all her doing. She'd gather this warmth and bring it to the injured man upstairs.

The door to Uncle Paul's room was ajar, and he was lying on the bed under the covers, an ugly purple stain on his cheek and a bandage on his forehead. His eyes opened and he beckoned her into the room. She closed the door and sat on the edge of the bed.

"How are you feeling?" she asked.

"I knew you'd come."

"I heard you call me in your sleep last night."

Her uncle's face looked weary, but he smiled. "I had a bad dream. I wanted you to rescue me." He touched the bruise on his cheek.

"Do you need a new bandage?" Sofia put a hand on his forehead.

"Your hand feels cool," he said. Reaching up, he put his hand on hers, then drew it down to his chest. He held it there, then guided it along his body so that she could feel his silken hair, the rising and falling of his breath. Back and forth across his warm skin he moved her hand. Her mouth felt dry.

His hand stopped moving hers. "Do you love me, *cara mia*?"

She hesitated. "Yes."

"Kiss me."

She kissed his cheek. He took her head in his hands and pushed his mouth into hers.

She returned his kiss. She knew she should have stopped this sooner, but her body was melting and could not reconstitute itself. She felt as if she'd set this desire in motion long ago, as if all he'd done was confront her with her longing. She let him pull her down on the bed, she let him undress and enter her, she gave in to her body's hum until all at once a taut string snapped and she sailed toward him like an arrow released from a bow. She flew into darkness, as if the world had vanished.

Sofia was shivering as she walked up Gun Hill Road. It was a warm spring afternoon, but she felt chilled and raw to the bone, as if she were naked. Her body was tingling with her uncle's scent of cured tobacco and spices. It felt as if she'd never cleanse that odour from her skin, never stop feeling his touch in the part of her that he'd entered. She was wearing him as a new skin that she could never shed. *That new skin should have been Stefano's.* It was her own fault, that she'd let it happen. *Incest.* The unpleasant word left a bitter taste, but she swallowed it. Life was going to pay her back for this.

She wondered if her uncle would brag about their escapade. Worse would be family parties — the two of them straddling this awkward secret. It was possible that he'd try again with her. *Soon it won't matter. I'll be married and my life will be different.* No — it did matter. Nothing could erase that afternoon. *A sexual apprentice. A foolish girl, a know-nothing.* Maybe she should realize that everyone makes mistakes. *No. Much worse. I did something wrong.*

And then there was Aunt Julia.

By flying on Zeppelins, the poor woman had found the only way to keep her husband faithful. Imagine the fun he'd had — he and his Navy pals from the *Los Angeles*. He was out carousing the night his son was born.

Uncle Paul could get her in trouble. He could tell Stefano what happened, and that the whole thing was her fault. She'd tell Stefano it was all a mistake, that her uncle was overwrought after his father's attack. On the other hand, she could get him into trouble, too. *We come from a line of anarchists.* The dangerous word began to interest her.

In early May, Paul flew on the *Hindenburg* to Germany. A week after he left, Sofia received a note from Aunt Julia in Long Island.

> ... *A letter postmarked Airship Hindenburg arrived today ... Uncle Paul describes it as a flying luxury hotel with extraordinary views of the night sky over the North Atlantic. It made me think of our trips to the park when you were a girl and how we gazed at the stars through your father's telescope. I imagined your uncle out in the gondola at night ...*

Necking. About to take someone to bed, Sofia thought.

> ... *viewing the spectacular Milky Way to the south, and the circumpolar constellations as they wheel above him. The state of the world is so dreary that the stars provide much badly-needed inspiration. After your*

marriage, the four of us must take an excursion to view the skies out on Montauk Point ...

Those days are done, she thought. She felt a pang of grief.

Stefano noticed her sorrowful look. He asked to read the letter.

"There's going to be a war," she said. "We'll never go look at the stars again."

"Don't be discouraged, *cara mia*." He held her in his arms.

"If there's a war, Leo will go."

"He'll be here for the wedding."

"They'll torpedo his boat."

Stefano held her at arm's length and looked at her.

"Sofia, you are torturing yourself. *Perché?*"

"I don't know why." She was lying.

He stroked her hair. "*Mia bella*, let the world go its way." He kissed her lips and she closed her eyes. "You must go to Lakehurst," he said. "The landing will be spectacular."

"No."

"*Cara mia*, it will cheer you up."

"Next year. When my aunt and uncle come home together."

5

Uncle Paul returned two weeks before Sofia's wedding. He wrote a note to her father, telling him that the trip was splendid, that he was writing an article about the Airship *Hindenburg* for *The New York Times*. Sofia, involved in wedding preparations, hoped to avoid him. She and Stefano had been shopping for furniture for the upstairs apartment — nothing too *moderne*, with the exception of the Philco upright radio and the trim little icebox-refrigerator. Her father had invited them to take what they liked from the living room. An overstuffed couch, an ornate cabinet — they couldn't afford the newer, more streamlined styles. Not yet. *The modernist furniture on the* Hindenburg, wrote her uncle, *melds form and function perfectly. No undue decorative clutter. The*

An Ordinary Star

German aesthetic embodies the modern age. Her father grimaced. *In German homes, perhaps*, he said.

Sofia knew her father was preoccupied, wanting to give her a hand, annoyed with her uncle's note, concerned about two of his patients who were close to labour. While Stefano and Leo painted the apartment, he sanded a bureau downstairs so that he could be near the telephone. At lunch, Stefano asked him if he'd spoken to Aunt Julia and Uncle Paul.

"I have only the note he sent," her father replied.

Stefano looked surprised. "You haven't spoken?"

"I tried this morning. There's no one answering their phone."

"*Nonna* never answers the phone," said Sofia. "She doesn't think her English is good enough."

"*Hello* is pretty basic," said Leo.

Her father felt sure they were downtown, visiting their son at boarding school. After lunch, the phone rang and he grabbed it. There was a long pause.

"I am so sorry," he said. He hung up. "Your aunt is in the hospital," he said to Sofia. "She's had a miscarriage."

"I didn't know she —"

"Four months." He paused. "Uncle Paul is very disappointed."

Sofia counted. Aunt Julia was pregnant when he left for Germany.

As her father had guessed, his brother and sister-in-law had been in Manhattan to see their son. It was there that Aunt Julia became ill.

"I've invited Uncle Paul to dinner," he said to Sofia. "Is that all right?"

Her stomach cramped into a hard knot.

"Of course."

"He can stay with us while your aunt recuperates."

Sofia went upstairs to prepare his room, putting fresh linens on his bed, smoothing them into place. *He's had so many women by now that he's probably forgotten the whole thing.* Downstairs again, she set the table with her mother's best linen and china. She cooked pasta and *vitello* and stuffed artichokes — as fine as any German chef's cuisine, afloat in the sky. The food's excellence made her feel defiant. She found a bottle of good wine. She invited Stefano, but he was working late that evening.

"*Figlia mia*, you've outdone yourself," her father said. "And on such short notice."

"It's no trouble."

Uncle Paul arrived, looking tired. They sat down to dinner.

"You will excuse me," her father began, "if the phone interrupts our dinner. I have a patient who's —"

Her uncle told him not to worry.

What if I'm stuck alone with him? thought Sofia.

"And how is Julia?" her father asked.

"As well as can be expected."

"This is very hard. As a doctor, I know —"

"I cannot wait to take her on the *Hindenburg* next spring. It'll cheer her up, I'm sure. Magnificent — the crystal in the dining room, the china — the whitecaps dancing in the sunlight. Manhattan from the air is splendid."

"You'll try again," said Elio. "She'll be happy."

"Of course. Of course."

"We have this wonderful meal to enjoy."

"You would have loved the food aboard the *Hindenburg*," said Uncle Paul. "With a top-notch dining room and bar — crossing the ocean in four days —" His eyes lit up and he poured himself more wine. "A whole year solidly booked and Washington refuses to sell the Germans helium. Does Roosevelt think Hitler is stupid enough to —"

The phone rang. Her father excused himself.

"My patient," he said when he returned.

Sofia took a deep breath. "Come back in time for Stefano," she said.

"I'll try."

Sofia invited her uncle to relax in the living room while she did the dishes. She'd take her time and hope he'd either get absorbed in the newspaper or fall asleep. As she scraped dishes, she heard him turn on the radio, heard the impatient *wee-ah* tuning of the dial until the newscaster's voice came clear. *The German Minister of ...* She put a plate of food in the oven for Stefano, then began washing the dishes. The broadcast continued. *Hailie Selassie plans to address the League of Nations...* Lost in thought, Sofia was absorbed in the routine pleasures of her task, the suds and warm running water, the soft towels for drying — a rite of cleansing that encompassed all the sorrow and annoyance of the mealtime conversation.

She could hear the announcer's voice. *Strikes are spreading across Spain as the army ...* She scrubbed the dishes, the pots and roasting pan as if they were her soiled life. She took more care with the carving knife, its blade too sharp to allow her mind to drift. Engrossed in the rhythm of the work, she reached for the towel on the rack overhead, dried her hands, turned around and found herself facing her uncle. She hadn't heard him come in. He was standing with his hands resting on the sink, encircling her.

"*Cara mia*," he said.

She felt the sweet unwanted warmth of his mouth on hers as his hands let go of the sink and grabbed her shoulders. She gave him a kick and a hard push. Reeling backwards, he almost lost his footing, but Sofia grabbed the big knife from the drainboard and thrust it inches away from him.

"I'll kill you," she said.

"*Putana* — wet as rain. I thought you liked it."

"This is my house, you pig. You do what I say."

They heard Stefano's key turning in the lock.

"I'll be going," said Uncle Paul.

"And don't come back."

Stefano made her sit down.

"That *cafone*," he said. "From the window I saw what he did."

"I showed him what's what."

"I should run down the street and break his neck," said Stefano

"He won't try again."

"What gave him the right to try even once? *Cara mia*, you must tell your father."

"No, I can't. Pop would tell *nonno*. The old man'll kill him."

"Which is what he deserves."

An Ordinary Star

She remembered her father's words. *Your aunt and uncle are in pain*, figlia mia. *They suffer from their illusions. What you see is illusion and suffering.* She told that to Stefano.

"Your father is a peaceful man," he said. "So I will be, also. Only that was no illusion, what I saw."

6

Sofia married Stefano at Holy Name Church on the 27th of June, 1936. Tina was their maid of honour, Gabriella a bridesmaid and Leo the best man. Father Mario performed the ceremony. Their guests included the Giornos (who provided the bouquets of coronations and baby's breath), the Malazzos (the undertaker making a rare sartorial appearance in a light grey suit), the Leones, the De Luccas, the Santinis and the Bernsteins. Her grandparents drove up from Orchard Street with Stefano's Aunt Francesca and Uncle Vito who'd borrowed a friend's Studebaker for the occasion. Uncle Paul — *who hasn't been well*, his brother explained — was staying in Manhattan at a friend's apartment on East 68th Street (implying that he was close to one of the best hospitals in the city). He drove to the church with Christopher beside him. He looked pale indeed, and not at all well. Aunt Julia came on the train from Long Island with *nonna*. The four of them sat together.

The Gun Hill Road Inn hosted the wedding breakfast, and afterwards the guests made their way to Dr. Gentile's home. It was a beautiful afternoon, the rhododendrons and peonies in bloom, the gazebo adorned with baskets of daisies and bluebells. In his role as best man, Leo flipped out his pocket knife and on the trunk of the ancient beech in front of the house, he carved a heart with the initials *S & SF* and the date — 6.27.36. Later they went indoors and young Christopher sat at the piano and presented the newlyweds with his gift — *Wedding Prelude*, which he'd composed himself. No one had heard him perform before, and as he moved his hands across the keyboard, the air became still and even the birds grew silent.

Eleven years old, and he was a sculptor pressing his hands into the contours of space, bending and shaping it with music. As she listened, Sofia drifted into Van Cortlandt Park and saw before her a carriage full of tulip-tree flowers. She was inside the mysterious day when her aunt and infant nephew danced the long hours of an afternoon into a dust of seconds. From her living-room window, she could see that the sky was enveloped in a haze of gold. She felt like an insect in a storm of pollen dust and she knew she was seeing as Christopher saw.

The air outside was fragrant with mock orange blossoms, their petals sifting down from the sky to the grass, and Sofia wondered if this, too, were part of the music. She stood in the doorway with Stefano, watching their guests depart, and all at once she understood that by her cousin's gentle intervention, time had vanished and the world had been made whole again. In the amber light, she and Stefano saw her aunt and uncle walking down the far end of Maywood Road. Aunt Julia was dressed in a short frock with a rope of pearls and an old-fashioned cloche hat, holding a tea rose from her mother Livia's garden, and Uncle Paul was as dapper as a movie star in vest and pinstripes and fedora. Walking with a skip in his step, he took Aunt Julia's hand and then leaned over to kiss her. He was proposing marriage in the flower-rain.

"OUR WORLD, TOO."

I

Aunt Julia was commissioned by *Women's Home Companion* to write about the stylish tubular furniture aboard the *Hindenburg* — *this is a fashion trend that is bound to make its way back to* terra firma, *once our sorry economy has improved*, she wrote Sofia.

She's floating off in more ways than one, Sofia thought.

Her aunt had invited her and her family to the *Queen Mary* launch in April. While on board, she'd be telegraphing items to the Ladies' Section of the *New York Herald-Tribune* on "Shipboard Science Made Simple." Sofia wondered what weighty items she'd try to explore. She concluded that in any case, it had to be better than staying home with *nonna*.

The letter contained a brochure, and months later, Sofia would continue to glance at it with mixed fascination and envy. At the top was a red strip with three German words in white letters — *Deutsche Zeppelin Reederei.* The cover showed a stylized businessman, a blue figure swinging his briefcase, striding across the globe. According to a flyer enclosed with the brochure, *in 1936 — its first year of operation — the Airship* Hindenburg *flew 1600 passengers* (one of them Uncle Paul) *for a total of 3000 flying hours.* Sofia read on. *We offer luxury accommodations, an elegant dining room, lounge, writing rooms and promenade.* Opening the pamphlet, she imagined the enormous slanting windows and the panoramic views of sea and sky. The lavish descriptions never tired her. *Now the sunshine is streaming in through the windows and you take your place in the dining saloon for a breakfast of crisp, appetizing rolls and aromatic coffee ... down below, you see the long shadow of the airship passing swiftly over the sparkling, foam-crested waves of the blue Atlantic ... the whole atmosphere is one of tranquility and peace ... In fact you seem to have been transported into another and more beautiful world.*

This was a feeling Sofia understood. Almost a year had passed since her wedding, yet she could still feel Christopher parting the curtain of time, revealing her aunt on her twenty-third birthday and her uncle skipping to a Bill Bojangles tune. She hadn't seen much of her aunt and uncle. When she did, she wanted to believe that the two of them had reconciled.

Her father hadn't encouraged her to invite them to dinner. He pointed out that inviting family meant you couldn't leave anyone out and he dreaded another conflict between Paul and *nonno*. No one could be certain that her combustible grandfather had been shocked into repentance, and everyone knew that Uncle Paul was a lit match in his presence. She deferred to her father with relief.

Aunt Julia and Uncle Paul were living with *nonna* Constanza on Long Island, just outside the city limits. Paul was teaching part-time at Brooklyn College. Aunt Julia was working on her freelance assignments, and Christopher, adept at using the subway, boarded at a school for the blind in Manhattan and met his father at the end of the line on weekends. *What a bad ride*, he'd say to his dad. *They all start whispering 'Make way for the little blind boy' as if I were deaf, too. I'd like to yell 'make way for the brain-damaged.'* He was a scholarship student, and he liked boarding school better than living at home. Better than his grandmother, too — only *nonna* Constanza had found a life of her own. She'd taken up gardening, pouring her copious energy into producing enormous crops of tomatoes and zucchini, lettuce and eggplant. She made friends. *I keep my two feet on the ground*, she said to her daughter and son-in-law. *The rest of you go fly.*

They did.

Knowing she couldn't, Sofia settled for the writings of the pioneering Dr. Hugo Eckener. *An emissary from the Isle of the Blest*, he'd written of his Zeppelins — and she wondered if airships could drift through the barriers of time and death. *Often when people greet [the* Hindenburg*] so enthusiastically as it appears in the heavens*, wrote Eckener, *I have felt as if they believed they were seeing in it a sign and symbol of lasting peace.* Sofia remembered the *Los Angeles*, so much like an apparition. She felt that when airships floated into view, time itself changed. Hours stretched like lazy cats and minutes sped up. Everything was blessed, and a wonder.

She read Aunt Julia's invitation to the *Queen Mary* launch. She showed it to her father and Stefano.

"We'll be waving goodbye to the great ships," said her father.

"How do you mean?" Sofia asked.

"The *Hindenburg* can cross the ocean in less than three days."

"I cannot trust the Germans with the future," said Stefano. "I am sorry."

Neither he nor Sofia could attend. Her father closed the office and went downtown to say *bon voyage* to her aunt and uncle. She imagined the popping of champagne corks, streamers and confetti and ladies with fox pelts draped over their spring suit-jackets, enormous smokestacks and New York Harbour alive with the hoots and blasts of whistles and foghorns. She imagined her aunt and uncle waving from the deck, sailing away into another life.

The first telegram came from the ship, addressed to Sofia's father. *Delightful second honeymoon.* This was followed by a short note. *In the quiet of an ocean voyage, one can experience many changes*, her uncle wrote. *We have had much time to enjoy and appreciate each other's company. Life is not always what it seems. Life takes us in mysterious directions. Sometimes the destination is in sight before the journey commences. But not always.*

Sofia eyed her father as he squinted, took off his glasses, wiped them with his handkerchief, put them back on and read the letter again.

"It must be the salt air," he remarked.

"Is Uncle Paul well?"

An Ordinary Star

"Relaxed. Not at all his usual self."

A few weeks later, he wired them from the *Hindenburg* on his way home. *Friends will meet us at Lakehurst stop don't put yourselves out.* Before leaving, Uncle Paul had given Sofia's father the names of a couple on East 86th St. in Manhattan. *For the landing,* he'd scribbled on the paper. "It would have been nice," said her dad, "if he'd remembered to leave their telephone number." Elio called the operator and located a Mr. and Mrs. Stafford who said yes, they were acquaintances of Uncle Paul, that they were driving to Lakehurst and they'd be happy to offer them a ride. They even had a friend in town who'd be willing to put them up overnight.

"And did Paul —" her father asked. Sofia saw his eyes widen. He hung up the phone.

"He has become so absentminded, my brother," he said.

"He may have asked someone else," said Sofia.

"Will you go with the Staffords?" he asked.

"Do they need me?"

"To spot your aunt and uncle," he said. "They don't know them at all well."

2

Sofia had wanted to see the arrival of the airship *Hindenburg*, and she began to look forward to the excursion. *It'll be a spectacle*, said Tina. *From miles around, people come to see the airships land. It'll be like old times, with your aunt and uncle. You don't have to visit with them.*

She hoped not.

It was a cloudy and overcast morning in early May when Sofia set out on her journey with the Staffords. Later she learned that the poor weather along the eastern seaboard had held up the *Hindenburg*'s arrival at Lakehurst, giving New Yorkers a lingering view of the world's largest aircraft as it drifted southward. *Even the Bronx got a look*, said Tina. *All along the Concourse, there were people out on their roofs.* The ship took its time, flying down the west side of

Manhattan, passing over Harlem and Central Park and Times Square, moving southward toward Brooklyn, distracting hundreds of baseball fans at the Dodgers-Pirates game in Ebbets Field, then looping back toward Lower Manhattan for a circle of Battery Park and the Statue of Liberty. As it flew, it drew into itself the nameless magic of the place below — cheers and glances of delight, the beauty of the tallest steeple or the best pitcher or the razzmatazz of the Great White Way. Up the East River and toward the Empire State Building *where my cousin works on the seventy-fifth floor*, said Gabriella later. *The ship got so close that she could wave at the passengers waving at them. Can you believe that? The big swastika passed right in front of her window.*

South toward the Jersey coast the airship flew. By the time Sofia and her companions arrived in Lakehurst, the impromptu grand tour of the *Hindenburg* was over and its landing postponed until the drizzle stopped.

Time stopped along with the rain. In the grey twilight mist, it might have been dusk or early morning. None of the spectators had any idea when the ship would land or even where it was — only that it had become a phantom. Some in the town of Lakehurst said that it was floating southward toward Atlantic City, but no one could see it in the gathering dark. Earth and sky flowed into each other as if they were nothing more than mist and rain. Everyone waited.

Mr. Stafford drove into the Lakehurst airfield, where hundreds of people had already gathered. He was a high-school science teacher — a squat, sandy-haired man with a tweed jacket, a moustache and pipe. His wife was a teacher, also. Fair and taller than her husband, she wore the kindly gaze of one used to soothing the hurts of children. Mr. Stafford took his wife's arm as he looked toward the enormous airship hangar. "What a place to teach a class," he said. "Practical science. Eyewitness history. I'd like to bring the whole school here." Mrs. Stafford agreed.

It was sandy, this airfield, and crowded with spectators and newsmen, all of them restless, as if they were roaming a vast and endless beach in search of the ocean. The three of them were standing to the northeast of the hangar and the mooring mast. They noticed the assembled ground crew of several hundred sailors, ready to assist with the landing. *Two hours they've been waiting*, said Mr. Stafford. *Rain's just about stopped now.* Sofia had brought Uncle Guido's binoculars. She took them out of the case.

Mrs. Stafford laughed. "Binoculars? For the *Hindenburg?*"

"So I can spot my aunt and uncle."

Sofia didn't want to miss them. She felt like a family detective, sent to unravel a mystery. More than this, she felt like a spy, observing members of her family in a moment of their private lives which belonged to them alone. It was rare for her to venture outside her neighbourhood without Stefano, and she felt exhilarated, as she did as a child on lower Broadway, waiting for the *Los Angeles*. Yet she missed the skyscrapers that walled in New York City like a fortress. Here she felt unprotected. Even with the Staffords by her side, the airfield was vast and unremitting, barren and featureless — its scale so huge that she felt mouse-like, skittering in the grass.

She looked around her. The sky was glowing with iridescent light.

"There she is!"

Sofia heard the shouts from the crowd, and she could feel the hum of the great ship's engines, hearing them as she lifted her eyes. The Zeppelin emerged from the haze to the south of them, elegant and graceful, gliding northward. A silver and gleaming apparition — and she saw confetti and streamers rippling in the slow dance of memory while ferryboats blasted their foghorns. It was so huge, the *Hindenburg*, that even at a distance, you were close. *More than eight hundred feet in length*, said Mr. Stafford. *And at five hundred feet above us — that is large.* Sofia was awestruck.

"Look at it turn," said Mr. Stafford. "Heading for the hangar and letting off hydrogen. Helps it come down nice and slow." He tapped Sofia's shoulder. "Now watch that circle, honey. Moving east now."

"A beautiful ship," said Mrs. Stafford. "Too bad about the swa —"

"It's dumping water," said Sofia.

"More ballast. That's normal," said Mr. Stafford.

Sofia enjoyed his patter. She didn't want to admit how overwhelmed she was by this enormous object drifting above them. Mr. Stafford put her at ease. He sounded like a radio announcer calling the plays at a ballgame.

"And now a right turn. Moving southeast for the final approach."

The *Hindenburg* was beginning its slow descent, moving forward. Sofia stared at the circular track around the mooring mast up ahead. Its huge circumference looked purposeful in a weird way, like the stone circles of a pagan ritual. Beyond the mast was the hangar — so outsized that it appeared much closer than it was. Over the ground crew the enormous

Zeppelin hovered — grand and eerie as a spaceship. The ship's riggers threw down ropes for the sailors below, but the sailors looked like tiny flies and the ropes were lit filaments of a spider's web and the whole of it shimmered in the eerie light as the men secured the port and starboard lines to cars on the circular track. The air was humming and Sofia smelled the fragrance of the earth after rain.

"Landing any minute now," said Mr. Stafford.

They were close enough so that Sofia could spot passengers on the portside promenade, standing by the windows, laughing and waving to the crowd below. She peered through her binoculars.

"I see my aunt."

Sofia let Mrs. Stafford look. "With the bonnet?" she asked.

Mr. Stafford looked. "That would be Paul beside her, then," he said.

With the binoculars, Sofia scanned a row of uniformed men walking toward the airship. Clipboards in hand, they formed a line, striding along with the single-minded resolve of ants approaching a watermelon.

"Customs and immigration," said Mrs. Stafford.

"I guess that means the passengers —"

The woman grabbed her arm. "Look!"

"What?" Then Sofia heard Mr. Stafford's voice above the din.

"There's a flame on the tail! Look!"

Sofia saw a thin blue ripple of light running along the backbone of the ship. Then she heard a loud, muffled *bang* that sounded like the kitchen stove when she put a match to the gas. No, worse, another explosion, louder this time — and

An Ordinary Star

at that moment, a flame shot hundreds of feet into the sky. It billowed into an ugly red-hot fist as the rear of the ship collapsed, lighting up like an enormous paper lantern, its skeleton etched in black against the fire.

The burning ship was drifting above the ground crew. She heard the sailors screaming as they ran.

An angry wave of heat came roaring toward them. Sofia felt her skin hot and blazing. How close were they — how far? She started to run. People were running all over the field, screaming for help.

Mr. Stafford grabbed her hand. "It's OK, I'm here," he said.

"My aunt and uncle —"

"The sailors'll help them. Come on!"

The nose of the ship, still buoyant, shot high up into the air, and the air itself shattered, as if the whole sky were a glass roof collapsing on their heads. They ran as fast as they could in the opposite direction, taking shelter behind scrub brush, safe from the firestorm. They turned and looked. High above, the ship's promenade windows were smashing open, broken panes and shards of flying glass floating down in an eerie spiral of light.

She raised the binoculars to her eyes, watching chunks of fiery matter float down from the elevated nose of the airship. *Luggage*, she thought. *Tubular furniture.* She'd allowed her eyes to go unfocussed and the scene before her was a blur. When she looked again, she could see that from high above the ground, passengers near the buoyant nose of the ship were jumping. She saw a falling woman, her hair on fire, her mouth wide open in horror, her hand just loosened from the grip of her husband's. A few feet away from his wife, that man, too, was burning, his clothes a sheet of fire as he fell. When Sofia put the binoculars down, these suffering humans blurred into light as if they were no more than floating embers, and she thought of their poor souls drifting away. She crossed herself.

"God help them," said Mrs. Stafford. She covered her face and wept.

"It's too damn high to jump," said her husband.

Sofia felt a cold chill in the pit of her stomach. Hesitant, she peered once again through the lenses. She spotted a newsman with a motion-picture camera who turned his rig away from the victims and on to the crumbled tail of the airship in flames. She saw a screaming torch of a man, his clothes burned off; rescuers running toward his collapsing form with blankets. It felt indecent to observe the final agony of strangers, obscene to witness the spectacle of innocent people as their lives were snatched away from them. She put the binoculars away.

"Dear, don't look anymore," said Mrs. Stafford.

Where are my aunt and uncle?

A blast of white flame shot right down the centre of the ship and out the nose.

"God help us," Mr. Stafford whispered.

From five hundred feet in the air, the nose of the airship collapsed in incandescent fire and fell to the ground, a smouldering mass of girders and scalded metal. The whole of it looked vast and hot and brilliant, as if a huge star had crashed into the Lakehurst airfield. The sky was lit with gaseous oranges, pinks and dazzling white — a roiling mass of fire and colour. Sofia felt it explode inside her with the certain truth that her aunt and uncle had perished. She started screaming.

"Aunt Julia!"

"It's all right, honey," said Mr. Stafford.

It wasn't all right. She screamed against his chest, but he didn't let go his grip on her until she began to calm down. After a while she felt too exhausted to cry.

Someone was shouting through a bullhorn: "Ground crew, give 'em a hand!" The fleeing rescuers were running back toward the wreckage, and she heard the wailing of ambulance sirens and the clang of fire trucks as they raced across the field.

"They're going back to find them, see?" said Mrs. Stafford.

Sofia dried her eyes, took her binoculars and scanned the scene. She'd try not to be frantic as she scrutinized passengers escaping through the windows, climbing out through the tangled girders, running away from the flames. *Where were they?* A yellow haze blurred her lenses, dissolving into a burning sleeve, a man's charred arm. *Captain, you're on fire!* Was she close enough to hear this? Another blur — someone snuffing out the flames. A blanket.

Through a gaping hole in the promenade window, she caught a glimpse of a woman seated, her hands folded in her lap. Everything was unspooling in such a slow and casual way, looping and unwinding as if nothing at all were the matter, as if the thread of life were endlessly spinning along. *There's a man walking up to that woman. Should I go tell him that the ship's on fire?*

Passengers were climbing to safety, members of the ground crew running to their aid. She stared.

The gangway stairs had dropped down from the promenade deck and were skimming the ground. Like a pair of sleepwalkers, her aunt and uncle were exiting the stairway arm in arm, their looks impassive, undaunted by the scalding rubble and smoke, the shouting and crying around them. They seemed removed from the calamity, as if the two of them were trapped — not in the wreckage, but in the moment before the airship was destroyed. Uncle Paul was dressed in jacket and tie, a fedora on his head, his briefcase in hand, reminding Sofia of the drawing on the Zeppelin brochure of the businessman striding across the world. He looked so abstracted that it seemed as if he'd stepped out of some ordinary airship, wandering by chance into this grand but catastrophic one. He had Aunt Julia by the arm, but she didn't seem to notice him, or anyone else. She was dressed in a floral-patterned frock, a light jacket, a brimmed hat with a pale blue ribbon and a clump of daisies. Her face was expressionless. She looked unscathed.

The pair turned to each other. A look sparked across the gap between them, as they hopped from the bottom of the stairway to the ground. Together they walked forward with deliberate slowness, as if they were leading a procession. *Over here, you two!* Sailors ran up to them and pulled them out of the way of the flaming cinders, leading them over the rubble to safety. Her aunt and uncle disappeared.

Sofia turned to Mrs. Stafford. "Did you see them?"

"No, honey, but —"

"They'll have an infirmary," said her husband. "We'll find them there."

But they aren't injured.

A sustained murmur, the awful sound of hundreds of people in shock. Firemen were circling the collapsed skeleton of the *Hindenburg*, turning water on the flames, and Sofia saw that dark smoke had blackened the sky. Her teeth were chattering. Mr. Stafford gave her his jacket. *This way, honey*, he said to her. He and his wife led her away. It felt as if they'd been there for hours, that it must be time for sleep and close to midnight.

Thirty-four seconds, said the evening news. *From start to finish.*

3

The disaster victims were taken to a hospital in the town of Lakewood, about ten miles away. Later Sofia forgot the drive in Mr. Stafford's car and the wailing of ambulance sirens and fire trucks along the country road. She had no idea what sort of place this hospital was or why the Staffords insisted that they go. *We have to check out everything*, they told her, glancing at each other as if they knew something that she hadn't figured out. Whatever that was, Sofia wasn't sure she wanted to know. She wondered aloud if her aunt and uncle had left with someone or had gone to a hotel. *We should talk to the authorities first*, said Mrs. Stafford. Sofia noticed that wary glance of hers directed at her husband and his nod at her words. *I don't know how they could be injured*, said Sofia, *since they walked away on their own.* The woman took her hand. *At very least, they'll be in shock*, she said.

At the very least.

"Someone here may know their whereabouts," said Mr. Stafford.

Sofia didn't want to be here. It wasn't a very tidy hospital — not like her father's spotless office with its glass and metal cabinet stocked with medications and dressings, a separate locked compartment for ampoules of morphine, glass jars full of gleaming sterilized instruments. Not at all. Here was a scene so jarring that she had to wait a few moments for its meaning to seep into consciousness, as if the place itself were a kind of medicine to clear the mind. She felt dazed as she looked around, and she found herself wondering why these injured people were lying in the corridor, their dressings soaked in blood; why they were propped up against walls, seated in what few chairs there were; why so few of them were lying on stretchers and cots. Maybe she could help find some chairs. Maybe she could assist the nurse who must be taking down names somewhere, deciding who the doctor should see first. Only this wasn't her father's office. It wasn't like anything she knew.

It felt as if her eyes were adjusting to a very dim light, as if light itself refused to penetrate the scene before her. The room was silent. Not a word of complaint, not a sound from anyone. One by one, she began to admit each of these horrors to her small room of sanity — each bloodied limb, the skin torn away; arms and legs, faces and torsos blackened with unimaginable burns — an entire room lit with the dim blue light of shock. Quiet. She watched and listened. There were orderlies and doctors, but she couldn't tell who was who. Some of them were giving water to the suffering who cried out for it. *They're going to die.* Her thought was as calm and indifferent as a falling leaf. A harried-looking man passed by with a hypodermic. *I have morphine*, she heard him say, *for anyone who wants it.* Sofia wondered if her father would approve. The man sat beside a patient whose eyes were terrified and full of pain. He was speaking to the victim with gentle assurance as he administered the drug, and in his compassionate voice she could hear her father speaking. She was shivering, as if she had a fever.

Across from her sat a dazed and badly charred man on the edge of a table, dabbing something on his burns, as if they were minor abrasions that would pass. When he was done, he offered the medicine to the woman next to him. Back and forth the bottle went. *Danke schön*, the man said each time.

Kapitan Lehmann, Sofia heard someone whisper.

She knew that name. He was a friend of her uncle's, or at least someone he knew. Christopher knew him — *a musical fellow, that's right*. He played the accordion.

"Are you looking for someone?" asked a nurse.

"My aunt and uncle walked off the ship. They looked unhurt."

"A lot of people seem all right," the nurse said. "And aren't."

"I saw some sailors rescue them," Sofia told her. The nurse urged her to look around.

Before they'd left the airfield, Mr. Stafford had spoken to a man with an Immigration badge, one of those advancing on the airship moments before it burned. The official had a copy of the passenger list and yes, Mr. and Mrs. Gentile's names were on it.

"And you're sure you saw the two of them?" he asked.

"This young lady did. Through binoculars."

"I only ask because of the confusion," said the official. "Some of the injured have been flown to hospitals in New York."

"They weren't injured," said Sofia.

"They'll turn up. If they don't —" The man looked exhausted. He'd gestured toward the makeshift morgue. "I don't know where else to direct you."

Which was why they'd driven to the hospital instead.

Later that evening, Sofia called Stefano and her father. *We saw Aunt Julia and Uncle Paul, but we've lost them in the confusion. They're alive.* It was the first long-distance call she'd ever made and she worried about the cost, but Stefano said *as long as you're fine — that's all I care about.* There'd been a bulletin on NBC Blue, her father explained, just fifteen minutes after the explosion. The announcement's speed had rattled him almost as much as the disaster.

They stayed with the Staffords' friends in Lakewood and in the morning, they drove down the road again toward the naval base. The sky was still blackened by smoke and dust and the entry points to the airfield were closed and under guard. In the distance Sofia could see the charred remains of the airship — smoke still curling from its mangled skeleton, its bent girders spreading outward from a huge metal disk like limp muscles trailing from the dead eye of a monster.

They located a military policeman. Sofia told the officer

that she was a relative of two passengers. He located a list of the dead.

"Thirty so far," he said. Her aunt and uncle's names didn't appear.

"It's not a final list," he added.

"I saw them," said Sofia.

"What's the name again?"

"Gen-*ti*-lay," she said. "Paul and Julia."

The man perused another sheet of paper. "From Long Island?" he asked.

"Yes," the three of them said at once.

"They're down as missing. Mr. and Mrs. Paul Gentile." He pronounced their name like the Gentiles in the Bible.

On the journey home, Sofia fell into silence. Mr. Stafford, proud of the radio he'd installed in the car, never turned it on. No one talked about the night before, but the Staffords observed the heavy traffic headed out of the city, moving toward the Holland Tunnel and the George Washington Bridge, blocked at every crossing as tens of thousands of people drove to New Jersey to view the disaster. Sofia wondered what there was to see. A charred ruin under guard — no one could get within a mile of it, she felt sure. From the back seat, she heard Mr. Stafford whisper to his wife. *Apparently, they're saying it might have been sabotage. A bomb on board or some such.* Sofia imagined a crewman with access to the hydrogen cells crawling out on the intricate catwalk inside the ship and setting the bomb. Who else could have placed it there? Except that a man on duty had to stay at his post and could not have escaped the explosion. He would have died at his own hand. That made no sense to her.

In any case, she wasn't sure it mattered.

She began to worry about Christopher. By now he would have heard the news, and no one would be there to reassure him.

She wanted sleep.

The Staffords insisted on driving Sofia back to the Bronx. It was late afternoon by the time they reached Maywood Road. The tall hedge in front of the house blocked Sofia's view. Tired and unfocused, her eyes began to draw in colour through the tight spaces of greenery — a bright blue splotch, a dash of yellow, a grey jacket and skirt — *oh, it's Mrs. Santini, and Mrs. De Lucca, too. What are they doing on our stoop?* She heard one of the women's voices — *what a terrible thing, that fire*, and then the other murmuring agreement. Leo's sailor cap bobbed over the top of the hedge. She heard Tina. Why was everyone home from work? Sofia came up the walk with the Staffords and ran right into her father.

"*Figlia mia,*" he whispered and took her in his arms. "Are you all right?" She assured him that she was, but he looked troubled as he walked her into the house. "Your aunt and uncle have gone home?" he asked.

"We haven't found them." She didn't want to say *missing*. The word that had reassured her this morning seemed ominous now. She told her father what she knew.

"*Basta.* Come inside. I'll call your uncle later."

The neighbours joined them. Their voices seem to come from a great distance, and Sofia felt as if she were viewing shapes and colours blurred and dimmed by fog. She began to understand why they'd gathered and what was about to happen. With the response of friends to a crisis, they'd brought food to her father's home — platters of roast chicken, cold cuts and crusty bread, lasagna and a huge bowl of salad. There was wine, but the gathering wasn't festive. Her neighbours were sombre, like mourners after a funeral.

"*Figlia mia*, drink," said Sofia's father. "Eat something."

"I'm not hungry."

Her father put his hand on her forehead. Tina made her a cup of tea and sat beside her. Her voice was quiet.

"Poor Sofia, we just got back from the movies. They had a newsreel of the fire."

"I saw a man filming it," said Sofia.

"No one's ever filmed such a thing," said Mrs. Santini.

"He turned away —" said Sofia.

Everyone was silent.

"— from the worst of it," she said.

Her father looked grieved. "*Basta*, Sofia. Don't talk."

"A man described the whole thing on the radio," said Gabriella, and the others murmured *yes* and *did you hear him?* "Right in the middle, he broke down and cried."

Sofia thought of young Christopher. She hoped he hadn't heard the newsman crying.

The front door opened and in came Stefano. "Don't get up, *cara mia*." He kissed Sofia. "We took our class to see the newsreel. *Madre di Dio*, such a tragedy." He hid his face in his hands, and then he looked up at her. "Your aunt and uncle. Where are they?"

"They wandered off."

Wandered off where? said his eyes. "They don't know what hit them, I'm sure," he said. *And neither do you."*

"I haven't slept."

"Wait a few moments. I'll take you upstairs."

"No, I don't want to be alone," she said. "I'll see the whole thing."

"Cara mia —"

"A man was on fire. A woman jumped from the window. Her hair was in flames. Two children —"

No, no, no, no, he whispered. He took her in his arms. Back and forth he rocked her, murmuring, stroking her hair. *Sofia. Povera Sofia. They didn't show that in the film. No, no, no, no.*

Her father spoke with Mr. Stafford before the couple left. Later he called his brother's home in Long Island. When no one answered the phone, he decided to contact the police.

"It's possible that your aunt and uncle have suffered hysterical amnesia," he said to Sofia. "It can happen in cases of extreme shock. It never lasts long."

Sofia was gazing out the window. "Shock because a friend caught fire."

"Who?"

"A man I saw in the hospital. Burns all over. A captain."

"The captain survived. Pruss is the name."

"Someone else. A Captain Lehmann."

Her father fell into a grieved silence. "He's dead, this Lehmann," he said at last. "On the news I heard his name."

He paused. "You are correct, *figlia mia*. Your uncle knew him."

Sofia went to bed, and as she began to drift into sleep, she was startled awake by the image of Christopher, his eight year-old hands on Lehmann's accordion. She wondered if anyone had spoken to her cousin. She wondered what he'd make of that poor man's death.

In the morning she found her father in the dining room, his newspaper spread out on the table, opened to an image of the flaming airship. She brought him coffee, but he let it get cold.

"No one deserved to die like this," he said.

"Would you like breakfast?"

"*Sì, grazie*. I am astounded. Someone has written '*A proud symbol of German power, fallen.*'"

"Would you like jam with your toast?"

Her father was staring at the wall, at the photograph of Uncle Guido.

"Tell that to their families," he said to no one in particular.

After breakfast, Sofia's father received a long-distance telephone call. He didn't speak to her or Stefano about it until he'd changed into his best dark suit, a starched white shirt, a blue silk tie. Hat, overcoat and briefcase — what he wore to testify in court or to visit the Medical Examiner's office. The thought of his going to the morgue chilled Sofia. *No. He wouldn't be wearing his good clothes out to Lakehurst. Not with all the smoke and ash.*

He told her he was going there. He'd put galoshes and an old coat in the car.

"I've been called by the authorities," he said at last.

They'd set up a makeshift morgue in the airfield hangar. In it were the few remaining bodies too badly burned to be identified.

"I saw them alive," Sofia whispered.

"Don't worry, *figlia mia*. We have to rule out certain things. That's all."

She thought it a long way to go, just to rule something out.

"Not if I can be of help," he insisted. "There will be grieving people. Families in shock."

Her father returned the next day.

"I'm certain," he said, "that my brother and sister-in-law are missing."

"I am sorry that you had to view the dead," said Stefano.

"Yes, but at least they are not among them."

"There was a write-up in the paper," said Sofia. She showed her father the article.

He glanced at it. "What do I want with this?"

"It says some bodies were so disfigured that they will never be identified."

"Not by any reporter," he said. He tossed the newspaper aside. "I happen to be a doctor. I think I'd know my family's remains if I saw them."

4

Other sections of the Sunday paper were more to her father's liking — and hers. Sofia found a special supplement on the upcoming coronation of George VI, whose brother, Edward VIII had abdicated the throne the previous December. The photos showed the royal coach and steeds and horsemen in plumed attire, the crown and sceptre of the new king, Westminster Abbey and Windsor Castle and the parade route through London. The event would be broadcast on the radio this Wednesday, May 12th. Sofia pondered the photos, along with the comment made by the Archbishop of Canterbury that for the first time, "the world would be the audience" at a British coronation.

She knew that in a matter of days, the grim news about the *Hindenburg* would pass, superseded by this glittering and hopeful event. As far as she was concerned, that was fine since most of the world's news was just plain miserable. To her father's dismay, Italy was growing closer to Nazi Germany while the Vatican's reprimands to the Third Reich went unheeded. Today, Sunday, just happened to be the first anniversary of Italy's conquest of Ethiopia through the use of poison gas, an occasion which Sofia's father allowed to pass without comment. *The whole world needs a vacation*, said Tina, who was collecting Coronation china and demitasse spoons. *They say Eddie's a fan of Hitler. When he marries Mrs. Simpson, maybe they'll issue a commemorative beer stein.* Tina was hopeless, said Gabriella, who was making a Coronation scrapbook. Sofia promised to listen to the broadcast.

"I am no fan of monarchy," said Stefano. "But the music will be worth hearing."

On Monday, Sofia went back to work. She attended to her father's patients and offered them the usual words of encouragement, and everyone was too polite to ask her what the disaster looked like or whether she'd seen the newsreel or heard Mr. Morrison's anguished broadcast. An international incident — that was the murmur and hubbub of the press and radio, the commentators carving and slicing the news like a Thanksgiving turkey, dressing it with dollops of speculation. The truth was that no one was certain why the disaster had happened. Because no calamity had ever been filmed as it unfolded, those who saw the newsreel had made history even as they witnessed it. A new plague was spreading around the world — a contagion of knowledge, and Sofia hoped for a cure, or at least a vaccine against constant distraction. In the waiting room were anxious mothers with their children. She had to concentrate on them.

Her father stopped by her desk with coffee and sweet rolls. He wore a look of consternation.

"*Figlia mia*, eat," he said.

She had no idea how to reassure him. She tried to work but she felt unmoored from life, locked in the moment when she saw her aunt and uncle stepping down the fallen gangway and through the tangle of girders and scalding metal. Unaccountably safe in suit and tie, in floral dress and ribboned hat, ready for business and leisure, sheltered inside that one enormous second before the disaster — was it possible? Sofia found herself wondering where her aunt and uncle had come from that night and if they'd been in the accident at all and whether she'd actually seen the destruction of the *Hindenburg* or only dreamt it.

Sofia's father had spoken to the New York and New Jersey police departments. They were searching for two people in a state of shock, putting out an alert for one or more individuals who might be suffering from amnesia. *They could turn up anywhere*, the detective said. *They may have wandered off to Canada.* The officials at the border had been notified. Her father insisted that there wasn't a scrap of forensic evidence to corroborate their deaths. *Are you certain of this, sir?* asked the detective. *I am a doctor — I am certain*, he replied. *What little remains*, the examiner assured him, *we haven't got the means to identify*.

Hoping to find clues, Sofia retrieved her aunt and uncle's souvenirs — brochures and menus and postcards. She found a telegram they'd sent from the *Hindenburg*. "Do you remember this?" she asked her dad. *"Friends will meet us at Lakehurst. Don't put yourselves out.'* Only he never asked the Staffords for a ride."

Her father had Paul's earlier note. *Life is not always what it seems. Life takes us in mysterious directions. Sometimes the destination is in sight before the journey commences. But not always.* He gave everything to the police.

Sofia wasn't sleeping well. In the middle of the night she'd wake up with a jolt, and she'd remember that a year earlier, she'd had sex with her uncle. Why on earth would she ever want to see him again? Wouldn't it be just as well if Aunt Julia and Uncle Paul had wandered off? *Not exactly.* Who would look after Christopher and *nonna*?

She'd go back to sleep and dream that she'd burst into flames, and she'd awake rolled up in her blankets. Sleep and wakefulness bled into each other like cheap cotton dyes in the wash. She'd recall the great *Los Angeles* crossing the pinnacle of the Woolworth Building, but in her dreams, America's own Zeppelin collapsed into the burning hulk of the German *Hindenburg* — a roiling orange fireball exploding over the spires of New York. *Hydrogen's too much of a risk*, the papers said. *Airships are finished.* She'd get up and pace the floor, trying not to wake Stefano.

On the night before the coronation, she thought about Christopher. A week had passed since the explosion, and she hadn't spoken to her cousin. It haunted her that the dead Captain Lehmann had taught him accordion as a child. Unable to sleep, she found her aunt's letter quoting his school composition after the *Graf Zeppelin* voyage.

... The more I played, the lighter I felt ... until one day, I "saw" two shadowy people in the light ... There was a dark-haired woman with a gentle face wearing a bonnet. She had on a print dress, and over it a jacket. There was a kind-looking man in suit and tie, wearing a hat and carrying a briefcase. The images came and went, as dreams do ... They looked like the people in stories that have been read out loud to me. I reached out to touch them, but they vanished.

They were dressed like that when they escaped the fire. She sat up awake for the rest of the night.

On the following day, the coronation of George VI was broadcast around the world. Sofia knew that six radio stations in New York City would carry the event. Unable to sleep past sunrise, she listened as the ceremony began. Later she turned the radio on in her father's office. There were no patients in the waiting room — none when the strains of Handel's *Zadok the Priest* began their long journey from Westminster Abbey in London, its jubilant chorus of *Long live the King* flashing across the ocean to every radio and every eager listener in every apartment and office and bakery and candy store on Gun Hill Road in the Bronx. Only the world had grown too large for Sofia Fiore. She put her head on the desk and slept.

IN ONE MOMENT

I

The police departments found no trace of the missing couple.

"I cannot give up on my brother," said Doctor Gentile.

"I understand," said Stefano. *Poor Elio*, said his eyes. *Two years pass and you cannot give up.*

Sofia's father ignored his Italian periodicals and turned his attention to medical papers on the subject of amnesia. *It was like this after the Great War*, he wrote in his journal. *Men were shell-shocked, but it was thought to be cowardly to show it. They'd end up using their fists, turning into drunkards, running away from their families. Have my brother and sister-in-law endured any less?*

"I blame our modern world," he said to Stefano.

The younger man looked surprised. "For their disappearance?"

"For whatever state of shock induced it."

"Yes, but *caro papà*, listen. No other passengers disappeared."

"I doubt if anyone else was as bitterly disappointed by the loss of the airship."

"But why would he run away?"

Elio was silent. "Countless times as a child, he ran away," he said at last. "He wanted so much to fly. Even then."

"Your poor father, how he suffers," said Stefano. "Only I have never quite believed his theory."

"Then you don't believe me, either," said Sofia.

"Why not you?"

"I'm the one who saw them walk away."

"I believe you, *cara mia*," he said. "But too much time has passed. Consider that they might have —"

Sofia knew that he couldn't bring himself to say that they might have perished during their escape. For two years, no one had questioned what she'd reported seeing that night. Instead everyone had written different endings to a story she'd begun, because without her aunt and uncle's return, her eyewitness account had no more weight than a dream.

At fourteen, Christopher was fair and lean, and he resembled *nonno* Domenico more than either of his parents. His face wore a sombre expression which would soften into wonderment as he spoke, as if he were always on the verge of some extraordinary insight. Sofia used to imagine that he wore dark glasses because he'd been blinded by whatever sunload of brilliance he'd pondered too long. Blindness aside, it had long been obvious to all the adults that Christopher didn't enjoy living with Aunt Julia and Uncle Paul. And neither did they with him, although they'd been reluctant to admit it. *He knows too much for his own good*, she'd heard her uncle say to her dad, and *he knows what's going to happen before it does*, said her aunt. Sofia had heard malice in her uncle's words, but she'd regarded her aunt's remark as nothing more than superstition. Until now.

She told her cousin that she'd seen his parents leave the *Hindenburg* alive. There was that composition he'd written, describing the clothing they'd worn that night. She read it aloud to him.

"It's almost as if you'd seen the future," she said.

He looked pained. "I didn't *see* anything. They were just *there*. Besides, I don't believe in time."

"I hope your piano teacher knows that."

"Everything happens at once," he said. "Time's an illusion."

He sat down at the piano and began to play a sonata by Mozart. He'd been learning the slow movement and now he seemed lost inside its melody, meandering through its minor key as if it were a neighbourhood in a strange part of town. Its tenderness appeared to give him solace. His face looked calm as he made his way to the end, as if the music had drawn him toward some conclusions of his own. He stopped. He sat with his hands in his lap, his head bowed.

"My parents have to find their way," he said.

"How do you mean?"

"In the world, I mean. Just as children do."

Sofia was stunned. She explained to him that raising children was, in fact, how most adults found their way in the world.

Pale with fury, he turned toward the sound of her voice. "Do you think I don't know why they shipped me off to boarding school?" he asked. "Long before I came along, I was killing their marriage. My father was out carousing the night I was born."

"What makes you think that?"

"He told me," he said.

Sofia felt chilled.

"You must wonder that I could be so stupid as to care."

"No, Chris — I don't wonder. They're your parents."

Christopher's look softened as he let his fingers rest on the keyboard. Sofia could feel the air stirring, as if the memory of the *Graf Zeppelin* were lifting him up from the ground. He began to play again.

We'll hear from Paul, said *nonno* Domenico, who sounded as if he were speaking about the plague. Only *nonna* Rosa wept. *Julia I miss*, she said. *And poor Paolo. I hope they're well.* *Nonna* Constanza spat on the ground. *Abandoning their son* — managgia, *they're better off burned to a cinder*, she said.

Elio read and pondered and made notes. Although he hadn't any clues.

Leo missed no one. He didn't tell his father that.

Life became as still as breath.

2

In sleep, Sofia forgot her aunt and uncle. She stared horrified at the eddies of blue flame snaking across the Bronx rooftops, at the fire ripping through mortar and stone as the airship collapsed over Maywood Road. In her throat, she felt the screams of the injured and dying. She woke up drenched in sweat.

Stefano held her. "*Cara mia*, you were crying."

"It's too late," she said.

On the night of the Hindenburg *fire, the world began to burn. It will never stop burning. Maybe Christopher's right about time. There is no end to any of this.*

"What is too late?"

"We're going to have a war."

She couldn't tell Stefano the rest of it. *Uncle Paul vanished because of me.* She thought of poor Christopher, who had no doubt guessed that his father had slept with her, who would blame her for his parents' leaving. There are moments, she realized, that burrow into your soul like worms in the bowel. When she looked at her husband, she'd taste her uncle forever. This was her punishment — that her uncle, although gone, would never loosen his grip on her.

On her way home from work the following day, Sofia turned on Barnes Avenue and saw a young man up ahead who looked like Christopher. It puzzled her that she hadn't seen him sooner. No, it couldn't be him — what would he be doing in the Bronx on a weekday? Dark glasses, his unruly hair as radiant as the golden monstrance in the church — it was Christopher, all right. Gripping a worn leather briefcase, he tapped a cane on the sidewalk, sweeping it back and forth like a battleship with its new device, radar. He was confident, walking like a monk inside a deep and trance-like concentration. For a moment he seemed insubstantial, a heat mirage that might at any moment disappear.

Then he did.

He turned down Maywood and strolled toward her house. Under the trellis he walked, and into the shade of the leafy beech where the bright spark of him blinked out like a firefly's light. Sofia realized that her eyes hadn't adjusted to the shade, yet the young man had vanished, as if he were air that the trees drew in through their leaves. A car drove by on the gravel road and the crunch of its wheels must have distracted her from the clicking open of the front door as Stefano let him in. Yet it seemed that he disappeared into a silence as profound as any blindness, so much so that it might have been of his own making.

She asked herself if time were a liquid thing, as slippery as dishwater. One by one, the days of the week had circled their way down the drain to Friday, to her cousin's arrival for the weekend. Only it was Wednesday. She felt certain that she was awake.

Sofia sat outside, on the bench on the upward slope of the lawn, a narrow strip of garden that separated their house from the neighbour's. From there she could peer into the front room. On Wednesday afternoons, her husband taught at home — reviewing scales with his students, running though each phrase of a violin piece. She could see an open window, a curtain nudged by a breeze, then Stefano and his violin. She could hear him playing a piece that sounded like a Beethoven romance. He was alone.

No he's not. This is a duet. Right now Christopher's playing the piano part somewhere.

Stefano appeared at the door. He waved at her, and then came outside.

"Was Chris here?" she asked.

"No, I'm alone. I had a cancellation."

"I saw him come up the walk. Then he vanished."

"He wants so much to be here," said Stefano. "It is possible he has sent himself."

Stefano brushed his lips against her hair, then walked her inside. In the cool shadows, he held her in his arms. "I love it when you're like this," he said. "Full of dreams. Who on earth has any left?" He kissed her and they went upstairs. On the second floor, she glanced into the guest room.

"In here," she said.

He looked puzzled. "You would enjoy this more?"

She would. She felt like an insect trapped in amber. Everyone was caught inside the hardened resin of some hurt or fear or desire — not just her. Only she was going to free herself. She was going to cast her uncle out of her body's memory.

"Let's make believe that it's the first time," she said.

"*Innocente.*" He laughed, then unbuttoned her blouse. "*Signorina*, first we get undressed," he said.

She kissed him, letting his tongue linger in her mouth.

"Like that?" she asked.

"*Perfetto.*"

3

Sofia became pregnant, and she felt as if Christopher had somehow blessed that spring day. She was four months along on the first of September, when her father told her that Germany had invaded Poland. She'd felt certain it would happen, yet in her mind she saw the great expanse of the globe swinging like an elegant chandelier through the dark of space. The lights began to go out, the brilliant lamp swinging in a hurricane, its crystal prisms smashing as they hit the walls.

"And Italy —?" she asked.

"Pray for Italy. Pray it chooses well."

Stefano would be livid. *You wait and see what Italy does.*

Italy declared neutrality. The next day, the two of them went walking in the Botanical Garden with Tina, her husband Joey and their little daughter Anne. The crimson dahlias were in flower, fat bees nuzzled in the snapdragon petals and the sky was morning-glory blue.

"How are you feeling, Sof?" asked Tina.

"Just fine, thanks."

"Lucky you — your dad's a doctor and your best friend's a nurse."

"And I drive a cab," said Joey. "I know the way to the hospital in my sleep."

Tina bent over to sniff a hollyhock. It buzzed and she pulled back. "I'd better *bee* careful," she said. "It's summer for another three weeks yet."

Is it? thought Sofia.

It felt as if summer were over.

That night Sofia dreamed that an enormous weight was crushing her, as if she were a cluster of grapes in a wine press, about to be pulverized into pulp and skin and seed. She felt no pain as the weight bore down on her, pushing her deeper into blackness, as if it would compact her into an object no larger than a speck. Then she heard *nonna* Constanza's voice. *Only a blessing can remove a curse* and she felt the woman's hands pushing hard on her stomach. It surprised Sofia that she didn't object as the woman continued to push. *This is Paul's child, and it mustn't be born*, said *nonna*. As the crushing weight ripped her apart, she awoke to the warm sensation of blood between her legs. *I mustn't wake Stefano*, she thought. Pain tore at her insides like a dog's teeth at scraps of meat. She gripped the sheets with her fists. She closed her eyes.

An Ordinary Star

In the fog of unconsciousness, she heard Stefano's voice shouting and then her father's. They took her in an ambulance to Montefiore, but she remembered nothing. She awoke to find Stefano beside her. She felt his hand on her forehead.

"I'm sorry," she said to him. "It's my fault."

"How is it your fault?"

"It runs in my family. The first child. Only Aunt Julia escaped."

He took her hands in his. "And your mother."

"She died young. We all have something wrong with us."

"No, no, no — we'll try again." He pulled out a handkerchief and dried her eyes. Then he dried his own.

I can't get rid of my uncle. I tried that day, but I can't.

Stefano told her that he loved her.

The world is on fire, said the radio.

By the time Sofia returned home from the hospital, every commuter on White Plains Road knew that Britain, France, Australia and New Zealand had all declared war on Germany. *World War Two* — she decided she'd better get used to the awkward sound of the words. Tina and Gabriella came by to comfort her with hot tea and homemade biscuits. When no one was there with her, Sofia folded the baby clothes and put them away. Leo decided it was time to go to sea. Stefano sat alone in his basement cubicle, writing music and preparing lessons. A few blocks away the el went rumbling along like an army, full of men on their way to work in Manhattan. One by one, the lights went out.

In the weeks following the outbreak of war, Sofia's father grew pensive and silent. He'd work late, then sit at home reading the *Times*, the *Telegram*, *Il Progresso* — whatever newspaper might offer sufficient information about the collapse of the Polish resistance or the sinking of British battleships. There was never anything to reassure him. After a while he'd come to the table, pour himself a glass of wine, eat some *pollo* and *insalate*. From time to time he'd glance up at the photo of his brother Guido or the daguerreotype of his soldier father. One evening, he turned to Sofia.

"Are you feeling better?" he asked.

"Today I lit a candle at church," she said.

He gave her a sharp look. "It's not your fault, you know."

She couldn't admit that she felt it was.

"Thank God *nonna's* in Long Island," he continued.

She hadn't forgotten the family superstition. Getting pregnant with the first child — it was like breaking the seal on an ancient jar of myrrh and aloes, perfuming herself with a fragrance intended for the dead. She'd never told *nonna* Constanza that a child was on the way. Yet when she miscarried, she'd remembered Aunt Julia's giving birth. She was certain she'd brought trouble on herself as her aunt had never done, as no imagined curse could do. Her own life was a bent twig, and although it was full of leaves and reaching sunward, not even God could make it grow straight.

Whenever she passed the church, she'd light a candle in memory of the lost child. Today as she did this, she recalled how, before her marriage, she'd gone to confession to admit that she'd slept with her uncle. For a moment, the priest had been silent. *Did he force you?* he asked, and she heard concern in his voice. *No*, she replied. Another silence, laden with shock. *He's your uncle*, said the priest. *Do you understand that he should not have taken advantage?* She told him that she did. *Were you willing? Yes.* He'd paused again, then asked if she were sorry. She was.

The sin was supposed to have been forgiven.

Her father sipped his wine. "It is common, with the first child," he continued. "The body has to learn how."

She shrank back, as if he'd touched a burn.

"*Figlia mia*, don't worry. I will have grandchildren at this table."

She twisted her napkin tight in her hands, then squeezed her eyes shut. Her father got up, pulled his chair alongside hers and took her hand between both of his.

Stefano had never written to his father about the pregnancy, and he told Sofia it was just as well. *I only hear from him now and again*, he said. *He's risen in the ranks of the fascisti, from the sound of things. His current lady-friend is the mayor's wife.* Sofia asked if the mayor didn't mind. *I'm sure he does*, said Stefano. *But he has no say. My father's the chief of police.* Captain Fiore had offered no congratulations on his son's marriage. *A man's first bride is his country*, he'd remarked. *You are always welcome to return.* Stefano had taken the letter, crumpled it in his fist and thrown it in the wastepaper basket. Sofia could still hear that paper's weightless fall into the back of her husband's mind.

Stefano walked into the dining room.

"Join us," said Sofia's father.

Sofia felt too weary to bring him food, and then she felt something warm around her shoulders. Stefano had wrapped her in an afghan, one that her mother had crocheted. She could feel her mother's embrace along with his.

4

Sofia was grateful for her family's comfort. Leo brought her something witty to read — as if he couldn't bear to be a smart-aleck himself, as if it were better for somebody else to make the wisecracks while she was upset. Unobserved, her brother looked more sombre then usual. When he'd realize he wasn't alone in the room, he'd clown and pop a jack-in-the-box smile, which then made him appear more moody than he was. His life was changing, and his next address would be a battleship. Certain that America would get involved in the war sooner or later, he decided to enlist in the Navy. *Better now than when a war breaks out*, he said. Their father couldn't grasp his logic, but Sofia understood that Leo was twenty-one and wanted space. She hoped that *nonno* Domenico wouldn't rant about his grandson joining the millionaires' war. Since that outbreak of hostilities in Europe, her father was in no hurry to engage *nonno* in conversation.

In November, *nonna* Constanza died of a heart attack. Having astounded everyone by managing on her own — making new friends, frank in her pleasure at living without her no-good daughter and son-in-law — she'd thrived on an engine of mobilized fury. On the day the engine sputtered and stopped, *nonna* was found by neighbours lying face-down in a green tangle of squash and pumpkin vines. Sofia wondered how Aunt Julia would feel when she realized that she'd missed her mother's funeral. She didn't have to ask what her uncle would feel. The news might even cause him to return home for good. She imagined a newspaper ad: *Come home, Paul. Your mother-in-law's dead.* She knew that no one would print it. She mentioned it to Leo as he helped her answer condolence messages. Her brother chuckled. He picked up a handful of Mass cards and shuffled them.

"Deuces are wild," he said. "Let's deal Uncle Paul a hand. And your pop," he said to Stefano.

"Don't be disrespectful," said Sofia.

"So quit laughing." Sofia bit her lip.

Stefano spoke. "I sent my father word about *nonna*."

"You *wrote* to that Fascist?" Leo made a face.

"I still write to my father," said Stefano. "That is what a son does."

"Maybe your dad knows Uncle Paul," said Leo.

Sofia frowned. "Do you think he's in Italy?"

"He is not that foolish," said Stefano.

"Let me tell you what I think," said Leo. "The two of them were Nazi spies. All that traveling around on German airships.

The Navy says there were hidden transmitters on the *Graf Zeppelin* and the *Hindenburg*. Gathering intelligence as they flew across the Western Hemisphere. You could probably paper the walls with all the information they collected, all the aerial surveillance. Uncle Paul speaks German. They both speak Italian. Look — they dumped their son. And that nice house they left behind? You think maybe Old Man Hitler paid the mortgage?"

"I had not thought of that," said Stefano.

"Well, think. All those phoney dispatches. 'Layman's aeronautics.' 'Shipboard Science for the Ladies.' Who'd read that garbage, anyway?" Leo screwed up his face.

Silence.

"I don't believe you," said Sofia.

"Sis — do you have a better idea?"

For a start, her aunt and uncle had *vanished*. Spies had substance — real, visible bodies. Maybe they'd had doubles who'd left the airship unharmed. Then how was it that their *doubles* disappeared? It was too confusing, too tangled in speculation. She told Stefano that she couldn't imagine Aunt Julia as a spy.

"I could imagine Uncle Paul," he said.

Maybe that's why he slept with me. He knew he'd never have to face me again.

"Then why would Aunt Julia have wanted another child?" she asked.

"Who says she wanted one?"

"When she lost it, they were both upset."

"*Innocente*," he said, his voice quiet. "What makes you think they lost it?"

"What else would they —"

"*Nonna* Rosa could have found someone, *sì?*"

"That's — unthinkable," she said.

"That is the world, *cara mia*."

Her body seized up with fright as if she could still feel those millstones pressing down on her, crushing the grain of a child. She started to cry. Stefano put his arms around her. "I should not have said that," he whispered.

5

Sofia's father decided to rent out her aunt and uncle's house in Long Island. He left most of his brother's furniture for the tenants and the rest — including Uncle Paul's books and papers — came back to Maywood Road.

The house — Victorian in mood, but not outlandish — became ponderous and shadowed. It felt to Sofia that along with the furniture, another family had moved in with them. Rather than adding to their storage space, the curved and ornate doors and drawers stuck and refused to open. One little drawer responded to Sofia's yanking — landing in her lap and dumping buttons, straight pins, two lozenges and an ancient business card. *M. Roland Laurier, Antiquaire, Paris/ New York.* Sofia pocketed the card. *Someday this junk may be worth money*, she thought. Her hopes diminished as the house began to look like a Coney Island souvenir shop, with bric-a-brac on every shelf and table — cut-glass candy dishes, a blue- and gold-edged *Hindenburg* cup and saucer and a leaden Statue of Liberty paperweight. There was a teaspoon and linen napkin filched from the *Graf Zeppelin* and a scale model (under glass) of the *Los Angeles* at its mooring post. None of them touched Sofia's imagination. Then she turned to her uncle's photos.

Most of them showed the pair in elegant dress, sipping wine on their airship voyages. They looked like movie stars. *Dearest Paul, such delightful company*, wrote Hearst correspondent Lady Grace Drummond-Hay. Her photo showed a sweet-faced woman with an intelligent gaze, an enormous bouquet of roses in her arms — from her grand tour around the world on the *Graf Zeppelin*, just before the stock market crash. Did Uncle Paul know her then? Sofia wondered if he'd slept with her. There was an autographed photo of Charles Lindbergh in aviator gear, standing beside the *Spirit of St. Louis*. (When had Uncle Paul met Lindy? He'd never mentioned flying in his airplane.) Another portrait was autographed in German. *Sehr geehrter Herr Gentile, mit freundlichen grüßen.* What did it say? It was signed *E. Lehmann (1933)*. The officer wore his cap at an angle, so that his eyes were partly shadowed. He looked like a serious man, a pipe clenched in his mouth. His gaze didn't meet the camera's.

Her father came into the room. "What are you doing?" he asked.

"Packing these pictures away," she replied.

"But why?"

"When I look at them, I feel bad."

"*Figlia mia*, I have faith they'll return."

"When they know all these celebrities?"

"My brother will tire of them," he said.

He asked Sofia to choose one or two photos for the wall. The rest he'd keep for his own perusal. He also wanted to read his brother's notebooks, written in a frenetic hand. Uncle Paul's output stunned him. He felt certain that its size alone was a mark of desperation that would provide a clue to the mystery of his disappearance. *And*, Sofia thought, *a reason not to believe Leo's theory. What kind of spy would leave so many notes?* She imagined her brother's answer — *A damn sneaky one.*

Leo was in naval training in Virginia. He sent cheerful letters complaining about the food. *Not like your grub, sis, but all my life I've wanted to see the world*, he wrote. *Just about anything is worth it. Truth is, I'm as lucky as they come.*

6

In June, 1940, Italy entered the war on the side of the Nazis.

President Roosevelt went on the air. He called *Il Duce* "a jackal" for plunging a dagger in the back of France. Sofia's father had felt sure that Italy would come to her senses, would join the Allies. *"Una disgrazia,"* he said that evening. In his study was a framed poster depicting Fascist Italy on the march. He took it off the wall, removed it from its frame, tore it up and threw the scraps on the floor. He didn't realize that Sofia was watching him. He sat at his desk, his face in his hands, his back to her.

They were inside the dark funnel of the war, spinning around its vortex, sure they'd be crushed. Sofia's father went to a rally. *Down with Fascism, we are Americans first* — thousands of men shouting, speaker after speaker rising to damn and curse *Il Duce*. Sofia wasn't there, but she knew that her father rose with the cheering mob, running to the centre of the stadium, a portrait of Mussolini under his arm. He tossed it on the heap where other men were throwing posters and banners, then their Fascist League cards and emblems, their copies of the racist *Il Grido della Stirpe*, paper swirling like leaves ripped from their branches in a hurricane. Someone lit a match to it and the cheering toppled over into rage, into jeers and curses and screams. According to Doctor Gentile, it felt like a public hanging, the condemned nowhere in sight.

Stefano told Sofia that he'd been walking near the edge of the crowd when he turned and saw Christopher standing beside him. The young man was transfixed, as if he could see what was going on. *Where on earth had he come from?* said her husband. Sofia could imagine his gentle voice, trying to steer the blind man away. '*What are you doing here?*' *And do you know how he answered?* said Stefano. '*This is a disaster site. I have come here to find my parents.*' *I thought he'd lost his senses.* Stefano took him by the arm and led him away from the crowd. '*Your parents aren't here,*' he'd said. It felt to him as if Sofia's cousin had stepped out of some other moment and into the present. He wondered who was doing the dreaming and which of these moments were real. The war was real — that much he knew.

When he told Sofia the story, his face was white.

When Christopher came for the weekend, Sofia mentioned that Stefano had seen him near the rally.

He looked puzzled. "What rally?"

"The anti-Fascist rally. Earlier this week."

"I wasn't there," he said. "I was downtown."

Sofia felt uneasy. "It must have been someone else he saw."

"I was trying to sleep," he said. "I dreamt about the wreckage of the *Hindenburg*. I had to rescue my parents."

"And did you?"

"I don't think so. Stefano led me away."

When she told this to Stefano, he said that the world's mind must have been dreaming them, that no one could be certain anymore of what was real. She was struck by the ease of his conviction. The war, he said, was turning everything upside-down, even though it was being fought across the sea. Things were bound to be different in wartime, he said with a wry look. Maybe the days would be longer, as with Daylight Savings Time, or the sun might do an impossible thing and rise in the west, in which case the hours would have to be reckoned with war-clocks calibrated for war-time. Sofia hoped not. The idea seemed dreadful, all the more so because she half-believed it.

Since they'd taken in her aunt and uncle's belongings, it felt to Sofia as if an odd breeze were blowing through the windows of her father's house on Maywood Road, as if some hidden presence were troubling the place. She didn't believe in ghosts and neither did her father (who was convinced, in any case, that his brother and sister-in-law were alive), but it felt to her that their dreams and memories were escaping from their well-used possessions like air from a punctured tire. She imagined the furniture saturated with the dust and sweat of so much passion that these stolid objects would give up their dreams to the mere weight of a head resting on a cushion, a back against a chair, an arm leaning on a writing desk. The world was full of such unclaimed dreams — each ordinary home a giant lost-and-found of the wondrous, each window open to the constant blowing of a new wind. How else was it that her aunt had been able to fly? Borne up on how much abandoned longing and desire?

Only she wondered what was going on with Christopher.

7

Her cousin was about to arrive for summer vacation, and Leo's room was so cluttered with her uncle's papers that she couldn't tidy it, let alone make space for Chris's belongings. Worse, it was hard to get past the stairwell to the room itself because the corridor was stacked with boxes, and she couldn't imagine poor Christopher swinging his cane through such a narrow passageway. *Selfish Uncle Paul. Damned inconsiderate.* She grabbed one box, gave it a kick and sent it straight to the head of the stairs. What in God's name was in it? She yanked it open. *Garbage.* Ashtrays. Playing cards. A tobacco humidor with a set of pipes. A leather tobacco pouch. A fake Ming vase too ugly to be displayed in the living room. *Get this crap out of my house.* She wanted to hurl the whole thing down the stairs. She wanted to smash its contents with a hammer.

What was stopping her?

Figlia mia, *they are not our possessions*, said her father.

Would he notice any of them missing? *He'd notice them sitting in the garbage pail*, she thought.

It felt as if there were no air up here. She was going to suffocate. Sofia opened a window in the stairwell. No, she was being pushed out — as if her absent aunt and uncle were taking over, squeezing her out of her living space. She scooped up the box and marched it downstairs. Heavy, but not too large — it would fit on the lower rungs of a baby carriage. There was a junk shop on Tremont Avenue, and tomorrow afternoon she was baby-sitting for Tina. Her father wouldn't care. She felt defiant. It was unacceptable to live as a refugee in her own home. She couldn't even tidy a room for her cousin because her aunt and uncle were foisting their clutter upon their son. Just one box — but she'd made up her mind. Next week there would be another box. And another.

She liked those walks with Tina's baby, striding up Gun Hill Road to the leafy Oval and along Bainbridge Avenue just east of the Concourse. At other times she'd baby-sit Gabriella's child, crossing Webster Avenue to the Botanical Garden, where she'd meander with the carriage through the summer primroses and lilies. In a place of so much flowering, she felt hopeful.

That afternoon, she packed the box under the carriage and walked south on Webster, crossing Fordham Road, ending up near Tremont Avenue. Nonna *Constanza's country*. This was where Aunt Julia grew up, where the two of them had shared her collection of leaves, her books about wildflowers and astronomy. Feeling an unexpected pang of grief, Sofia continued walking, tracing with her senses a map of pungent smells, of colours hot enough to taste. There were pushcarts all along Arthur Avenue — a neighbourhood ripe with the odours of cod and tripe and freshly-butchered chicken; a sprawling, noisy market that rolled up its sleeves, glistening in the heat like sweat on a huge forearm. She walked, lost inside the rhythm of her walking and the rolling of the carriage wheels. Walking, walking, until the familiar neighbourhoods of the West Bronx began to dissolve — their stores and squat apartments and tidy stoops — into ineffable strangeness.

She had to find the junk shop. The wind pushed at her feet, spinning the carriage wheels around — although moments ago there'd been no wind at all. On Tremont Avenue, people eyed her as she skimmed the ground — fruit vendors and shoppers with grocery bags; the *macellaio*, his window hung with plump chickens and bulging sausages. *No junk shop. I was sure it was on Tremont.* In spite of the wind, it was a hot day, and the sun heated up the brittle edge of afternoon as if it were paper and could burn.

She turned down a quiet street of small apartments, their stoops and sidewalks full of children, and she knew that she had walked here before — not only in memory, but inside this very moment. Upward she glanced at mothers leaning out of windows, eyeing their kids' play and shouting back and forth. She heard the jingle of an ice cream vendor pulling up to the curb, the kids crowding around the freezer at the rear of his bike, mothers with their tots wandering off with Dixie cups and wooden spoons, the older kids licking cones and slurping ices. Up ahead, a truck with a carousel in tow played music. She noticed a man with a straw boater and a clutch of balloons. About to buy one to tie to the carriage, she saw the vendor chatting with a young girl leaning out the window, two stories up.

"You can't come upstairs," she said. "My mother's out."

"Here, catch." The man let go of his clutch of balloons and the girl reached out to grab them. Her plump, rosy arms, the *squeak* of rubber against the window sash made Sofia dizzy. She looked again.

A young, dark-haired woman wearing a cloche hat was standing a few feet away from her, watching the spectacle up ahead. Sofia knew who it was, but also *when* it was. She glanced toward the shadows of a nearby sycamore. There stood a bearded gentleman, his arms folded, eyeing the woman. She wanted to call out to her aunt and uncle, but she realized that she would be calling across time and they wouldn't hear her. She could go right up to them and say hello. Then she remembered what her father had said once about sleepwalkers: *Never wake them suddenly. Guide them gently to their beds.* Except that if anyone were sleepwalking, it was her.

She felt in shock.

The first moment of her aunt and uncle's courtship — it was still alive, right around the corner almost, near Fordham Road, in fact. She remembered reading somewhere that the spirits of those dead people who hadn't finished their work on earth would sometimes return to haunt their houses and loved ones. This wasn't quite the same — it was *she* who'd found *them*, and she had no reason to think they were dead. *There must be something for me to learn*, she thought. *Something*

I didn't see the first time around. She wondered if at that same moment, her aunt and uncle were also experiencing their second chance at life. It was possible. Almost anything was. Including the fact that the past had awakened like a sleeper in the middle of a dream, stumbling out of bed in the dark.

With the onset of war, most things had grown too strange to fathom. Stefano'd taken her to see newsreels at the Melba and the RKO, but she found it hard to comprehend the scenes of destruction, the chaos that had overtaken the world. Today it felt to her as if some enormous explosion must have blown the body of time itself apart, heaving a chunk of her early life into the rubble of some ruined city. She began to wonder what other events would be hurled into periods of history where they didn't belong or perhaps into lands that no longer existed. Even as she approached the house, she could hear Stefano's violin through the open window — a sonata composed two centuries ago in an Austrian town, springing to life in Williamsbridge, the Bronx. Except that with music, you expected this.

She walked up the path. Under the beech tree sat Christopher. He appeared to be sleeping, his grey shirt blending into the silvery folds of the huge trunk. He turned toward the sound of her footsteps.

"Look who's here," he said. "Out for a walk?"

"Teresa got a tour of Tremont Avenue."

"I just had this incredible dream."

And I just escaped one. Maybe the same one. She explained that she was rushed, that Tina would be coming by soon, and could he listen for the baby while she fixed some lemonade? She paused. *Oh my God. The box.* She'd never found the store — was she going to have to lug that bric-a-brac into the house all over again? *Not this minute.* She ran inside.

The music stopped. Sofia opened the front door and she felt the sound of Stefano's violin before he began to play again. A warmth spread through her body, taking the chill of consternation from her bones. The sound swelled and ripened, working its way into the grain of things like a fine polish into wood. Colours seemed brighter, her mother's crystal more beautiful, the sunbeams stranger and more evanescent. Sofia tiptoed into the living room.

Stefano sat playing with his back to her, his jacket off, his shirtsleeves rolled up. How unguarded he was, his back like a blank wall on which someone was bound to scribble a four-letter word. Or take a potshot with a beebee gun. A dark blotch of sweat was spreading across the back of his shirt. Sofia felt uncomfortable, as if she had no business watching his exertions, seeing what his music cost him.

He was playing Beethoven, his arms drawn into the powerful rhythm like a canoeist heading into rapids, the tight cords of his arm and shoulder muscles pushing the phrases ahead. How physical a thing his music was — she'd never known this before. Even as he played a slower passage, it seemed as if his back were bearing an immense weight, a burden that might crush him. Yet whatever he carried, the music bore. On it, he shifted the weight of his life, stacked it and hauled it and drove it around like lumber on a flatbed truck, as if he were hoping to build himself a sturdier dwelling than the one he had.

At the end of the movement, he stopped. He put down the violin and turned to face her.

Sofia put her arms around him. She could smell the salt of his sweat and feel the dampness of his shirt, as if that, too, were part of the music — an unheard emanation, spilling over into scent and touch. She'd sensed this with Christopher, too, whose music couldn't be contained by sound. It overflowed into the optic nerve, blessing the eyes and filling the pores of the skin. It belonged to life itself.

"*Cara mia*, you look tired," said Stefano.

"I've had a long walk," she said.

"Where to?"

"I ended up in another year. I saw Aunt Julia and Uncle Paul. Before they married."

Stefano stroked her hair. "*Magia,*" he said. "It happens."

"Isn't the past supposed to be — *past*?"

"You can't see it anymore. That doesn't mean it isn't here."

Yet sometimes you *could* see it. Sofia remembered her father's telescope. Light that began its travel in the era of the Caesars, stars through which you could gaze at distant time and contemplate a past still present to the eye. She felt as if she'd spent such an afternoon. In sunlight.

She prepared the lemonade, then walked to the front door to prop it open. Outside, the huge beech tree was shining like a lantern. *It's facing west, that's all.* Only every leaf was brilliant gold and the earth was fragrant with jasmine. Christopher was curled up, sleeping on the bench that surrounded the trunk of the tree. Teresa was asleep in the carriage beside him.

Where was the box? It wasn't under the carriage. It was nowhere in sight.

In the living room, Stefano picked up his violin and drew his bow across time.

CHRISTOPHER

I

On weekends, Christopher practiced the piano in their living room and light began falling on everything in random and unexpected ways. At midday the sun would drape speckled light along the back of the couch like a giant antimacassar — light that should have progressed by then to the fringed edge of the lampshade on the end table, but Christopher liked to say that he had surplus light to spare, and he brought it into the house through his music. He felt certain that the business with the sun was an illusion, that he hadn't pushed its sidereal motion ahead of schedule, that light wasn't bending around him as if he bore the gravity of a dark, invisible planet. She sensed that he was preoccupied, as if he were trying to solve a difficult problem on his own. He told her that he hoped to apply for a scholarship to Julliard. He was also trying to compose some music.

"Now tell me what *you* hope for," he said.

"If I say it, it won't come true."

In his face, she saw compassion. "May I take your hand?" he asked.

She put her hand on his and he clasped it. His grasp was warm — strong and confident and full of unmade music. She imagined his hand cupped at her ear, like one of those shells that roared with the sea.

"Last summer," he began, "I dreamt you saw my parents when they were young. They'd met on the street."

Sofia was aghast. "You didn't."

"That day you left the carriage by the tree. I was napping just before you came."

"That's where I'd come from."

"From my dream?"

This is too strange, she thought.

"It was a good dream," he continued. "I felt it was your gift to me."

"But Chris —"

"You had a box that disappeared, right? And I know where it went."

"Tell me."

"I dreamt you left it with my parents. All those years ago."

"I was looking for a junk shop," she said.

Chris laughed.

2

Sofia wondered if Christopher's gentleness had made a difference — along with his Chopin études that happened to drift upstairs whenever she was alone with Stefano. She became pregnant, and in the spring of 1941 she gave birth to her daughter, Petra Livia. She was a healthy baby, and her grandfather never tired of taking her in his arms. He gazed at her through his spectacles with a loving and yet distanced eye, as if she were a patient's baby, as if he'd noticed that she was shy and would rather get to know him a little at a time. He stroked her chin and when she smiled, his serious expression dissolved. "*Che bella,*" he'd whisper. One afternoon the radio was on, and Sofia stood in the doorway, listening to a familiar song — *I'm Getting Sentimental Over You*. Her father was holding his grandchild and dancing with old-fashioned grace to the music of Tommy Dorsey's band. It was the first time he'd danced since her mother left them.

Welcome baby Petra stop love to Mom and Dad stop your Uncle Leo, said the telegram. Petra was baptized, and Stefano's Aunt Francesca and Uncle Vito arrived with *nonna* Rosa and *nonno* Domenico from Orchard Street. *Nonno* looked sombre. Since Uncle Paul's disappearance, he'd visit with Sofia's father from time to time, but he'd stopped picking fights. Both he and *nonna* had grown quiet as if they were hiding from an armed enemy, holding their breaths, waiting for danger to pass. *The war will end with a workers' victory*, said *nonna*, but she no longer sounded convinced. Today she was speechless as she held her great-granddaughter. Her wary gaze softened and her eyes became those of a much younger woman. *Nonno* reached out toward Petra with a work-roughened hand and she gripped his finger with all five of hers.

"*Bene*, a fighter," he said.

Christopher was playing the piano when Sofia brought Petra over to him. He stopped playing and held out his arms to take her. His face was lit with joy.

"I remember *flying*," he said. "When I was this small."

"Your mother skittered above the ground like a leaf."

"You *saw* her?"

"In Van Cortlandt Park. Time collapsed like a circus tent." She remembered her father's words. *What you see is illusion and suffering.* "Don't tell a soul," she added.

"Why not?"

"I did, and no one believed me."

"I believe you," he said to her. "Because I remember."

Sofia took his arm (or thought she did) and led him out the door. They walked toward Gun Hill Road, heading westward up the hill — Chris sweeping his cane along the sidewalk, Sofia pushing the baby carriage. They were in no hurry but as she reckoned time, the stroll to Van Cortlandt Park took minutes, and Sofia knew that they wouldn't be gone long enough for anyone to miss them. As they approached Jerome Avenue, she touched Christopher's arm and guided him along the path into the park. The air was quiet in a pristine way, as if sound had not yet been created.

"There's no one here," Chris whispered.

"Are you surprised?"

"It's Saturday. You'd expect lots of people."

"Feel the breeze." In the distance Sofia noticed a fuzzy cloud of light that sharpened into a form as gauzy and nimble as a dragonfly. Green as spring — a woman in a long-waisted dress, pushing a baby carriage down the path. *Aunt Julia's sixteen years away*, Sofia thought. The woman approached the park bench, took the child out of the carriage, and before Sofia's eyes she floated off, her gold scarf trailing behind her. Green and gold, an apparition. Sofia stared at her aunt, transfixed.

Christopher held tight to her arm. "That wind," he said.

"Isn't it lovely?"

"Is my mother here?"

As he spoke, Sofia glanced at the empty carriage by the

park bench, her aunt's green hat on the blankets. She wanted to walk him toward it so that he could touch his mother's hat, but she was afraid it would dissolve into air.

"She *was* here," said Sofia.

"She flew right past me?"

"Yes," she answered. "I don't think she recognized the two of us."

Christopher looked as if he might weep and then Sofia felt the wind again. Down from the sky they began to fall — soft green blooms, large and gold at the heart like exotic birds in flight, and they touched her cousin's cheeks and brushed his eyes. He told her he'd caught one in his hand, but Sofia knew that the trees were bare, that these flowers did not belong to the visible world. They echoed the tulip tree which wasn't yet in bloom, which didn't even grow in this corner of the park. Down they came, these lush blossoms, swirling in eddies.

"My mother is alive," said Christopher.

From Jerome Avenue and Gun Hill Road, parents and children moved into the park. Long silent lines of them, slow and graceful, passing like wind through the flowers on the grass.

Christopher thanked Sofia. He kept the tulip-tree blossom in a glass of water beside his bed. He loved holding Petra and rocking her. There were days when Sofia felt certain that his feet were about to leave the ground.

The war in Europe and Asia haunted them, and Sofia worried about Leo. *We're not in the fighting yet, thank God*, she thought. Home with Petra that spring and summer, she'd turn on the radio. *Japs occupy French Indochina*, said the newscast. *Is that near India?* Sofia thought to check her father's atlas. As she prepared lunch, she glanced out the window and into the backyard garden where Christopher was sitting with Petra in his arms. The garden was sunlit, flourishing with mint and tarragon, oregano and thyme. Sofia breathed in its scents and forgot the Pacific war. Feeling close to Petra, she could feel herself drifting into the warmth and light that played on Christopher's body, into the fragrant intensity of leaves and flowers, the hesitation and then the joy of his hand as he touched the soft bristle of a rosemary shrub. She felt him saying to her infant daughter, *here, smell my hand*. Oil of rosemary — oil of everything he'd touched. Petra smiled. Then Christopher stood and lifted her up and his feet left the ground. He vanished with her baby.

"Petra!" she screamed.

Moments later, they came inside.

After Petra settled down for her nap, Sofia strode into the living room. Chris was seated at the piano, playing a Bach partita, its brightness rippling out of his fingers. He stopped and the notes dissolved like the last golden streaks of a Roman candle.

"You are one lousy baby-sitter," she said.

He made his way over to the couch and sat beside her. "What did I do?" he asked.

"You *flew*," she said. "The two of you disappeared."

"I don't remember anything. I'm sorry."

"You didn't hear me scream?"

"No." Christopher looked perplexed. He reached out,

found Sofia's hands and held them. "I'm sorry," he said. "I was just — somewhere else. And so were you, if you saw me — *flying*."

"I'll never take you to the park again."

"Maybe I was flying to Paris," he said. "I dreamed my parents were there."

Sofia wondered if they'd ever again have a sane conversation.

"So you were taking Petra overseas. Well, don't."

"I *wasn't*. I'm going when the war's over. To study."

He raised both his hands, as if he were lifting an invisible object, and then he moved them toward Sofia's face. She held still as he found her cheeks and cupped his hands around them. His fingers explored her eyes, her nose, her chin. It felt gentle and harmless and she wasn't aroused. She could sense that he needed to draw a map of her face, as if he were a traveller looking for directions. She felt his finger trace the outline of her lips.

"You're beautiful."

Sofia drew back. "You need to stay on the ground," she said. "Or stay away from Petra."

"Will you dance with me?"

Dancing is a kind of flight, she thought. She turned on the radio to Glenn Miller's show. The orchestra was playing *Moonlight Serenade* as she took his hands. Together they skirted the floor. Chris had a natural grace, an ease of movement which impressed her. She felt his trust and confidence in the easy grasp of her hand, in the relaxed feeling of his hand on her waist. The music stopped. Christopher lifted his hands, moving them toward her face, and he traced its outline with his fingertips. Then he pressed his mouth against hers and she felt the salt taste of his tongue. She pulled away.

"No, Chris. I can't."

He looked bewildered, not sure what to do next. A moment later he threw his arms around her and she felt his hot tears stinging her skin. He wept in silence, in the way that trees give up resin, as if his tears belonged to a larger order of things than private grief. She tried to comfort him.

"You'll find someone, Chris. Your own age. Don't cry."

When she took his hand again and held it, all she could feel was air.

3

After Pearl Harbor, Sofia felt everything change, as if a fifth season had been added to the year. The new season's climate altered the beauty of the others — with its daily lightning-storms of news, its icy grief. Over the year, Maywood Road became tinged with sadness. The change was subtle, like the first chill day foreshadowing winter. Some men left for war, and in Bernie's Deli, Sofia would notice a stunned neighbour picking up a parcel Bernie had wrapped — her hands shaking because at home was a devastating telegram and the touch of any paper at all was more than she could bear. Harry passed along most of these stories of bereavement, but Sofia soon learned to read her neighbours' faces. Mr. Wiseman, who owned The Budget, lost his son in the Philippines and he closed the store for the rest of the week.

An Ordinary Star

Closed due to sorrow, read the black-edged sign on the door. His shelves were as depleted as he was — they lacked sugar and flour, coffee and tea. Whether they wanted to spend their coupons or not, Sofia or Tina would drop by, hoping to cheer him up.

Stefano had to register for the draft, but his nearsightedness disqualified him for service. Instead he signed up for volunteer work as an air-raid warden. Sofia was grateful for the hours he'd spent at his music stand, squinting at tiny, unreadable notes. It was bad enough that her brother was overseas. *Somewhere near Morocco*, said his last letter. She found a map and pinned it up in the kitchen. It was too depressing and she took it down.

"And what can I do to help?" asked Christopher.

"You must prepare," said Stefano, "for the day when the war ends."

Students older than himself were enlisting. Christopher looked adrift. "I hope my parents are safe," he said to Sofia. "Wherever they are."

Sofia did volunteer work at the church, collecting and sorting clothes for refugees. The new year came, Christopher turned seventeen, and Stefano lost students to the war. As she tried to live an orderly life, it seemed to Sofia that the hands of every clock were spinning out of control. There were no intervals of armistice or cease-fire that might have measured the passing of time. Each day some part of the world collapsed in exhaustion as another part of the world awoke to battle. Rangoon, Timor, Sevastopol, Tobruk, Lidice — the unfamiliar names choked her throat with smoke from fires burning, places where it had become impossible to tell the day from night.

Like everyone on Maywood Road, Stefano put blackout shades on the windows. The lights on Burke Avenue to the south of them went out, cars crawled down Gun Hill Road with their headlights off, and night settled in around stores and apartments, the neighbourhood church and subway stop. The ordinary world began to vanish.

"You've gotta' wonder," said Tina, "why the hell Hitler would attack the Bronx."

"It's New York City," said Sofia.

"And they can't bomb Yankee Stadium in the dark? How dumb is that?"

Sofia wasn't sure. She was beginning to think that few things added up and that in the long run, practically nothing mattered.

She busied herself around the house, and her father saw her dusting the ornate furniture. "We won't have all this forever," he said.

"Thank God."

"After the war, we'll sell your aunt and uncle's," he said, "if they haven't returned by then."

Her father's hair turned silver, like an old man's. He'd begun sorting through her uncle's photographs and journals, but the handwriting tired him. Small and cramped, it required a magnifying glass. *In time*, he said, *I will read it and make sense of all this*. He said it with less conviction than before. He was more concerned these days with Leo overseas and the war — the fact that his beloved Italy had allied itself with the Nazis. Sometimes when her father thought he was alone, he'd turn off the news and sit slumped forward, his face in his hands.

He seemed burdened by memories, but when Sofia asked him how he was, he always said *bene*. He'd told her once that his family had been his joy, that there had been no other happiness as great, that on the whole he'd been satisfied with life. She wasn't always sure she believed him.

His consolation was his grandchild, Petra. He loved to baby-sit. He talked to her in Italian. He held her.

Was anyone happy?

In bed, Sofia recited verse to Stefano.

> *Nel mezzo del cammin di nostra vita*
> *Mi ritrovai per una selva oscura*
> *Che la diritta vita era smarrita...*

"But you are sad, *cara mia*," he said.

He read to her from Browning — *How do I love thee? Let me count the ways* — and Shakespeare also. *Shall I compare thee to a summer's day? Thou art more lovely and more temperate.* The old words had a rhythm, a music independent of their meaning, or so it seemed to her. Yet they brought no solace.

"Once we were a happy family," she said to him. "At the dinner table, my father used to teach us about Italy. Once, my mother —"

"Once you had no one to love you, *mia bella*."

"Have you gotten over the loss of your mother?" she asked him.

"I never will," he said. "But I have other consolations."

"Do you think Christopher misses his parents?"

Stefano hesitated before he spoke. "He is not — whole, your cousin. Yes. He misses them."

She wasn't sure she agreed with Stefano about Christopher. To Sofia he seemed happier. When he'd come on weekends she'd see him alone, the radio on, the voice of Bing Crosby or Frank Sinatra filling the room. With his cane, he'd trace a box-step on the carpet, and she was amazed at his ease of movement. Ever since she'd waltzed with him on that strange afternoon, he'd taken to dancing, and his liveliness made her hopeful. Sometimes he'd hum along or sing a few bars with the crooner, and when he sat down to practise a classical piece, the music sang, as if he were still dancing. He no longer seemed disheartened and sad. He'd won his scholarship to Julliard and at Sunday dinner he'd chat about his strolls in Central Park, about going to concerts, about playing duets with students in his summer music class. At last he told them what had happened.

"I've met a girl named Evelyn," he said. "Her parents were born in Paris."

"There's your steamship ticket," said Sofia.

"She's a native New Yorker," said Chris. "And guess what?"

"She looks like Rita Hayworth," said Stefano.

"As if I'd know. Her parents survived the *Hindenburg* fire."

The room went silent.

"She was in boarding school at the time. She knows about my parents."

An Ordinary Star

"You must have a word with her father," said Elio. "Perhaps we —"

"Her parents don't want to meet me. They don't believe that the blind should marry."

"I hope you haven't proposed to her already," said Stefano. Everyone laughed, including Chris.

"Not yet," he said.

Christopher practised the piano all summer while Sofia worked outside in the garden, hoeing and digging beans and lettuce, corn and tomatoes, eggplant and squash. In the warm sunshine she could hear him spinning a luminous thread of sound. *He could make someone so happy*, she thought.

She preferred her cousin's music to the radio — the war news humming like a hive of angry bees. As cheered as she was by Christopher's good mood, she always felt as if something terrible were about to happen. By evening-news time, it almost always did. The war wasn't going well. America had surrendered in the Philippines. Japan had captured Singapore and Burma, and the Germans were in Libya and Egypt. She harvested greens, then picked a clump of fresh mint and made tea for Tina and Gabriella. They sat in the backyard watching the kids toddle around the garden.

"Is that your cousin playing the piano?" asked Gabriella.

"I think so," said Sofia. "Or it's something he's dancing to."

"He *dances*?" asked Tina.

"He's got a girlfriend."

"How about that? Good news for a change."

In the background, Sofia could hear the phone ringing. Moments later, Stefano came outside and beckoned to her with a puzzled look on his face.

"It's for you," he said. *It's long distance*, he whispered as she walked inside. Sofia felt sick. *Something's happened to Leo.* The receiver shook in her hand as she raised it to her ear. As she did this, Christopher stopped playing — an abrupt stop, as if her action had unplugged his hands from the keyboard.

"Mrs. Fiore?" the operator asked.

"Speaking."

"I'll put your party on the line."

That was the last Sofia heard. No breathing, no voice, no foggy, distant sounds, none of the static or click of disconnection. Yet she sensed the presence of someone on the other end, trying to talk to her.

"Hello? Hello?" She felt reluctant to hang up the phone.

Someone's there. She raised her voice. "Where are you calling from?" *And from when?* She imagined a voice travelling across time like the last sputtering of a long-dead star. She felt unnerved and she hung up.

"Who called?" asked Stefano.

"There was no one on the line."

"It may have gone dead," he said. "They may call back."

Sofia went outside again and told her friends what had happened. Tina put down her teacup and stared at her. "The guy's a pervert," she said. "Master class."

"*What* guy?"

"Sofia, are you a dunce? Have you considered your uncle?"

"Of course I have. But why on earth would he do that?"

"You'll pardon me," said Tina. "But in the real world, people do lousy things. They cheat on their wives. They dump their kids. So now he's discovered the telephone. Hot breath."

"He wasn't *breathing*."

"Oh, by gum, he's good at this," said Tina.

Sofia didn't laugh.

In church, she lit a candle and prayed for the safe return of her aunt and uncle. She thanked God that hope could become a sound, that it could take the form of a ringing phone. She also prayed that Evelyn's parents would open their hearts to Christopher. *Believe me, God*, she said, *if Chris doesn't take that girl to bed, he'll disappear. Little by little — one splotch of colour after another. It runs in our family, as you may have noticed.* Sofia imagined another dimension in time and space, one that blotted up drifting souls like her cousin and his parents, absorbing their spirits into a seamless earth and sky. *The lost and missing are floating all around us. In and through us, too, like thoughts.* Sofia felt afraid.

NOWHERE

I

In April 1943, Christopher and his classmates gave a performance at Carnegie Hall. Evelyn's parents were attending — and she'd persuaded them to meet Chris and his family afterwards. He'd prepared a programme of Brahms and Mozart — played with enough passion and tenderness, Sofia thought, to electrify the stiff-looking pair of Upper East-Siders in the front row. She eyed them. Evelyn's mother was blond and pretty — with an abstract, almost featureless expression, as if a hurricane had blown away whatever slight imprint life had made on her face. She wore a pillbox hat with a veil and a fur wrap over her jacket. Her husband, likewise fair and well dressed, was a stocky man with an air of disquiet, his eyes shifting back and forth as if he feared an unpleasant run-in with some old business rival. She recalled that they'd survived the *Hindenburg* fire, and she wondered if this was the cause of the hurricane that had emptied the woman's face, the anxiety that kept the man so restless in his seat.

Yet when Evelyn got up to sing, she had her parents' absolute attention. Like her mother, she was slight and pretty, stylish in a navy skirt and jacket. Her hair was platinum blond and she wore it in a pageboy that bounced light, as if she were transmitting a coded signal, an urgent call to attention. The effect was dazzling. Something larger was at work in her, an intensity of spirit that must have attracted Christopher. *He would have felt it on his skin*, Sofia thought. *As warmth, not light.* She sang in a beautiful contralto — a program of Italian songs, *Caro mio ben* and *Amarilli*. Sofia imagined her mother's delight, as if for a moment, the songs had returned her to life.

Sofia's father listened, rapt. After the concert, he strode over to praise his nephew *and this wonderful singer of Italian songs*. Evelyn's dad shook his hand and introduced himself as Roland Laurier. Sofia recognised the name, but she couldn't remember where she'd heard it. The man was in the shipping business and dabbled in antiques. Mr. Laurier complimented Christopher. When the young pianist was encircled by his classmates, the man lowered his voice and spoke to Elio. "I hope it wouldn't be impertinent to ask," he said. "Were the boy's parents handicapped?"

"Not at all." Elio paused. "Had they been blind, they would not have travelled on the *Hindenburg*."

Mr. Laurier stroked his chin. "Indeed," he said.

"Christopher tells us that you were on the airship. The night it —"

"Yes. I regret not having met them."

"I'm certain that he met my brother," said Sofia's father afterwards. "There weren't that many people on board." Sofia agreed. *I recognise his name*, she thought. *Laurier or Lorraine or something French.* There'd been a card she found in her uncle's bureau drawer a few years back, and God knows what she'd done with it. *One of these days it'll turn up. An antique seller, I'm sure.* To her mind, there were things more important than the *Hindenburg* and Uncle Paul's whereabouts. She wanted to see Christopher happy, and she didn't care if Mr. Laurier was lying to her father. For one thing, her cousin's love for Evelyn lessened the risk that Chris might make another pass at her in the living room or float away in some waking dream with Petra in his arms.

"I try to imagine Evelyn at our table," said her father. "But I cannot."

"She sings those beautiful *canzone*," said Sofia.

Stefano started laughing.

"Now what is so funny?" asked Elio.

"I am thinking of Leo. Off the coast of North Africa. What sort of bride will *he* bring home?"

"*Madonn'*. I hope an Italian girl."

Sofia's father looked disconsolate. She knew that he was not prepared for so much change. Without saying as much, he'd assumed that one day, everything would return to what it had been before the war. Sofia knew that from his perspective, Petra would be the oldest of the grandchildren to come — her own and Leo's and Christopher's — and the little ones would soon be sitting around the table in Sunday dress, practising Italian, sipping *espresso* and eating *biscotti* as *nonno* quizzed them on the glories of ancient Rome. Sofia thought of Leo's most recent letter. *I'll be on the destroyer, watching as Italy falls — as they hang that bastard Benito by the balls, ha-ha.* The language had displeased her father, but Leo had been at war for over a year, *and he is a sailor, after all*, said Stefano.

"It is a new world," said Elio at last.

Christopher agreed. Because of his excellent debut performance, he'd been invited to attend a two-week music programme in Rhode Island that summer, one sponsored by a wealthy patron of the school. Evelyn had also been selected. He'd soon have to make a decision.

"Do her parents know about it?" asked Sofia.

"You have her reputation to consider," said Elio.

"We'll check to be sure they're chaperoned," said Stefano. Later he spoke to Elio. "I hope you will let him go," he said.

"We'll see."

"Poor Christopher has had so little in life."

"Soon we will have an empty table," said Elio.

"For two weeks only."

Elio looked away, as if he didn't believe that either.

In July, Christopher left from Grand Central Terminal carrying Elio's worn valise and a briefcase full of music. Evelyn was going to meet him at the kiosk in the main hall. The Lauriers had warned their daughter that if the two were found by

An Ordinary Star

themselves on the estate, they'd both be sent home. That satisfied Sofia's father, and he let Christopher go.

Rhode Island — Sofia tried to imagine this bucolic place. She was preparing a salad for dinner and listening to a Sunday broadcast of a Verdi concert with Toscanini conducting. She was so engrossed in her thoughts that she didn't notice when the music stopped. Then she heard cheering. Puzzled, she went into the living room. *Bravo!* yelled Stefano. He leapt up to hug her father. "Italy's out of the war." He kissed Sofia.

"*La guerra è finita.*" Elio embraced his daughter. "Smile, *figlia mia*. Your brother's out of harm's way."

Sofia brought out the wine and glasses for a toast. Her father poured.

"*Pace*," he said. "*Al nuovo mondo.*"

They drank. Stefano lifted his glass again. "I will drink to peace for my father," he said.

"*Bene*," said Elio.

To Evelyn and Christopher and their happiness. As she raised her glass, Sofia watched her father saying goodbye to Rome the Eternal, to *Il Duce* and to the blossoming of a new Italian day. His face looked as drawn as the last drops of water from a well. She knew he understood that the old world was over but he didn't look ready to celebrate. It was as if her mother had died all over again. It was as if the well were dry and her family's table as deserted as a ruin.

Italy's out of the war. Sofia knew that in spite of his suffering, her father was grateful. She wondered if Christopher had heard the news. It was July, it was 1943 and by the following morning, it felt to her as if the old, tired world had flipped over like a pancake on a griddle, its top side browned to perfection. *That's Italy. The bottom side is Germany, and it's next.* She'd forgotten about Japan, then imagined another pancake. *Both sides for Japan.* She wanted to run errands, to see her neighbours at The Budget on Burke Avenue, to ask them if they'd heard the news and when and how.

She went to Bernie's Deli, jangling the bell as she pushed the door open. Just then the light shifted, as if a cloud were passing before the sun. Time slipped into the falling light of afternoon, and summer fell asleep and rolled over into the short days of winter. *Is it going to rain?* Sofia glanced at the front counter, at the marinated herring, the *mozzarella* and olives; at the fresh-baked *challah* and poppy-seed rolls on the shelves behind. Ahead of her were customers — Gabriella's mother talking to Mrs. Malazzo, but Sofia was no longer in the world that had just greeted the end of Mussolini. Everyone looked chilled, as if they'd been walking in the snow, and she found the silence disturbing.

As she waited in line, words found their way into her ears, but they were not the words she'd expected. She heard *accident*, and *blind* and *yeah, right up on Gun Hill Road*, and she became aware that the woman on line ahead of her was whispering to Harry. Sofia shivered as he took the customer's order, wrapped her packages with butcher paper and tied them with string which he looped into a bow.

The woman left. Beckoning Sofia forward, Harry lowered his voice. "Her husband saw a guy fall onto the train tracks. Gun Hill Road station, around midnight. Blind fella'. Prob'ly tripped." He paused. "First thing I thought was, *that sweet man*," he said. "You know who I mean."

"My cousin?"

"Yeah."

"Saturday he left for Rhode Island."

"We should thank God," he said.

Tina was working as a nurse once again and when she came home from the hospital, Sofia called to ask about the accident.

"Only that he was one lucky guy," she said.

"How?"

"He fell and rolled under the ledge. Train just missed him."

"Do they know who he was?"

Tina hesitated. "You worried about your cousin?"

"He should be in Rhode Island. But —"

"Chris doesn't even live in the Bronx. Worry if they're talking 96th Street."

Sofia decided she was right.

She wondered why this stranger's mishap had troubled her as much as it did. The accident hadn't been reported in the papers and even Tina's matter-of-factness felt imagined. What Sofia knew to be true was the overwhelming fact that Mussolini's empire had collapsed. She told herself that planet Earth was jiggling on its axis, that this was one of those ineffable days in history.

A week passed. Evelyn had promised her a note from

Rhode Island, but she'd heard nothing.

"Don't worry, *cara mia*," said Stefano. "Chris and Evelyn may be lovers. At this very moment, he may be getting her pregnant."

"*Stefano*. That's *horrible*."

"It is not horrible."

"But do you realize —"

"There are worse things in this world," he said.

I'm sorry to be tardy, Evelyn wrote at last. *We are making grand music. Christopher is thriving in the sun.* Sofia began to hear his piano and her voice spinning lazy tunes into each other. *She's teaching him jazz.* Light sashayed across the living room, as if they were dancing. She knew they had become lovers.

When they came back to the city, Christopher called Sofia and told her what she'd already guessed.

"I live nowhere now," he said. "Evelyn is my true home."

"You mustn't forget your family," said Sofia. "We're your home, too."

"We're thinking of moving to the Village."

"Are you crazy? You'll give my father a heart attack. Evelyn's dad'll kill you."

He laughed. "I'm crazy."

"You'll be awfully far from the Bronx," she said. "Sunday dinner."

"It's not far. The subway goes to Gun Hill Road."

"Are you careful on the train?"

"*Careful?* I've been riding alone since the age of *nine*."

"We're still your family, Christopher. We don't want scandal."

"I love you dearly, Sofia."

The phone clicked.

Stefano laughed when she told him. "There are no scandals in the Village. That's a good idea they have."

When Sofia's father asked how Christopher was, she told him only that he was in love. He didn't smile. "My nephew is in love with the child of dishonest people," he said. "I researched the passenger list on the *Hindenburg*. The Lauriers are nowhere mentioned."

"Maybe they were spies," said Stefano.

"*Figlio mio* — don't jump to conclusions."

"They may have travelled under different names."

"It's possible," said Elio. "But it doesn't make them spies."

Sofia's father hoped that Christopher would be careful. *Surely he'll bring Evelyn to dinner soon*, he said. *Then we can talk some sense into them.* He'd decided he liked the young woman who was so devoted to Italian song, who for no reason he could fathom also loved jazz. *My heart goes out to Chris*, said Stefano. *Now, at least, he has comfort.* As for Sofia, her cousin's words had touched her. *I live nowhere now.* She felt certain she'd encounter him — unmoored from gravity, floating over the treetops, disturbing the air. Even with love, she wasn't sure that he was made for this earth, any more than his mother was. At night she dreamed of tulip-tree blossoms fluttering down from a grey winter sky.

2

In October, Italy signed the surrender. Days later, Stefano received a telegram. He looked at it, crumpled it into a ball and threw it aside. When he left the room, Sofia picked it up and read it. It was from a cousin in Apulia. *Tuo padre è morte*, it said.

Poor Stefano. She glanced at it again.

Fucilato. Executed.

"They're taking revenge," said Stefano.

"I understand," said Sofia.

He sighed. "I do and I do not. This is my father."

Stefano sat with his face in his hands, his eyes covered, as if the news were a harsh light. When he sat up again, he looked stricken.

"So Captain Fiore has been shot," he said.

"*Cara mia*, we'll have a mass said."

"They hang the corpses from the lamp-posts."

She thought about his mother. No funerals for either of his parents, no wreaths for him to lay on the graves on their anniversaries. Her father came into the room and Sofia told him what had happened. He sat down beside Stefano, and put his arm around him.

"*Figlio mio*," he said. "You are my son."

"*Sì. Capisco.* I understand."

"When I die, you'll come to pay your respects. Every year you'll bring the wreath. *Capisce?*"

Sofia's father gestured to her to bring some glasses. He opened a bottle of wine and they drank together.

Sofia knew that Stefano's grief weighed like a stone on her father's heart. *How young my own father was, figlia mia, when he was killed,* he said as he gazed at his photograph of the uniformed man. *Younger than I am. It doesn't seem fair to have lived longer than one's father.* In his spare time, he'd taken to sitting at the dining-room table, gathering together photo albums of his scattered family, eyeing the ancient demitasse cups and spoons from her mother's Sunday table, perusing his yellowed books of Italian history and essays. These would be for his grandchildren, he said. He'd stir some anisette into his coffee and Sofia could smell the fragrance of a lost world filling the room.

"And then there's the mess upstairs," he added.

With Leo expected home soon, Sofia felt relieved when her father roused himself to tidy her brother's bedroom. He went through Uncle Paul's boxes and threw out most of the yellowing papers. Left was a collection of school notebooks which he packed in a Macy's shopping bag and took into his study. Sofia got busy cleaning the room.

Petra was toddling along behind her, and she started sneezing on the dust. *Poor baby.* Sofia dug into her apron pocket for a handkerchief. She pulled it out and wiped her daughter's nose. A small card had fallen out of her pocket. *Roland Laurier, antiquier.*

"Mommy, what are you looking at?"

Laurier. Evelyn's dad.

"Mommy?"

"Nothing, sweetie." She put the card away.

Sofia watched her father put aside everything — his grandchild, his archives, the end of the war in Italy, his son returning home. He had become a rescuer once again, sleeves rolled up, digging through the soul's debris that had buried his brother and sister-in-law. He'd acquired a magnifying glass but when Sofia peered into the room, she observed him doing a doctor's work, his face grave and intent, as if he were perusing his charts. Beside him, he kept a pad of ruled paper and from time to time, he'd jot down notes. He never discussed what he was reading, and it was understood that no one else would be allowed to look at Uncle Paul's writings.

She tapped on the door. When he let her in, she gave him

the card. She told him she'd found it in Uncle Paul's bureau, but quite a while ago.

"Why did you not tell me sooner?"

"I forgot I had it. Just now I found it in this pocket."

Her father looked at the card. "It's possible," he said, "that Uncle Paul made a purchase from this man."

"Except that Uncle Paul didn't like antiques."

"*È vero.*"

"And the furniture's junk. About as Parisian as I am."

"Your uncle's no judge of quality," he said.

"Laurier's no antique dealer."

"*Figlia mia*, what makes you so sure?"

"If he travelled on the *Hindenburg*, he went under a false name. I'll bet this card is false, too."

Her father didn't answer. He found a paper clip and attached the card to his notepad. He sat at his desk and continued reading her uncle's notebooks, and Sofia wished that she could read over his shoulder, in order to find out how her uncle and Roland Laurier were connected. *Except that if anything illegal were going on, Uncle Paul wouldn't have written it down*, she thought. How was she going to find out?

Her father continued reading after supper, and well into the evening. When Sofia got up in the middle of the night, she glanced downstairs and saw that his light was still on.

3

Two weeks after Italy signed the armistice, Sofia's father received a letter from Leo explaining that he'd have to remain in Italy a while longer. *Guess what, Pop — they're sending me to Bari*, he wrote. *You can give me some of your relatives' names to look up.* The place had been protected by the Allies, he said. They never bombed it, keeping it intact for the day their troops would land and start marching northward. *The clean-up crew*, he added. *Flushing out the Germans.* Bari was the main supply port on the east coast of Italy, and they'd ordered him to help supervise the on-and-off-loading of the ships. *It's because of my Italian*, he wrote, *that they want me here. Maybe I'll meet a beautiful signorina, and never come back! Arrivederci, papa!*

"At least he hasn't lost his sense of humour," said Sofia.

"Will he ever get started in life?" Her father looked rueful.

"Sure. He'll teach Italian," she replied.

"*Madonn'*, he'll be sick of it."

"He can look up his cousins," Sofia said. "And aren't there places to visit in Bari? You told me there's a nice cathedral."

"*Cara mia*, the war is still on, I'm afraid," said Stefano.

No one heard him.

The days grew chilly. It was almost winter when the Germans struck.

When Sofia stepped into the living room that night, she could feel a silence opening to engulf her, like a vast human mouth the moment before it begins to scream. She heard the radio, a word here and there. *Bari*. She stood in the doorway and listened, glancing at the photographs, the armchairs with their ancient antimacassars. *Luftwaffe*. She could not bring herself to set one foot in front of the other. *Trying to cut the American supply lines, trying to halt the British advance up the east coast.* In her mind flashed an image of the old city, a protruding finger of land encircled by water. On either side was the Port of Bari. *Ship after ship, loaded with ammunition* and *like a dreadful fireworks display* and *another Pearl Harbor*.

Her father sat slumped over in a chair. Sofia sat down beside him. He didn't stir, didn't hear her enter the room.

Townspeople set afire, leaping into the sea.

He looked up, but he gazed at nothing. "The streets are so narrow," he murmured. "Closed in."

She touched his arm. "What, pa?"

An Ordinary Star

"Like a box with a lid."

She tried to make sense of it, and then she realized that the old quarter must have been blown apart. She'd never seen these ancient streets that meandered through her father's soul as if he himself were a city. He hid his face in his hands.

Leo, he whispered.

Your son is alive, said the telegram. *He will be returned to convalesce.*

Her father grew old, and very quickly.

"I will never see my home again," he said.

"Leo's coming home," said Sofia.

He stared out the window. "Did you know I met your mother in Bari?" he asked.

"As children. Yes."

"It is ashes." He spoke as if Sofia hadn't yet heard, as if the disaster had just happened. She knew then that it would always be like this. He would live inside the last frail moments of the world he'd known, his hand forever reaching out to turn the radio on. Yet he would pause before the destruction of the place he loved most on this earth, and he would die in that place of hesitation. He turned away from her and hid his face.

And I am old now, also, thought Sofia. *I am a house of cinders. My roof is the sky.*

4

A new year, and her father's hair was white. *That very city is my flesh and blood*, he'd said, but Sofia never saw him weep. He received correspondence from the Navy about Leo's condition. *He was exposed to toxic fumes*, the naval doctor wrote. Because he was a doctor himself, her father wondered why they couldn't tell him more. Leo would be returning soon. In the meantime Elio retreated to his study and continued to scan his brother's writings with the fastidiousness of a surgeon. He seldom spoke.

When Sofia walked by his open door — his desk at a right angle to the entrance, his brass lamp lit under the green glass shade — she'd notice him turning pages and making notes. One Saturday afternoon, she heard the *clank* of the chimney flue in her father's study, and then the rustle and crackle of burning paper and smouldering wood. The door was ajar and she saw him poking the logs, starting a good fire. *A chilly day. It's snowing.* No, he had the air of a purposeful man, not one approaching the hearth with tea and a good book. He'd stuffed the cracks between the logs with wads of paper. Beside the fireplace was a trash can and in it was a speckled notebook cover without its pages.

She wondered what her uncle had written, that her father had to burn it.

An hour later she passed by again and saw him seated at his desk. He'd stopped turning pages. He was glancing at something, reading it with a look of incomprehension. He picked up his pad and his pen, began making notes, then put his pen down. He hid his face in his hands.

When her father sat up again, Sofia saw that his eyes were wet. He continued reading. Too grieved, she thought, to burn whatever it was.

At dinner that evening, her father looked distracted as he poured wine.

"We cannot forget the ordinary world," he said.

Sofia wondered what he meant.

"That is easy enough to do," said Stefano, "with a war on."

"Easy and foolish," said her father. "Imagination can be a curse."

"If you mean Hitler's," said Stefano.

"If you call that imagination."

"But then there's Einstein," Stefano remarked. "Such an extraordinary man."

Her father didn't argue the point. Sofia cleared the dishes and brought in dessert. She found the conversation very odd. She wondered what was on her father's mind, what he might have read in her uncle's notes that had caused this digression. *The sun is an ordinary star.* Was her father pondering that? *He's thinking about death*, she told herself. *How we mustn't forget the things that pass away.*

At that moment, he turned to look at her. His face was grieved, his gaze so stricken that it made her afraid of what he was about to say. Between the time he opened his mouth and the time that the sound of his words entered her ears and were sorted out into thoughts by her brain, she felt as if her entire world were teetering on the edge of collapse.

"It is no gift that man can fly," he said.

He pressed the napkin to his lips, left it on the table in a wrinkled heap and pushed out his chair. He excused himself and left.

Whatever it was that upset him has been burned, Sofia thought. *Thank God.*

She'd never considered that her uncle might write about their sexual encounter — a single event would be too commonplace to set down on paper when the man had had so many. It relieved her to retreat to the kitchen and do the dishes. She felt comforted with her hands in the warm, slippery water. Stefano went upstairs to hunt for some music that he wanted to practise, while her father took his seat in the living room, tuned the radio to the news and listened. Two weeks earlier, the Allies had landed at Anzio, Italy, and he'd

An Ordinary Star

felt hopeful. From the kitchen, Sofia could hear the newscast. *It's February fifth*, announced Edward R. Murrow, *and the Soviets are mounting an offensive in the Ukraine*. She found herself thinking that the Allies were winning the war, that soon it would be over and Leo would return to them. *What kind of shape will he be in, my poor brother?* They had no idea how serious his condition was or how long it would take him to recover. *Persistent hacking cough and fatigue*, said the last letter they'd received from the Navy.

Sofia finished washing the dishes. The newscast had ended, and she could hear the strains of a Bach cantata on the evening concert that followed. Her father seldom listened to that programme, unless he dozed off in the middle of the news. Upstairs she heard Stefano tuning his violin. *If he wants to practise, he won't appreciate the radio.* She went into the living room to turn it off.

Her father was sitting in his chair, his back to her, his arms hanging limp at his sides. Turning toward him, she saw that his face was pale and white as parchment, his mouth slack, his eyes wide open, as if in terror.

She shook him. "Pop!"

Nothing.

"Stefano!"

He came running. He touched her father's face and hands. He called an ambulance. The attendants arrived to find that Elio Gentile was dead. *It must have been a heart attack*, said one. Swift and crushing — how was it that he didn't cry out in pain? Maybe he did. Maybe the radio was on too loud or the water in the kitchen running too hard. In any case, Sofia didn't hear him. *Daydreamer. You weren't listening*, she told herself. *It would not have mattered if you'd heard him*, cara mia, *he died so quickly*, said Stefano. Never one to impose on anyone, her father would have taken pleasure in his understated exit. It was all scant comfort. She let Stefano attend to the details of the funeral.

"*Cara mia*, these are hard times," he whispered.

"It was too sudden."

"*Sì*. He was too young, your father." He held her cold hands between his.

The funeral couldn't wait for Leo's return. Should they try to send him a cable? *Don't*, said the undertaker Mr. Malazzo. *What can he do on board a ship, in the middle of the ocean?* They decided to leave the bad news for when he returned. He'd be sent to Kingsbridge Hospital where the vets were, so they didn't have to worry that he might barge into the house, dancing in the front door and yelling *Pop, I'm home*, just as if he'd come back from the ballpark. *Poor Leo*. Even if he'd returned home fine, she knew he'd never hop-skip into a room again with that way he had, as if the rhythm of his dancing could turn on every radio on earth.

What anguish for her father — dying alone, knowing he would never see his son again. She remembered his look of terror and she felt as if her father's house had just collapsed on her. She gasped.

"*Cara mia*, what is wrong?" asked Stefano.

Her Uncle Paul would never see his brother, who'd loved him so.

"Everything," she answered.

An Ordinary Star

Elio Gentile was buried at Woodlawn Cemetery, alongside his beloved Livia. Stefano brought wreaths for both their graves. Afterwards the neighbours came with trays of ravioli and sausages, chicken and *vitello*. They remembered *il dottore* with kind and quiet toasts, and this consoled Sofia. She tried to comfort poor *nonna* Rosa and *nonno* Domenico — the two weary elders who'd lived to see the death and disappearance of every one of their children. They'd come to church and wept throughout the mass. Who could console them in their suffering? *We live for our children*, said Domenico. *It is not correct that they should perish first*, added Rosa, as if she were a teacher who'd caught a mistake in addition, as if she had an eraser that could rub it out.

"*Mio figlio* was a man of the people," she said to the neighbours.

Domenico said nothing. He clasped Sofia's hands between his. He embraced her before they left.

Christopher came, holding Evelyn's arm. He looked as if he'd been crying. In him Sofia could feel an eddy of sorrow rippling out from the loss of his parents, filling this moment of grief. He was tall and as grave as a statue, and yet Sofia could see light passing through him, as she once did with her mother. He embraced her, but all she could feel was the slight brush of air.

"You can still visit us," she said to him.

"I want to go to Paris."

"You will."

"Soon. Very soon."

His comment troubled her. He and Evelyn didn't stay long. In a corner by himself stood Stefano. He spoke to no one.

Sofia felt grateful for the family that she and her daughter could provide for her husband, who had none. She thought about her mother, as if Livia might be here among the guests. She began to sense the largeness of her absence, as if her death had been nothing more than a shift into a ghostly room, the loss of a soul that her family could feel but never see. Her father had been that room, the place that held her mother in a loving conversation that would never end. Now he was gone and he had taken her with him. The house was silent.

A few days later, Sofia went alone to pray at her father's grave. She dreaded the look of the raw ground, the gash in the earth where he was laid to rest, yet she wanted to be alone with him in the winter silence, under the soft grey sky. As she approached the gravesite, she noticed that it had begun to snow. Then she looked again at the tiny white petals that were falling on her hair and her dark coat and on the raw earth where she knelt. She scooped them up in her hands and smelled their delicate scent, and then they melted. She let the snow flurries powder her coat, wondering at their beauty, wondering where she was.

As she walked through the cemetery in the falling snow, she saw a shadowy figure up ahead, a man with a cane and dark glasses. *But there's no sun as it is*, she thought. He seemed ghostly and without colour, and then she realized that he was blind, that she might be seeing him as he saw the world. *Maybe that's Chris*, she thought. *We are close enough for that to happen.* At that moment he faded from view, dissolving into air. She wondered if she'd stumbled upon the year when her cousin would leave this world. *I should call him when I get home and see how he is*, she thought. When she got back to Maywood Road, she felt foolish. *All you do is worry.* Something else needed her immediate attention.

5

Leo had been sent to Kingsbridge Veterans' Hospital in a wooded part of the West Bronx, not far from the bend of the Harlem River into Spuyten Duyvil Creek. *Puddles*, Leo used to call them. *Faucet drip. You couldn't sail a bottle-cap in either one.* Now Sofia imagined him recuperating from a dread of water.

His ward was a bleak but tidy place with its row of iron beds, its chairs and tables in a corner. Sofia looked around. They'd been told that her brother had a problem with breathing, but she saw no oxygen tanks. She eyed three men playing cards, two others absorbed in checkers. Another grey-haired fellow sat alone, leafing through a magazine. All six were listless but breathing unaided. The lone man looked up and started coughing. His eyes connected with Sofia's.

"Leo," she whispered.

How thin he is. What's happened to his hair?

Leo seemed perplexed at first, as if he hadn't expected to see them here. Then they embraced.

"I got this cough," he said. "Right after the fire."

Sofia asked him if he were feeling better. After he'd spoken, she told him about their father's death.

Leo stared out the window and started coughing again. Stefano got him a glass of water.

"Bari burned down," said Leo. "We had to go jump in the sea."

Sofia remembered the airship, its passengers falling from a terrifying height, their frail bodies crushed and burning.

"The air smelled like Italian food," her brother said. "I couldn't breathe." His voice was hoarse.

"Fire takes oxygen out of the air," said Stefano.

"It's like it's still happening to me."

"You'll get well, thank God," Sofia said.

Leo was silent, and then he spoke. "Pop died?" he asked.

"Your brother was exposed to poison gas," said Stefano.

"The letters never mentioned poison gas."

"Never mind the letters. My uncles were gassed in the Great War. I know that cough. It is possible his lungs were burned."

"Do you think Leo knows?"

"Sure he knows. The Germans bombed his battleship. He smelled it."

"*Like Italian food*, he said."

"Garlic. That is the smell of mustard gas."

Sofia couldn't get hold of the idea. She thought of her lost Uncle Guido, equipped with a gas mask, driving an ambulance through the battlefields of France. *Mustard gas* — it sounded horrible. Left over from the First World War. She thought there was some law against it.

"Not on Leo's battleship, that gas," she said.

"Why do you say that?"

"It's too cruel. Mussolini used it in Ethiopia. America —"

"*Cara mia*, we are at war," he said.

"Poor Leo. Maybe he caught cold in the water."

She began shivering in the chill rain of memory. She heard the clang of fire-bells, and she could feel in her throat the rotting air at Lakehurst. *Where are my aunt and uncle?* She squeezed her eyes shut.

Stefano took her in his arms. "*Innocente*," he whispered. "Your brother will be well. Don't cry."

It may be just as well that Pop is gone.

Leo had moved like air through a curtain of death, and now he was as pale and insubstantial as their mother had been. Home he'd come — his body alive with the worst that could happen.

Sofia felt this same dread sometimes, this same deathlike pall over her life. She still had waking dreams about the *Hindenburg*, but she endured them, as if this and her uncle's disappearance were the price for having slept with him. A shard of memory that she'd pull from her skin, a stab of pain that made her wince — she tried to put them aside. She was grateful that the penalty had not been worse.

Leo remained unwell. *Some men are malingerers*, the doctor said. *Others need more time. There's nothing wrong with him that time won't fix.*

Sofia didn't believe it.

6

For a week after Elio Gentile's death, Sofia avoided his study. It still felt like her father's private space, containing a gentle and studious life the way a stoppered bottle holds a fragrance. With the funeral over, Sofia had to retrieve her father's will. She found the folder in a desk drawer, but the desk was too cluttered for her to spread out the document and read it. In front of her was one of her uncle's notebooks, still opened to the page her father had been perusing, his leather bookmark lying across it. There was also a notepad, its used sheets rolled back to expose a blank page dated *February 5, 1944* — the day her father died. His fountain pen was lying on the pad.

On the last afternoon of his life, Elio Gentile had written only three words: *Non è vero.*

It isn't true.

Sofia grabbed his magnifying glass and scanned the open page of her uncle's notebook. *What patience my father had. You need the Rosetta Stone to decode this.* As she began to make out the words, she wished for hieroglyphics.

How can I ask forgiveness? her Uncle Paul had written. *I have done an unspeakable thing.*

I will return to Julia. I must try to find her again in the air.

It was dated April, 1937 — a year after Paul had seduced her and just before he and Aunt Julia set sail on the *Queen Mary*.

Sofia was horrified.

Non è vero, her poor father wrote, on the last day of his life.

If Uncle Paul had been sorry, he could have told her. Only he fled — the coward. She'd guessed right, that her aunt and uncle must have found love again on their leisurely journey. Even so, her uncle knew damn well that if he never came back, her father would read this.

Sometimes life took years to heave up a wrong — like a chunk of some irreparable ruin, buried under a ton of earth, yanked loose by a derrick's teeth. It wasn't true that life shrugged everything off. On the sand foundation of her one mistake, life had built an unstable house where the mortar had begun to crumble from the shoddy brick. It didn't take much to knock it down. It crushed her father.

Only she wasn't certain that it was this news that killed him.

What about the stuff he burned? She went to the fireplace, opened the screen and poked at the ashes. There was nothing left. Returning to his desk, she spotted Mr. Laurier's business card attached to the ruled notepad. On it were pages filled with her father's handwriting — all of them rolled back, leaving the blank page with its three words. She sat down to read what had come before her father's last sentence. *His pouch must still be in a box. Must find.* That mystified her. Also *Sofia guessed right. Antiques — yes and no.* And *In on it? A girlhood crush on my brother. I will read on.*

And so he had.

Sofia ripped the pages off the pad and bunched them up in a ball. She did the same for Uncle Paul's mention of their sexual encounter. She yanked open the screen, pulled down the flue, heaved a few split logs on the fire and stuffed the paper in the cracks. *Just because I was stupid enough to sleep with Uncle Paul doesn't mean I was stupid enough to be in cahoots with him. What the hell was Laurier doing with my aunt and uncle? Whatever it was, chances are my dad died knowing.* She threw in some kindling. *Uncle Paul, you abandoned us. You killed my father, and your memory will not live on.* She ripped up the rest of his notebooks, bunched up the papers into wads and stuffed them between the logs. Tomorrow she'd find his photographs and burn them, too. She lit a match to everything and watched the fire crackle and spit, the paper glow with embers as her father's speculations crumbled into ash and her uncle disappeared forever.

Stefano walked into the room. "*Cara mia*, you're covered with soot."

"I was burning papers."

"But you're crying." He dried her eyes with his handkerchief. "You're missing your father, *sì?*"

"*Sì.*" She paused.

For a moment Sofia had felt the truth edging its way through her body — a raw and freighted kind of truth, like a prisoner making a jailbreak when he doesn't deserve escape. She decided not to confess a thing. As Stefano embraced her, she understood that her body had grown used to this secret of hers as if it were one of those dull muscular aches that comes from lifting the same load over and over. Stefano might sense its presence in the touch of his hand on her skin, but he would never see it, never know of it. It wouldn't matter. *Everything is present to us if we open our eyes. Stefano knows that nothing disappears.* She thought of her soul as she'd imagined it when she lost their first child — as a bent twig that would never grow straight. She glanced out the window at the beech tree, at its delicate tracery of branches sleek with ice. Her soul was just as resilient, just as strong.

Before they went to bed, Sofia peered outside again. "Look," she said to Stefano. The evening sky was as bright as day.

"As if the sun were falling apart," he said.

"Are we under attack?"

"*Madonn'*. I think we would have heard sirens."

"Still, it's too bright for evening."

Stefano took her in his arms. "It is not an attack," he said. "The sky was like this when my parents appeared in the Battery on the day of the eclipse. The last time I saw them."

Outside their window, an icy branch cracked in the wind.

How disjointed her life felt. *You could shuffle time like a deck of cards*, she thought. *It's all there, all at once.* The thought made her uneasy.

That night, she dreamed she was walking to the Gun Hill Road subway when she saw Christopher running up the stairs. He was wearing dark glasses and carrying his white cane, but he seemed to be chasing someone. Up ahead, she could see Uncle Paul and Aunt Julia as they'd looked on the night of the *Hindenburg* fire. Christopher called out their names. She heard the wail of an ambulance siren and then screams.

She woke up to a red dawn tipping over the window ledge like a cup unbalanced on a saucer, its light about to spill on the carpet and leave a bloody stain. Stefano was shaking her.

"There's been an accident," he said.

THE BOX

I

Sofia's head aches from the tight bandage, but memory leaks like a stain through the gauze. Recalling the past exhausts her and she's drifting in and out of sleep. She feels lips that brush her forehead and hands that hold hers. Now and then a voice murmurs *Mom, it's me, Petra,* or *it's Julie — Daughter Number Two, live from New York.* Or *honey, its Tina. Joey's parking the car outside. How'ya doin', sweetie?* Sofia wonders if she's dreaming them. She's sure about the nurse who comes to change the drips, who always says *how are you today, Mrs. Fiore?* as if she might answer *fine and dandy* from behind her oxygen mask. She hears a soft blur of old, familiar sounds — Gabriella and Eddie (or was it their daughter?) talking, Tina and Joey and Harry's son Bernie, their big Bronx voices as hearty as good bread. Like tastes and smells — a richness to the very sound of their names. *Petra, sweetheart*, says Tina, *I'm so sorry about your mother.*

Her old friend's making chit-chat, patting her arm, talking to her daughter. *Me and your mother, we go back a long way. Potsie and jacks when we were kids. Egg-creams at Old Man Bernie's before he modernized and ripped out the soda fountain. Oh gee, I could go on.*

Tina's hand feels warm and Sofia doesn't mind the chatter. She wishes she could talk. They never lost touch, and she'd always thought there'd be one more coffee, one more chance to catch up. *Only time's run out*, she thinks. Time's skidding every which way, and she's lost control of the wheel. *Hey, kiddo — don't worry*, says Tina and she opens her bag and pulls out a matchbook. *All the candles you can light.* They were going into Holy Name Church to pray for Sofia's mother, but now she's the one in need of prayers. Her friend's hand is stroking her forehead, and she hears her saying *take it easy, kid.*

Only she can't remember if Tina's still alive.

She's sinking and rising like a rudderless boat bobbing on the edge of a rough sea. A swish of memory floods the deck and she gets seasick on the great rolling ocean of her own life. A nurse comes to adjust whatever's going through the tubes. *It's OK, Mrs. Fiore.* She cleans her up. *Tina's gone now*, Sofia thinks, uncertain if she ever came.

When Sofia wakes up again, she remembers the day before she fell.

There she is, on the sunny back patio of Petra's music store

An Ordinary Star

in Linden, New York — a hangout for musicians passing through town on their way to the city, a cubbyhole for lovers of classical and jazz CDs. It's early and the store's just opened. She's here because she has a doctor's appointment at noon, and Petra's insisted on driving. She could have driven herself, but she also knows that her daughter's worried. She's old, after all, and something in her blood's no longer working as it should. It's not a malady she'd ever heard of, not a big-name disease-of-the-month with an ad campaign and a flower. As it turns out, she feels weary today, glad she accepted the ride. As she relaxes in a shady corner of the patio, she can hear one of Petra's CDs — a woman's scat-singing, a rich contralto weaving its way through the scales.

What would my father have thought of this music?

She peers through the glass doors into the store. As she does, the front door jangles open to the tapping of a white cane — a rhythmic staccato with a hint of swing. Mesmerized, she watches as a hand reaches up to touch the doorframe. The man ducks his head, edging his way inside with the care of someone determined to avoid a misstep. He's a tall and sturdy man in wraparound shades, his thinning white hair still edged with blond. Even with the care he takes, there's a largeness about him that feels relentless, too much so for the size of this place. His presence fills the store like a flooded river rising. Sofia stares, glad that she'd spoken to Petra. *If cousin Chris shows up, don't send him out here. I haven't got the energy this morning.*

"May I help you?" asks Petra.

He turns toward the sound of her voice. "You are Petra Fiore?"

He introduces himself. His voice is hesitant, as if he seldom speaks English, and Sofia strains to catch his words. *How many years has it been?* she wonders. On more than one occasion, she and Stefano had gone to visit him in Paris. He seldom came to New York.

"I only dropped by to say hello. I will call your mother later."

"Did you know my father passed away?"

"I did," he says. "Forgive me — I am late in paying my respects." He hesitated. "And how is your mother?"

"She's slowing down. She still enjoys your music."

"Thank you. In case I miss her, let me leave my CD. Evvie has sent her something, also." He puts his hand in his jacket pocket and pulls out a flat rectangular package. Then he leaves.

At noon, Petra locks the store and comes out on the patio.

"So my cousin's here," says Sofia.

Her daughter hands her the CD. "Evvie sent you something, too."

Sofia takes the package. She puts it in her purse and walks out to the car.

From long ago, the sound comes rumbling — the racket of the el along the track above White Plains Road, the cars screeching through the iron latticework of struts and beams, the wooden railings gripped by businessmen and held by office girls with soft, gloved hands. How often she'd climbed the steps to the top of the platform, then to the subway on the upper level, moving through the cranky turnstiles, glancing at

An Ordinary Star

the wrought-iron streetlights and the boy with red suspenders shouting the *Daily News* headlines. A commonplace thing, unlike that terrible evening when she and Stefano went to sleep with the winter night as bright as the day.

She can still feel him shaking her. *Christopher fell,* her husband's words. *A man's been arrested,* said a cop on Gun Hill Road. *There are witnesses.* Then a fireman's voice: *God was with this blind fella. Rolled right under the ledge.* The man who pushed Chris in front of the train had been drinking. He went to prison. At the trial, Christopher reported that just before he was assaulted, a man had asked his name. *Do you have reason to believe that someone wanted you dead?* asked the judge. *No, Your Honour,* said Christopher.

Sofia remembered summer, when this subway accident had skidded and crashed through the barrier of time. She felt afraid.

The police searched the prisoner's apartment and found a stash of bills and Mr. Laurier's letterhead. When they got a search warrant for his shipping business, Laurier shot himself in the head. *He had people moving his goods,* said the FBI, *to Germany.* Sofia wondered what he was shipping that made him take his life. She never found out. Nor did she ever learn why Chris was assaulted, and she's long since grown weary of the question.

Christopher uses the name Chris Giles and he's made something of a name for himself as a composer and accompanist. His new CD is called *Golden Sky.* In the car, Petra puts it on. As Sofia listens, she remembers his wedding gift — music breaking open like a fragrant orange, peeling time away from the present moment. She regrets that time took Stefano, that he isn't here to reminisce. She sees that vision of her aunt and uncle in love, hop-skipping down Maywood Road to a Bill Bojangles tune. *We're old now, Chris*, she thinks. *Did you ever think we'd live to be this old?*

Petra stops for a red light. She reaches over and turns off the CD.

"Mom, what's the matter?" she asks.

"I'm all right, dear."

"You're crying."

"I was afraid I'd never see Christopher again."

She cries because the things that are clearest in her mind are the oldest things she can remember. There's the view to the east down the slope of Gun Hill Road, a street of frame houses and neighbourhood merchants, their striped canvas awnings rolled down against the sun. She'd shopped on Burke Avenue with her mother, and in those days Bernie's Deli, De Lucca's Meats and The Budget had everything they needed. On her own shaded street it was so quiet that you couldn't even hear a train or trolley — only from time to time a passing car. When she was young, life moved at a stroller's pace through this part of New York City. Or, in summer heat, it sat and waited. Then on her wedding day the sky changed colour and flowering trees filled the air with a fragrance rare for this part of the world.

Long ago she went walking, wheeling Tina's daughter in the carriage, crossing Tremont Avenue and ending up on the

An Ordinary Star

other side of time. It hadn't surprised her. As a child, she'd seen her aunt fly. She'd watched sunlight passing through her mother as though she were stained glass in the solemn cathedral of her family. One day she stood in the moon's shadow as her father floated toward the distant stars. She cries because she's old now, afraid that no one will believe her.

Later that afternoon, Christopher calls her at home, apologizing for too long a silence. He wants to take her out to lunch, and she's pleased. In her older years, she's come to prefer face-to-face visits to the telephone. More than that, she's grown confident in speaking her mind and she finds it hard to be blunt with a disembodied voice. Just as she's ready to hang up, Chris interjects.

"I need to ask you a personal question," he says.

Not over the phone, you don't.

"So are you going to ask me in person?"

She's sorry the minute she says it. *How inconsiderate of me*, she thinks. *He's blind*. She remembers that in his youth, Chris would blurt out anything over the phone, including his passion for Evvie. From his point of view, the telephone made everybody blind.

Chris ignores her question. "Did you burn my father's papers?" he asks.

"How come you've waited so long to ask?"

He paused. "All these years I've felt foolish. About the accident."

She listens.

"That evening, I had a nightmare. I could feel heat and the

smell and crackle of a huge fire and the sound of your voice screaming. I called to see if you were all right, but the line was dead. So I came uptown to find out if your house had burned down. When I got off at Gun Hill Road, the sidewalks were so icy that I had to go back home. I should never have come."

"I did burn those papers," said Sofia. "That night."

"What made you do that?"

"You want to know what your dad wrote," she says.

"I used to think that my father was in love with you. But I can't imagine —"

"If you can't, I won't."

Silence.

"Forgive me, Sofia. I am not sure what prompted this."

"Lunch," she says. "What time will you pick me up?

2

"What prompted this' is the fact that you still don't understand the accident. Who does? Maybe your father's spirit came to warn you away from the tracks.

It's early morning. Getting up, Sofia moves with care and deliberation — sitting, then tucking her feet into the plush slippers that her granddaughter gave her, standing with no particular haste, slipping into her bath robe. She pulls the bedroom curtain back to see the sunlight, and she crosses herself — thankful, at her age, for the grace of another day. She remembers her cousin who's never gazed at her with loving eyes. *One day you'll see God's face*, she thinks. *So no more nosing into my head, OK?*

She pauses before the bureau, touching the framed photograph of Stefano. *Caro mio.* Then she puts her hand on the

353

smooth, cool whiteness of the porcelain knob, turning it, pushing outward. As she does, she hears a tinkle, a pretty sound that makes her think of wind chimes on a summer's day. Her jewellery — a pendant carved in jade, a rope of pearls, a string of cut-glass birds from Rome — her husband's gifts, hanging from a bracket that he made for her. She listens, as if he were telling her to take it easy. The sound holds his gentleness, and will hold his memory forever. The thought makes her smile, but as she's about to walk into the corridor, her eye catches something on the bureau — the package that Evvie left for her. *Later*, she thinks. *It can wait.*

No, it can't.

Who said that? The voice was charming, yet firm.

Bemused, she sits down, picks up the package and unwraps it. Under the brown paper is a worn leather pouch. Attached to it is a note in Evvie's handwriting. *Dear Sofia ... Some time ago, an English acquaintance sent me a box with Christopher's father's name on it and the address of your house in the Bronx. She says she found it at a flea market near Weymouth, outside London. She thought its contents might interest Chris, but I think otherwise. It is you who would be interested, as you will see.*

The pouch is a roomy one, and it contains a yellowing envelope, still sealed. It is addressed *For Sofia*. The handwriting's tight and cramped — written in fading, fountain-pen ink. Sofia puts on her reading glasses, and she realizes that her hands are shaking. Inside the envelope, there's a letter that falls from her hand to the floor. She notices it, but doesn't bother picking it up. In her hands she's holding a thing she's never before held in her life.

An Ordinary Star

A wad of hundred-dollar bills.

She's never seen this much cash, and she's too frightened to count it, as if moments ago her Uncle Paul had robbed a bank, unloading the cash — and the crime — on her. More mysterious is a bank note folded several times into a square. It turns out to be a large certificate written in German script. She notices a number in the upper left-hand corner: 1000*rm*. A denomination of some kind, none that she knows. It must be a financial paper, something from a bank. *Stock?* No one in her family held stock in the Depression years. *A bond? Maybe.* A familiar word stands out on the page. *Berlin* and then 1935. She folds it up again. Even she would know that it was worthless now.

What were you up to, Uncle Paul? She whispers the words, as if he's in the room.

Her hands are shaking as she picks the letter up from the floor.

May 6, 1936
Cara Sofia, when I return, I hope it is your wish
 that we will be close once again. I apologise for my
 thoughtlessness in not protecting you ... should you
 face a problem, accept this with my love and sincere
 apology.

She rips up the paper and throws the scraps in the wastepaper basket. Her eyes sting with tears. After all this time, it stuns her that his words could make her weep. She starts to place the bills and papers back in the pouch and realizes all of a sudden that the feel of the ancient leather is encoded in the memory of her hand — dark and soft, worn even then. A tobacco pouch, and against her fingers the ribbed glass of the humidor, the wooden lid that screwed on tight, the whole of it resting in a wooden stand with slots for the pipes and impressions where the bowls sat. A boxful of bric-a-brac she'd kicked across the hall. Long ago she'd scooped it up in her arms and vowed to sell it for junk.

She'd put it under Tina's baby carriage. That damn *box*.

Lost in a hole in time.

I don't need the aggravation. Not right now. She puts everything back in the pouch and leaves it on the bureau.

Sofia makes her way down the corridor to the bathroom. *I ought to put some plants in here*, she tells herself. *All that light and steam goes to waste.* She smiles a little. *The orchids and gardenias I could buy with that cash.* The room's large and white-tiled, trimmed in a green-ivy pattern, the towels soft and green. It was Stefano's idea — an idyllic place, with a stylish sink and bath. It wasn't that long ago when she'd sit in the bathtub and read in Italian. Roman verse, also — *O Fons Bandusiae*, an ode by Horace, the only one she'd memorized in Latin. She used to recite it in memory of her father, who shared a passion for books with her and with her brother Leo who died too young. *I think of your grandfather every day*, she said to Petra once. *He made our lives beautiful. He made us more than we were.*

Her father wouldn't have approved of his brother Paul's investing in German anything, let alone giving her the bond. *If* nonno *Domenico had known, he would have turned Uncle Paul into dog chow. Only I never received the envelope. He changed his mind about sending it to me when he knew we wouldn't be 'close once again,' after I came at him with the knife.* She takes a deep breath. *Calm down.* She imagines a snowball tossed into a bonfire. The angry thought melts away.

It's so long ago, she thinks. *What does it matter?*

The words come back. *Your aunt and uncle are in pain, cara mia.*

She still honours her father's wisdom, knowing that it's because of him that she remains calm at moments like this. In her final years, she appreciates the care he taught her in the use of words. She'd learned to live inside the cloister of her own thoughts, to abandon speech when it wouldn't do. Stillness mattered and silence worked in her as yeast in bread. Her thoughts would iron a shirt to a crisp whiteness, simmer her homemade soup to a boil, pat down the soil of a new plant. In this way, she'd found that everything she touched gave rise to some larger awareness, a presence she could feel but never name. Over the years she'd loved her children and cared for them, but they'd never entered her true abode of silence.

For so much attentiveness, she's grateful now. As she opens the bathroom door, she feels alive to daylight and to the smoothness of the doorknob and to the sweet anticipation of a warm shower. In her face reflected in the mirror, she sees a thing that startles her — a readiness to leave this earth.

Not before I meet Chris for lunch.

She walks into the bathroom, turns on the shower and slips out of her bath robe, her body glowing. All at once she's a young woman, and handsome Uncle Paul has his eye on her. *Salute, mia bella.* She kisses him. He pulls her down on the bed.

You bastard.

In the shower, her foot gives way. Sofia's head hits the side of the tub and she tumbles into blackness.

It's as if a rock had struck her, smashing open the memory of the afternoon she'd slept with him, the image of her red jacket hanging on the back of the guest-room door. It had been warm that first week of April, and she'd walked back to work without it. Later that evening, she retrieved it and went up the street to return some laundry starch that she'd borrowed from Gabriella's mother. On her way home she shoved her hands in the pockets and pulled out a scrap of paper. *Sofia*, it read, *if there's any problem because of this afternoon, go talk to my mother. She'll help you. I'll provide money, if needed. Paul.* Danger throbbed in her head. *Nonna* Rosa was making her wedding gown. His *mother* — and he was telling her to ... she wondered if a bigger fool than herself had ever lived.

Two weeks later when she'd missed her period (she'd always been punctual to the day), she took the train to Delancey Street and strode over to her grandmother's for a fitting. It was so dark in this tenement stairwell that her hands still remember groping for the railing, inching up to the second floor, making her way along the hall by feeling the embossed tinwork on the walls until her fingers hit the second doorframe on the left. *I need help*, she said to *nonna* Rosa, who looked at her with surprise and puzzlement when she explained the situation — including the fib that Stefano was her lover. *In three months you'll be married*, figlia mia. *Less.*

Sofia started to cry. *I'll show. I can't.* Three days late wasn't anything, *nonna* assured her, but Sofia wasn't prepared

An Ordinary Star

to take a chance. *I'll give you some tea*, said *nonna*. *But what if you're ill and your father finds out?* Sofia didn't care. She took the tea home and drank it. Later she felt sick and began to bleed. It was a heavy period and the cramps kept her up all night, but she was grateful. *You are too pale*, said her father. *You need more iron in your diet.* She would have eaten a railroad track to get that iron, so relieved she was that her father suspected nothing.

Only life caught up with her, and when it was time for the first child, she had a dream of *nonna* Constanza crushing her stomach with her hands. *This is Uncle Paul's child and it must be destroyed*, she said in the dream. Sofia bled and she is bleeding now. The terrible story continues, the rock keeps right on going through time and space, finding windows and smashing them, its trajectory deflected by strong wind and the luck of its target to have turned a corner, ducked into a shop, pulled the car away from the curb just in time. Today her luck has fled her. Where did that damn box come from? What was all that money *for*? Yet did it matter? When had she not felt the broken glass when the window shattered, the shards embedded in her skin? When?

3

"The surgery was successful," Petra whispers to Julie.

What surgery? Inside Sofia's head there's a faint throbbing, as if a tiny fist were banging on the inside of her skull. She hadn't invited anyone into her head and the very idea upsets her. The knowledge that she's lost a part of her already-dwindling life to anaesthesia makes her feel worse than helpless.

Two warm hands clasp one of hers. Her daughter Julie's a dancer, as slender as bamboo. She has a loft in the city, somewhere below Canal Street. She's supposed to be rehearsing. *Cousin Chris is on his way*, she says to Petra. *I got permission*, Petra answers, but Sofia's not in the mood to wonder what part of her body they've got permission to mangle next.

"Is she sleeping?" whispers Julie.

An Ordinary Star

"We have a surprise," says Petra.

When Sofia looks, she sees that her older daughter is holding Stefano's violin. She can't remember when she last heard Petra play, but it's been a while. Julie's standing beside her sister. She cups her hands in the shape of a lotus, bows before her mother and then — dances. Right there in the ICU, in front of the nursing station and three other beds, she swirls and pirouettes and pivots on her toes as Petra plays a lilting melody. The tune's called *Figlia Mia*, one that Stefano had written for her birth. Julie's leaps are soundless and the ward is so still that even the monitors seem to hum along in lazy, switch-off mode. As Petra plays the final bars, Julie folds herself on the floor like a flower closing its petals, then rises up again, as wondrous and still as a heron on a single leg. Floating on water — Sofia can feel herself drifting along the sidewalk, she and Aunt Julia dancing through the modern world. They're rising from the ground, into the wonder of forgotten time, into the sun etching everything in gold. *So this is what they got permission for.*

Julie bows. She sits down and pulls a tissue from the box. She dries her mother's eyes.

It's late now, and her daughters have left this hushed room, these four beds, the desk where the nurses come and go like shadows. The light is dim; there's something that looks like Venetian blinds and tinted glass on the windows. No voice rises above a whisper, no footstep is heavier than a cat's; even the bleeps from the computers that attend to her are soft and muted, *cluck-cluck-cluck*, like a hen. She thinks that somewhere there must be an invisible knob that lowers the volume on everything, as if to prepare her for the silence of God. Her daughters have made her feel dignity, but she knows she's become a child in the womb again, nourished through tubes, her body drawing in red cells, white cells, platelets, water, a sedative of some kind. At the other end is a catheter so she won't mess the bed. *How I miss my mother*, she thinks. *We never talked. I don't know how she faced this.*

4

Christopher's sitting beside her.

They've taken me off the respirator, Sofia thinks. *I've got to talk to you.*

"I won't leave you," he says. "Don't be afraid."

He sits by her bed, finds her hand, and holds it. The nurse helps him seat himself so that his ear is close to her mouth.

"Evvie's package," she whispers.

"Yes?"

"Cash. Your father's."

He looks startled.

"A German bond." She's too exhausted to continue. She manages a few more words. *On my bureau* and *ask Petra*, but she's not sure he's heard her. She feels drowsy. She must have drifted off to sleep, but when she awakens, Christopher's still there and he's saying *will you go and look?*

"Poor Mom," Petra says to him. "What a shock."

She's comforted that her daughter understands her well enough to guess that the package is the reason for her fall. Only she's certain that Petra will want to know more. She'll look for clues to the mystery — she'll search the trash can in the bedroom and maybe even piece together that ripped-up note from Uncle Paul. *They must have done some work for Laurier, my aunt and uncle. Shipping something, and he paid them a lot of money.* She's too tired to think. Christopher lifts his hands, moving them to find her face. He lets his fingertips rest on her forehead. Only she isn't sure if it's then or now, or whose touch it is after all. No, it's her cousin's because he's blind, and because he touches her as he did years ago, with the hesitation of a white cane mapping an unfamiliar road.

When Sofia wakes up, Christopher's sitting by her side. He leans over and strokes her hair.

"Petra found the money," he says. He looks grieved.

"In a junk box," she whispers, sure this could mean nothing to him.

"I remember the box," says Chris.

What road had it travelled since the day she went strolling and the box disappeared? How was it that she'd finally received what her uncle had never given? Chris takes her hand and in his touch she feels herself relaxing, letting go of *how* and *where* and *what on earth* and the grievous memories that the box contained. That it reappeared is mystery enough.

5

After the days of the airships, Uncle Paul and Aunt Julia moved like wraiths through the haunted sky. They flew and returned but never came back. Sofia remembers her brother Leo who also returned but never came back, who coughed his lungs to death from mustard gas and died at Kingsbridge Hospital. She longs to see him and Stefano. She pulls and struggles, as if she were a prisoner in handcuffs.

"Mom, don't." It's Petra's voice.

Julie presses the alarm and two nurses come running. "It's OK, Mrs. Fiore," says one while the other takes a set of plastic restraints and cuffs her wrists to the bars of her bed. Sofia keeps breathing, feels Petra's hand on her forehead. *She was trying to pull out the iv*, she hears Julie say to the nurse. She drifts back into twilight, wandering inside herself.

What's wrong? asks Stefano.

Shadows are falling, walling her in.

I've done only one thing I regret. She feels it lodged in the marrow of her bones, a story that had multiplied in every cell, that had entered her blood and consumed her. She watches Stefano's face.

Povera *Sofia, what does it matter? Our lives are done. Forgive me.*

All these years she's waited.

It's OK to talk to her, the nurse says. *She can still hear you.* In the shadows, Julie lights a votive candle. *Forget about permission — this is big, Sof*, says Tina as she pulls out her matches. *Light 'em all.*

Only night's collapsing on the world. She hasn't time.

Sofia moves away from the city, across the river to the Lakehurst barrens. The airship's in flames, its nose shooting five hundred feet into the air, its terrified passengers jumping to their deaths. Aunt Julia! Uncle Paul! As the nose crashes in a fiery heap, she's convinced her aunt and uncle have perished and she starts to scream.

It's all right, honey, says Mr. Stafford.

She blacks out, comes to, watches the couple leave the airship. They look unaware of danger, trapped in the moment before the calamity happened. *What you see is illusion and suffering*, says her father.

An Ordinary Star

Aunt Julia and Uncle Paul are standing high up by a shattered window — he in his smart business clothes and she in her spring frock. The fire below is spitting rage, but their faces are still, as if they're prepared for what has to happen. Uncle Paul turns to Aunt Julia and takes her hand. The sky bends open as they leap and tumble into the chasm of time, never to be heard from again.

So they are gone. So everything is gone.
Gone where?

She's floating under the black sun, through a moment of grace in the moon's shadow. She is going to find them.

ACKNOWLEDGEMENTS

Many individuals and institutions have made it possible for me to research and complete this work. In particular, I would like to thank Laura Tosi of the Bronx County Historical Society for her assistance in finding archival photographs of the Williamsbridge neighbourhood. Thanks also to Alan Janus of the Smithsonian National Air and Space Museum in Washington, D.C. for information and documents pertaining to the airship *Los Angeles*. I am grateful to Lawrence Lyford of the Lakehurst Naval Air Base in New Jersey for showing me the historic airfield and hangar and to John Iannacone, a survivor of the *Hindenburg* fire for recalling details of that event. Original research provided by Prof. Jerome Krase of Brooklyn College at CUNY helped me to understand the social structures of Italian communities in early twentieth-century

New York City. The Mid-Manhattan branch of the New York Public Library offered access to a huge photo-archive of the city's downtown. The extent of support for fascism in the U.S. is documented in John P. Diggins' work, *Mussolini and Fascism: The View from America*. For historical information on the WWII mustard-gas episode in Bari, Italy, I consulted *Disaster at Bari* by Glenn E. Infield. For eyewitness history, an audio interview with my mother Antoinette provided me with the peddlers' dialect chants along with much detail about the street life of the old Bronx. In memory, I thank her.

I am grateful for the generous support of the Ontario Arts Council and the Toronto Arts Council. Thanks also to my editor and publisher Marc Côté for his faith in this novel from its earliest beginnings as a story. Janis Rapoport took the time to read the shorter version, and I would like to express my gratitude for her helpful suggestions and her generosity. Thanks also to my agent Jack Scovil, and to Mary Ellen and Meg for a place to stay in Manhattan. Most of all, I am grateful to Brian, my spouse and extraordinary friend.